SANCTUARY
STORIES

Bilingual Press/Editorial Bilingüe

General Editor
Gary D. Keller

Managing Editor
Karen S. Van Hooft

Associate Editors
Ann Waggoner Aken
Theresa Hannon

Assistant Editor
Linda St. George Thurston

Editorial Consultants
Barbara H. Firoozye
Ingrid Muller

Editorial Board
Juan Goytisolo
Francisco Jiménez
Eduardo Rivera
Mario Vargas Llosa

Address:
Bilingual Review/Press
Hispanic Research Center
Arizona State University
P. O. Box 872702
Tempe, Arizona 85287-2702
(602) 965-3867

SANCTUARY
STORIES

Michael Smith

Bilingual Press/Editorial Bilingüe
TEMPE, ARIZONA

ISBN 0-927534-50-9

Library of Congress Cataloging-in-Publication Data

Smith, Michael, 1943-
    Sanctuary stories / by Michael Smith.
       p.   cm.
    ISBN 0-927534-50-9 (paper)
    1. Central America—Social life and customs—Fiction. 2. Hispanic Americans—Social conditions. 3. Central America—Social conditions. 4. Hispanic Americans—Fiction. I. Title.
PS3569.M537828S26 1994
813'.54—dc20   94-34230
                                     CIP

PRINTED IN THE UNITED STATES OF AMERICA

Front cover photo by Jeffry D. Scott

Cover design by Nancy Kennedy

Back cover photo by Neil Goldstein

CONTENTS

Foreword

THESE STORIES AND ESSAYS were inspired by the refugees who came to the offices of the East Bay Sanctuary in Berkeley, California. Although in fictional form, the stories are based on real experiences of real people. As a good muckraker, I have sometimes placed the burden of suffering of several individuals onto the shoulders of one. As a good pacifist, I have fought to keep the violence to tolerable limits. In the essays I stick to facts; the characters are not compilations, the events are not exaggerated.

These are not horror stories but stories of simple human dignity. These are the stories of the humble, the poor, the tired, Indians, farmers, factory workers, people denied the opportunity of education, university students, cops on the beat, soldiers, and guerrillas. These are the stories of people who, despite the violence of poverty as well as terror, have retained their humanity. I am privileged to have known them.

Rafael

WHILE THE BEAUTIFUL, YOUNG PEOPLE occupied the street above, Rafael and I huddled in our basement office. Summer still lingered outside, warm and bright, and the university students strode purposefully to class, dawdled over cappuccinos and scones in the Music Box Cafe, or chatted carelessly while they waited in line at the automatic teller machines to withdraw a few crisp twenties for the evening.

Wintry gloom chilled the basement, and Rafael kept a grimy hand around his paper cup of instant coffee for warmth. Practically on top of us, the always-stylish young people jogged in gleaming spandex outfits yet managed to smell fresh and clean. Rafael wore hand-me-down blue work pants and a clashing red, orange, and green plaid polyester shirt he had picked up for 50 cents at the flea market. He and his clothes reeked of yesterday's sour sweat and last night's alcohol.

Rafael was hung over. He didn't look good. His thick black hair, pushed straight back from his forehead, was greasy. His eyes were yellow and red where I expected white. His cracked lips often parted in a nervous grin, exposing yellow teeth. His upper and lower gums were inflamed, his breath fetid. I tried to maintain a healthy distance between us.

Rafael had come in from the Central Valley because his work permit had expired. He had worked in the tomato fields all summer, in the tomatoes as the farm workers said, and soon it would be time to work in the grapes. He'd gotten his permit renewed, gotten drunk with old friends, and was killing time until the next bus left for the Valley.

We didn't have much to say to each other at first—I had other things to do, and Rafael was hung over. We were just killing time until Rafael began the return journey, both of us wishing that he was already on his way. For lack of anything better, we half-heartedly talked about the weather, about how hot it was in the Valley in the summer, over 100 degrees every day. I mentioned that being a Central American he must be used to the heat, and that saw him off on an unplanned journey.

He reminded me that he was a Kanjobal Indian from the highlands of Guatemala, from a little village in Huehuetenango Province, 2,500 meters above sea level. "The air is always fresh in the highlands and when it rains it becomes cold. Look, once I crossed the mountains on foot. It took me three days. It rained and was cold and my boots were bad and my feet always wet and cold and by the end of the journey the boots fell apart."

That fragment reminded him of how cold it was in his house at night and how his father would laugh and tell them that it's good to be cold because the only place where everyone is always warm and no one complains of the cold is hell. He remembered how everyone in his family had to carry firewood, even his sisters and mother, and once when he was very small and carrying a heavy load on his back he had been too sick to make it up the long hill. His uncle Francisco found him and carried both Rafael and his bundle of sticks. In his fever he had thought that his uncle was a giant, and for a long time he was afraid of his uncle while at the same time thought him a saint.

4

A patch at a time Rafael sewed together the family quilt with the thread of his quiet voice, and I learned things about him that I hadn't known before as well as things that I'd filed and forgotten, as I had done with the folders of so many others.

Rafael, his father, and older brother worked on a large plantation near their village. Each was paid a dollar a day. There were seven in his family—father, mother, and five children. They lived in a one-room house built of sticks and mud with a thatched roof and a dirt floor. Running water remained in the creeks and electricity was still undiscovered, not only in their house but in their entire village. They owned a small patch of land on the side of a hill high above the village. It was very steep, that land, but on their one day of rest a week, the one day they didn't work on the large plantation, they made the long climb to tend their corn and beans. Life was hard but peaceful.

Rafael could not remember a time when there were no rumors of fighting, but the fighting was always far away in the mountains and didn't affect his peaceful village. Army patrols came through the town rarely, but they came more often than the candidates for governor of the province. The soldiers only spoke Spanish, which few people in the village understood. When they searched the houses and questioned the men, very few people could respond. This angered the soldiers, who beat those who didn't answer quickly or respectfully enough. That was normal.

Rafael laughed until he had a coughing fit—from which I rapidly retreated—when he remembered the excitement the fabled guerrillas caused when they came to town. When they entered his house with guns and took a half sack of beans and a half sack of corn that his father had hidden under the roof, Rafael alone was not angry with them. He was too much in awe to be angry. Later they held a meeting that everyone in the village had to attend. The guerrillas told everybody that if they helped them then after the revolution the men would receive four or five dollars a day and maybe even the big plantations would belong to them. Although everyone liked that vision of the future, no one went with the guerrillas. Most people in the village were afraid, and they simply wanted things to remain normal.

After a short time Rafael and a few of the other young boys began to sneak out at night to attend meetings in the hills with the guerrillas. Soon they began training using sticks as rifles. In those days Rafael was always tired because of the training at night and the hard work during the day.

One night Rafael's older brother waited for him outside the village and caught him as he came back from his training. His older brother beat him and told him to quit the guerrillas because, even though they spoke Kanjobal, they were outsiders who wanted to change things and the people in the village were peaceful farmers who wanted life to go on as it always had. Rafael's brother didn't want changes. If there were changes, the people of the village would suffer as they always had when there were changes.

The army came again. Rafael and his brother were high on the hill above town working their land, but their father had stayed home sick with diarrhea. The patrol took all the men suspected of supporting the guerrillas down to the river where they beat them to death with clubs and then hanged them from trees. Rafael's younger brother ran up to their fields to warn Rafael not to return because the army was looking for him. When he caught his breath, he told them that Uncle Francisco had told the army that the guerrillas had come out of their house with corn and beans and that Rafael often met with the guerrillas. The soldiers wrote Rafael's name in a book and took Rafael's father away. One of the twelve dead men hanging in the trees was Rafael's father. From that day on Rafael stayed in the mountains with the guerrillas. He was fourteen years old.

When Rafael was nineteen, he returned to his village in charge of a guerrilla unit. They were fleeing from the army and took over the village because they needed a place to rest and eat. He was glad to see his family again, especially his mother even though she scolded him for running off. He was even glad to see his older brother, who was then married and had children of his own. He had thought of his family many times during the cold nights in the mountains, and he had often thought about killing his Uncle Francisco.

When he came face to face with his uncle he couldn't kill him right away as he had so often planned. His uncle seemed to have aged, and perhaps it was because he had changed that Rafael couldn't kill him right away. "Where in my memories he was strong and straight and almost a giant, perhaps even a little arrogant, when I saw him again he was old and bent. He was small. He was my father's brother and looked like my father had looked when I saw him for the last time, the morning before the soldiers killed him."

As Rafael talked I didn't hear his words so much as see him. He was dressed in machine-made clothes from Taiwan, but I pictured him in his village in the highlands, dressed in an embroidered shirt and pants woven by his mother, a knitted scarf or a straw hat with ribbons dangling from the back to show that he wasn't married, dressed in the kind of clothes that some of the university students above us paid a small fortune for in the import stores. As he talked, he kept his hand wrapped around his now-empty coffee cup. His never-loud voice had grown softer and softer until it grew so soft that I had to lean closer to hear him, close enough to smell the old alcohol mixed with coffee. He didn't move in his chair, but his brown pupils darted from side to side in his yellow eyes. There was an ever-so-slight twitch beneath his right eye, and although it was cold in that gloomy basement, his skin gleamed with invisible sweat.

"My uncle, when I saw him, was nothing more than a poor Indian like my father, like my brother, like me. He was neither a giant nor a saint. How could I kill him? It would be like killing the wrong man, not the man I had dreamed of killing. Yet I had to kill him. Many nights in the mountains I had told the members of my platoon that my uncle had collaborated with the army, and he was guilty of the murder of my father and eleven other men. We had orders to kill everyone who denounced their neighbors to the army. I had to kill my uncle.

"I went up to our land in the hills that night because from there I could see all the land below. I watched for the army that chased us, and I thought of my uncle. I squatted on the hill. I wrapped myself in a blanket to hide from the wind. I looked out into the darkness, waiting for the sun to appear, waiting for the time when I would kill my uncle. It grew very cold, and I remembered many things. My uncle was my father's older brother, and I remembered that when I was young he would sometimes scold my father the way my brother scolded me. I remembered another time when my uncle, my father, my older brother, and I went into town together. It was the first time I could remember going into the town, and it seemed so grand compared to our little village. My uncle scolded my father for buying so much rum and told him that he should also buy something for his sons. My father bought me a yo-yo from a street vendor. It was supposed to light up when you worked it. It never lit up, and I never learned to work it well but still it was like a treasure to me. One half was blue and the other clear. The clear half was supposed to light up. It had a little light bulb in it. My uncle tried to teach me how to work it, but he himself could not remember how the vendor did it. My uncle had large strong hands, but he was clumsy and could never seem to catch the yo-yo when it came back to him.

"I knew I had to kill my uncle.

"My uncle had many children. I grew up playing with my cousins, fighting with them, going to church with them. When I killed their father, they would hate me the way I had hated my uncle those years in the mountains. Perhaps, some day, they would kill me.

"Before dawn, when the sky was gray, I heard the helicopter come. With its machine guns it shot at the hills on the other side of the valley where no one was. I watched the red tracers fly from its machine guns, and it was like watching a machine from another world, a spaceship. I was afraid. If it came to the hill where I was I could do nothing. I didn't have a rifle. My platoon had only three rifles for fourteen of us. I had only a stick like the one I had trained with five years earlier and a machete. What good are those against a spaceship? As it grew lighter I saw a cloud of dust far away where the army trucks approached. I ran down to the village to warn my unit. I took the AK 47 rifle from one of the men and went to my uncle's hut. He was sitting there in his hut in the darkness, waiting, with two of my men there to guard him. I told the men that the army was coming and we had to leave. I ordered the other men out of the hut in a loud voice. I was very angry. When the sunlight came into my uncle's hut, it lit up his face. I looked into my uncle's eyes for a long time. Eyes like my father's eyes. As he looked at me, his eyes grew weak and afraid as my father's eyes must have done when the army took him down to the river to kill him. Neither of us spoke. I could hear the roosters crow, the helicopter far away, a child crying in the next hut.

"I went to say goodbye to my mother, and even though I had a rifle in my hands, I felt like a small boy as she scolded me. I embraced her, and then I ran for the mountains with my men. We fled across the mountains for three days. Sometimes the army was very close, and although we were very cold, we could not make a fire for fear that they would see it. It rained often, especially at night. I didn't sleep those three nights. I was wet and cold. My boots were coming apart. The mud was deep. We lost five men. I don't know if the army caught them or they just got lost. The first day one was gone. The next day two more. We were sad and cold but most of all we were afraid. Often we were angry because we were afraid. I scolded the men for being slow or for getting lost, and they threatened to report me for being a bad leader when we escaped and joined the main group. I couldn't sleep those three nights because I was so cold and wet and because I could not stop thinking. I thought about my father, my uncle, my mother, my family, everyone in the village. I saw them all, over and over again. I was sad because I knew that I had seen them for the last time.

"After three days we were across the mountains. I escaped from my men. I did not go to the guerrilla camp because I knew that they would punish me. I crossed into Mexico and came to the United States."

I walked outside to see Rafael off. The bright sunlight made us blink, made our eyes water. The students passing by seemed unaware of Rafael. He was invisible to them, and yet they gave him a wide berth because he looked and smelled like yet another of the many homeless people who hung out near campus. We shook hands.

"My mother sends me letters," he told me as I held his hand in both of mine, reluctant to let go. "She does not read or write, but every three or four months she goes to the town and pays a man there to write a letter for her. She tells me that she receives the money I send her and that everything is normal there. Her last letter arrived just before I left the Valley, two days ago. My uncle died of the flu in the spring, and the army came and took many men away. No one has heard from them since. They took my older brother."

The White Van

JUAN DOE WAS A TRAFFIC COP in a nice neighborhood in Guatemala. He liked his job. He was a bachelor who lived alone in a poor neighborhood where few people had reliable employment. A traffic cop's salary wasn't much, but it was steady and there were perks. He got to wear a uniform and he got to lord it over his neighbors, buying one a beer, bullying another.

Although he was an avid reader of crime comics and often fantasized about employing his brilliant mind and steely body to capture a master criminal and his gang, in the eight years that he was a cop, Juan neither chased, apprehended, nor arrested anyone, not even a graffiti artist. He stood in the intersection of two busy avenues and a seldom-traveled, narrow street and directed traffic. He was proud of his intersection, feeling that the extra small street added responsibility and prestige to his position. His pride sometimes made him a little arrogant when he cited an illegally parked car or wrote an accident report, and perhaps a little condescending when he gave a lost soul directions to a nearby street or business.

Juan's days were filled with the long commute to his station and from there to his intersection where he stood tall and kingly in the bustling traffic, perhaps trying to suck in his substantial stomach when he'd grown fat. His evenings were filled with beer and rum. His conversations were about football and girls, both from the viewpoint of an observer rather than a player. The civil war and the repression were remote from his life. If people in his barrio or acquaintances he met for a drink in the corner bar had antigovernment opinions, they simply would not talk about such things with Juan Doe, a policeman. Better to talk about safe things, such as football, girls, or the correct interpretation of a dream so that one could pick the winning lottery number.

In his eighth year as a policeman, Juan Doe noticed an attractive woman who passed by his intersection at sunset. He recognized her the next few times she passed by at the same hour, and because she was young and pretty, he began to watch for her. Because he had a trained policeman's mind he soon noticed that she came by on Mondays, Wednesdays, and Fridays. On those days he would look for her lovely figure in the thinning crowd walking out of the setting sun. He would feel good when he caught sight of her, and sometimes, in spite of himself and the stern policeman image he wanted to project, he would smile. Or he would grow angry when some stupid driver snarled traffic and a bus packed with evening commuters blocked his view so that he missed her approach, only noticing her after she had turned the corner and was already disappearing down the darker, emptier street.

Although he never said one word to her, and she did not once so much as nod at him to show that she was aware of his existence, she became a regular part of his life, and he looked forward to her visits to his intersection on Mondays, Wednesdays, and Fridays, the way a house-bound person looks forward to the trash collector's weekly visit, or the way a teenager looks forward to those Saturday night dates with his steady girl.

Sometimes Juan fantasized that instead of turning the corner she would cross the little street and stop at the bustling avenue with the clear intent of crossing so that he could gallantly halt the traffic for her. Often, as she disappeared down the dark street, he would speculate as to what she did and why she passed by on Mondays, Wednesdays, and Fridays only. Did she work at a bank? No, bank employees didn't carry purple day packs as she often did. And too often she wore jeans or slacks. Was she a housewife returning from the market? No, she seldom carried shopping bags, and besides Juan didn't want her to be married. Was she on her way to visit her boyfriend, carrying the ingredients in her pack for the dinner that Juan Doe wished she would fix for him some romantic evening? But then why did she never pass by on Saturdays? Neither did she pass by on El Día de Los Novios, Valentine's Day. Juan Doe eventually realized that she didn't pass by on any holidays. Thinking back over the few times she had missed her regular days, times when he had thought that she might have been sick, Juan decided that they had been holiday absences. So, no, she wasn't on her way to a date. She was a worker like he was, on her way home. But perhaps he had it wrong, backwards. Policemen are trained to look at situations from all angles. Juan prided himself on his acuity and open-mindedness, which on rare occasions had led him to discover who the criminal was in his comic book mysteries. He decided to look at the situation from another angle. Perhaps she was not on her way home from work, but on her way to work when she passed Juan Doe's corner. Perhaps she was a poor woman who lived in a poor neighborhood as Juan Doe did, and she only came to this nice neighborhood to work, as Juan Doe did. Perhaps she was a babysitter or took care of some old person. Juan found that solution to be most satisfactory.

One fine Monday evening as he watched her walk slowly toward him, turn, and disappear into the twilight, he noticed a white van about a half a block behind her. The van crept to the corner, turned, and slowly disappeared into the gloom. Juan would have thought nothing of it except that the van, despite the darkness, had its lights off. Because he was unusually bored after the girl disappeared from view, he idly speculated that she might be the daughter of a rich industrialist or the mistress of a government minister, and guerrillas in the white van were after her, wanted to kidnap her, and hold her for ransom. Perhaps he, Juan Doe, would save her. He tried to suck in his belly at the thought and resolved to be on the lookout for the opportunity to be a hero and win the girl of his dreams.

That idle speculation grew more serious the following Wednesday when he saw the woman pass his corner on schedule, with the white van at a discreet distance behind her, again with its lights off. He yelled at the driver to turn his lights on and quickly signaled the traffic in that direction to stop, but the traffic was heavy at the moment, and his abrupt change of signals only managed to create a bottleneck in the intersection from which the white van easily escaped by turning right. However, because of the van's slow pace he was able to dash his way through the suddenly stopped, honking cars and note the van's license plate number before it disappeared into the gloom behind the girl.

That evening, when he returned to his station, he reported the white van for driving without lights, running a stop sign, reckless driving, and snarling traffic. The sergeant said that they would track down the van and give the driver a citation.

The girl didn't come by the intersection on the following Friday even though it wasn't a holiday. Nor did she come by on Monday. Juan Doe never saw her again although several weeks later he saw photographs of her.

A policewoman investigating the kidnapping, torture, and murder of a female student at the University of San Carlos interrogated Juan Doe at the station house. Witnesses had seen a white van in front of the student's house on a Wednesday night, the last night she was seen alive. One of the witnesses even remembered the last three numbers of the license plate because they were the last three numbers of a lottery ticket he had just bought from a street vendor.

14

He was certain that seeing the numbers on the license plate was a sign that he had the winning number, and even though his number hadn't been among the announced winners he'd kept the ticket, equally certain that a mistake had been made that would soon be corrected.

Those last three numbers matched those of the complete license plate number Juan Doe had reported to his sergeant. Unfortunately, Juan Doe could not give the policewoman any information about the occupants of the van because it had been dark. But no matter. With the complete number they would soon track the van down. The policewoman handed Juan photos, and for the first time he saw the pretty girl close up. Several photos had been taken at home with the family, some at school with her friends, some by herself. She had been very pretty. The last photos had been taken after she had been tortured and killed. They were ugly.

The policewoman and her partner returned to the station several days later to tell Juan that they had linked the white van to several other kidnappings and torture-murders of students and professors at the university. They had traced the white van to the Policía de Hacienda, the Treasury Police. They took Juan Doe to their station where they took a deposition from him.

The case became famous. It was covered by all the newspapers in Guatemala, and the crimes were linked to the highest levels of the Policía de Hacienda. Juan Doe didn't normally read the papers, but he began buying them to look for news about the case he had gotten involved in and also to look for photographs of the pretty girl who had become a part of his life.

Several high officials were charged with the crime, and they swore revenge on everyone who had anything to do with the case. First, the judge who was to hear the case disappeared. Then several of the police investigators were murdered under mysterious circumstances. Then the judge's body was discovered. The last time Juan Doe bought a paper there was a photograph on the front page of the policewoman who had questioned him. She had disappeared a few days earlier, and her body had just been found in the municipal trash dump. Buried inside the newspaper was a small article whose headline caught Juan Doe's nervous eyes: BODY IDENTIFIED BY LOSING LOTTERY TICKET.

Later that same night, while walking home from the neighborhood cantina, Juan Doe was instantly sobered when he looked back and saw a white van suddenly lit up by a street lamp. The white van, with it lights off, discreetly followed him up the street.

Manrico

MANRICO LUNA WAS NOT THE BRAVE HERO of fiction, the mysterious knight who defeated all the other knights in the tourney, then sang his way into the heart of the most beautiful lady in the land. He was neither fearless nor dashing. He didn't even look like a hero. Not at all handsome, his face combined the usual features for an ordinary result. And his body, well! Rather than tall, he was short. Instead of muscular, he tended toward flab. It was all too obvious that he had never in his life popped steroids and pumped iron, for he had a sunken chest, a pot belly, and skinny arms and legs. Due to a lack of martial arts training he was neither agile nor quick.

When young, Manrico and four compañeros, in tight-fitting Mexican costumes, played mariachi music at cheap night clubs in San Salvador. However much Manrico enjoyed the life of the troubadour, he didn't make enough to have the pants and jacket of his costume let out often enough to keep up with his not so gradual expansion into the form of a pear on toothpicks. He finally gave up that troublesome costume when he met his wife, Eleonora. They moved to the town Manrico grew up in, and Manrico got a job driving a truck for the widow Doña Azucena.

Despite Manrico's handicaps in the hero line, he earned the friendship of most people who knew him by simply being a nice guy. He earned the respect of his friends when the civil war broke out in earnest by trucking supplies to displaced people as a volunteer for the Red Cross. Manrico knew that many people who tried to help the poor or worked for organizations like the Red Cross were suspected by the government security forces of being Communists, subversives, and guerrilla collaborators, but he didn't think that he would have any problems because he had always avoided getting mixed up in politics. Anyone in town would vouch for him. Besides, Manrico was a capitalist. He owned two shares of PIROT, a U.S. electronics factory in El Salvador.

News of Manrico's extensive portfolio must have eluded Section Two, the intelligence branch of the army, for they took him from his house one night and installed him in a special building used for interrogating subversives. Eleonora went to the Red Cross, which somehow managed to get Manrico released the next day. Manrico was shaken by the experience. Like everyone in El Salvador, he had heard rumors of the terrible tortures committed by Section Two. When they first began to interrogate him, he had been terrified of what they might do to him. He had almost wished that he knew the names of Communist terrorists in the Red Cross or the location of guerrilla weapons caches so he could tell his interrogators what they were so anxious to learn. But he didn't know and hadn't confessed. Although his captors had taunted him by telling him that he would never leave that place if he didn't tell them what they wanted to know, he was quickly released.

Manrico was fortunate to have been released after only one day, having suffered only a minor beating. When his bruised ribs healed sufficiently, he went back to his truck driving job.

His employer, Doña Azucena, bought produce in the small towns to sell in the cities. Hers was a small operation.

She had one old truck that any number of people would have been glad to drive in that poverty-stricken region. Although she told everyone that the only reason she kept Manrico on was because he knew how to keep the old rattletrap running, she wasn't fooling anybody. She liked Manrico. He was almost like one of her lost sons. Because she liked Manrico, she advised him to stop working for the Red Cross. She even blustered and threatened him, telling him that if he got arrested again, she would fire him because she was just a small businesswoman who couldn't afford to get mixed up in politics. Although Manrico paid no attention to her threat, he did heed her advice, for a while. But long after his bruises healed, his spirit still nagged him. He missed working for the Red Cross. He had enjoyed taking food, water, blankets, medicine, and clothes to those poor refugees who had suffered so much, those sad people whose faces lit up with gratitude when they saw him drive into the camp. The children always surrounded his truck, shouting and laughing, and when he got down from the truck they mobbed him. Those receptions always gave Manrico a warm feeling. He felt that he was doing something important, that he was important. It was something that needed to be done, and if he didn't do it, could he be certain that someone else would? And if Section Two threatened the next volunteer, scared him off, then who would do it?

Manrico Luna was the first to admit that he was a coward. He did not like pain or discomfort. He complained like a child when he had a cold, and he grew weak when he had to miss a meal. And for a month he fussed like a big baby over his bruised ribs. Yet Manrico Luna was that kind of ordinary human being who wanted to keep on doing what was right, no matter how frightened he was. And so he decided to volunteer for the Red Cross once again. He told himself that Section Two had already arrested him, interrogated him, and released him. Now they knew that he was neither a Communist nor a subversive. They would have no reason to arrest him again. They knew that he was merely a simple man delivering food and clothing to displaced people. No one would blame him for that. And if through some error they did arrest him again, he was somewhat confident that the Red Cross would get him out again. And besides, the beating the interrogators gave him hadn't been so bad. He could withstand that much again in the name of a good cause.

The second time was worse. Much worse. The second time they used the capucha and the bucket of sand, while not neglecting, of course, to beat him with fists and rifle butts. They tortured him for ten days, all the while denying to his wife, to the Red Cross, to human rights agencies, to anyone who inquired about him that they had him, even suggesting to his wife that he had run off with another woman, and to the human rights groups that the guerrillas may have kidnapped him.

Manrico had heard of the capucha, but he hadn't had a working intimacy with it until the second time they arrested him. Two men wearing masks so that Manrico wouldn't be able to identify them in the unlikely event that he was re-leased would take Manrico from his cell to the interrogation room. They asked him the same old questions, and when he gave them the same old answers they beat him with their fists. They warned Manrico to tell them what they wanted to know, but he couldn't. He believed their warnings, believed that they would hurt him, but he couldn't tell them where weapons were hidden or that Fulano de Tal was a terrorist and a guerrilla, because he didn't know. That's when they used the capucha.

The capucha is a rubber hood that is slipped over the head. It is tight, so tight that the victim cannot breathe. There is little physical pain, but there is terror.

The interrogators tied Manrico to a chair, which was bolted to the floor to prevent him from 'moving. They slipped the capucha over his head. Manrico could not see. He could not breathe. No matter how much he struggled, he could not suck air into his lungs. The torturers hit him in the head or in his fat, soft body while he struggled to breathe. The blows were frightening because Manrico had no warning when the next one would come. The blows to the head hurt but after a few moments Manrico's attention was so concentrated on his attempts to breathe that he hardly noticed them. The blows to the belly, on the other hand, made him gasp even harder for the breath that would not come. Quickly an overwhelming panic took hold of Manrico. He was terrified that he would never breathe again. When the torturers saw the growing panic in his straining body, they taunted him. They told him that he was going to die. That he had breathed his last breath. They laughed as they taunted him and continued to hit him. There had been moments in Manrico's life when he had thought that he was about to die, times when he had a severe cold, once when he had a bellyache. In those moments he had fantasized that he would meet death calmly, bravely, acceptingly. But tied to that bolted chair, unable to breathe, he was certain that he was about to die, and he could not compose himself. He gasped uncontrollably for air that did not exist. He strained, every muscle in his body taut. He was conscious only of his burning lungs and the rubber mask that prevented him from breathing. He struggled harder and harder as he sensed the end. His body arched, his hands and feet strained against the ropes. He was dying. He lost consciousness.

Moments after they removed the capucha he came to. He gasped. He sucked air into his burning lungs. He panted. He breathed uncontrollably. His torturers laughed at him and showed him the powdered insecticide as they sprinkled it into the capucha. As they slipped the capucha back onto his head the gritty powder dissolved into a sticky paste on Manrico's forehead and cheeks. The sickly smell burned his nose and split lips. He tried to keep his mouth shut. He tried not to inhale. But he knew that it was futile. His only hope was to pass out without attempting to breathe. He tried to remain calm but a punch in the stomach started the uncontrollable gasping. Manrico could no longer control himself. He sucked the disgusting poison into his mouth, his throat, his lungs.

The next day they asked Manrico to sign a confession stating that he was a terrorist guerrilla who delivered weapons and other supplies to the FMLN, and that the Red Cross was a front for the guerrillas. Manrico swore that it wasn't true, that it was a lie. He refused to sign. That's when they began with the sand bucket.

They tied his wrists to a beam above his head. They raised the beam so that Manrico was then suspended a few inches above the floor. As Manrico couldn't grasp the beam with his hands, and as he was fat, his wrists soon began to hurt. They lowered him when he thought he couldn't withstand the pain any longer. The pain was awful but it was nothing compared to what was next. Next they attached one end of a thin cord to his genitals. They tied it tightly to his genitals so that the pain was excruciating but, again, that was nothing. Then they tied the other end to a bucket of sand, which they placed on the floor between his feet. There was no slack in the cord. When they raised the beam, the weight of the sand bucket pulled on Manrico's genitals. Despite the soundproofing in the room, Manrico's screams could be heard by other prisoners in their cells. After a few seconds Manrico passed out from the pain. Then they lowered him. When he came to, they raised him again.

They tortured Manrico for an hour that day. When they finally took him back to his cell he could barely walk. During the next eight days, they alternated between the capucha, the sand bucket, and two days of rest when Manrico did not gain consciousness sufficiently to please his torturers. When he wasn't being tortured, he lay in a ball on the floor of his cell, slipping in and out of consciousness. They gave him no food, but they gave him water twice a day. They often had to kick him into consciousness to get him to drink the water.

On the tenth day, because of pressure from human rights organizations, they released Manrico.

Doña Azucena took him home in her rickety, old truck. Each bump in the road, each bounce of the truck, each too-sharp turn or too-sudden stop sent shocks of pain through Manrico. Doña Azucena and Eleonora helped Manrico into bed, where he stayed for several months before he was able to move about. It took another few months of rest before he was able to drive the truck again. Finally, when he was able to drive without pain, when he felt fully rested and recovered, he went back to work. He did not join the Red Cross again. He was terrified of being picked up and tortured again, but he was also stubborn. Using Doña Azucena's truck he delivered supplies to the refugees as a private citizen rather than a member of the Red Cross, and he made fewer supply runs than before. He hoped that those precautions would be sufficient for him to escape the notice of Section Two. At the same time he was fatalistic. He was certain that one day they would grab him again.

Manrico didn't know why he continued working with the refugees. He was truly terrified, truly afraid that Section Two would kidnap him and torture him again. The torture had been horrible beyond belief, and he did not want to suffer anymore. Manrico wasn't a hero. He was just an ordinary man who looked even less like a movie hero after his recent torture.

One night Manrico heard a strange sound outside his house. Ever since the torture, he had been a fitful sleeper, often waking at the slightest unidentifiable sound. Some nights he could not sleep until nearly dawn. That night Manrico had tossed and turned in bed, unable to sleep. When he first heard the strange sound, he froze. He listened intently. He thought he heard a voice outside in the street, a voice calling him to come out. Or was he dreaming? He woke his wife. She heard the voice, too. He crept to a shuttered window and peered through a crack. In the light of the dim street lamps he made out several uniformed men. Their faces were blackened and they carried rifles. They hid in the shadows. One of them fired his rifle into the air. Manrico knew that sometimes the security forces created a disturbance outside a house to get the occupants to look out to see what was going on. When they saw their targets at a window or a door they would open fire and kill them. Those men were stalking his house, waiting for him to show himself. They had called his name. They had fired

into the air to get him to come to a window. Without stopping to pack money or valuables, Manrico and his wife
slipped out a back window and ran for the trees along the
river. They ran for all they were worth. They ran for their
lives.

Raimundo

ONCE UPON A TIME so long ago that it was hard for him to remember it clearly, in a land so far away that he no longer even dreamed of going back, a boy named Raimundo lived with his family. Raimundo was never lonely because he had many brothers and sisters to play with. He never cried except at funerals or once when he swallowed too much water when he and his brothers were roughhousing in a muddy puddle behind the house. He was never afraid—well, hardly ever, because everyone loved him and the world seemed good. The world seemed so good that he had no reason to be afraid. True, when he was very young he had been afraid of the dark and could not understand why there had to be darkness, but his father took him by the hand one star-spangled evening and pointed out to him the guardians of the night, the many people just like the people from the village who could be found among the stars if you looked hard enough. "See those stars over there, the ones that make a half circle," Raimundo's father said, pointing with a gnarled, calloused finger. "That is the belly of Tío Panzón. He is sitting in the doorway of his house, his hands folded over his enormous belly, his head drooping. You see, he is

25

asleep. But if you are in trouble in the night you need only to shout and Tío Panzón will awaken and he will protect you." Tío Panzón wasn't really Raimundo's uncle. All the children in the village called him Tío Panzón because he was such a comic, comforting character. He often played with the children, his big fat belly bouncing as he ran. When he grew tired he would sit on a chair in the door of his house and sleep.

"And see those stars in a line over there. That is La Flaca." La Flaca, too, was loved by all the children in the village. She was very old and thin, and in the morning she brushed her long gray hair in the sunlight behind her house while she hummed or sang softly to herself. La Flaca was the midwife. She had helped deliver all the babies in the village, and because they lived in a village, where there was no doctor, when the children were sick with the fever or diarrhea, La Flaca would cure them.

"If you look closely enough at the stars," Raimundo's father told him, "you will see all the people of the village. They also live up there in the heavens where they watch over us at night. Look closely. Who else do you see?" Searching for the guardians of the night among the stars became a favorite game of Raimundo's. Together with his father, he traced in the south the figure of his solid older brother, Ángel, with his machete hung from his belt. Low on the horizon they pointed out José, the carpenter, with his hammer raised. They even made out the figure of Father Grande with his big straw sombrero and his peasant's sandals.

Raimundo lost his fear of the dark by playing among the stars. Although he never really saw more than bits and pieces of the guardians in the stars, Ángel's belt, José's hammer, Father Grande's sombrero, he told his father that he saw every detail clearly. Although they agreed that they both saw La Flaca brushing her hair and Father Grande smiling, Raimundo could never quite make those things out. Still, he told his father that he did. Perhaps it was because Raimundo wanted to believe that the guardians were there in the stars and hoped that they would all become clear

when he became a man like his father, or perhaps it was because he loved his father so much that he said he saw them.
Although Raimundo never saw the people of the village in
the stars, he searched the night sky so much that even the
faintest of those lights became his friends.

Raimundo grew up unafraid. He romped in the fields
that surrounded his small village. He splashed and swam in
the pools created by the rain. He played football in the harvested fields. When he grew older he helped cut cane and
pick corn and beans. That was hard work, especially cutting
sugar cane, because it was hot and there were so many in-
sects in the dense, tall cane, and the sharp leaves of the
cane cut his hands. But his father and older brothers were
with him and they helped him. Sometimes they talked about
football games they would play on Sunday after mass. Sometimes they would talk about Father Grande. Sometimes Raimundo's father would tell them a story.

Raimundo's father was named Isaías. He was a religious
man. He was a humble farmer who rented a few manzanas
of land where he grew vegetables to feed the family and a
few cash crops to buy essentials. He also worked on the
large plantations with his sons during the busy seasons.
Although Isaías had been working since he was a young
boy, he had managed to squeeze in a few years of schooling.
Because he was kind and wise, he was a leader in the village.
Because he could read and write, he became a lay preacher.
As there were not enough priests for all the people in
all the villages, men like Isaías would read from the Bible
and lead discussions among the people. They talked about
the meaning of a particular passage in terms of their own
lives rather than in terms of a people who lived long ago
and far away. That was what Father Grande did in every
village he went to, and that was what he encouraged the
catechists to do. Until Father Grande taught them to think
of the Bible in terms of their own daily lives, they had
thought of God as a patron of a large plantation or the
comandante in the cartel. But Father Grande taught them
that God was of the people, even the poor people.

At home Isaías often remarked on how wise the people were if once they got to thinking. And he often talked about the passages he had selected for discussion. But try has he might, Raimundo, as he sat on the hillside at night looking at the familiar friendly stars, could not remember the words. He could clearly picture his mother as she washed and ironed his father's only white shirt before each Bible study session. He could clearly picture his father as he carefully shaved or trimmed his graying mustache. He could clearly picture his father, when at last he was ready, putting on that sparkling white shirt. That shirt was so clean it seemed to shine with its own bright light as Isaías stood at the head of the congregation and read in his gentle voice. Sometimes Raimundo was certain that his father, in his bright white shirt, was up there among the bright stars of the Milky Way, his Bible in his hand. But he could never completely make him out.

Raimundo tried to form the Big Dipper into Father Grande's sombrero, and below the Big Dipper he tried to find the sandals where, as a child, he had told his father that he had seen them, floating above the horizon. Many long nights during the dry seasons in the mountains, Raimundo gazed at the stars and remembered his childhood. How happy the family had been when Father Grande stayed with them, sleeping on a straw mat on the dirt floor of their house. The one thing that Raimundo remembered his father saying was, "It is a curious thing that the government says that the bishop of the neighboring see is a saint because he lives in a big, fine house with servants and from time to time donates a few beans and corn to the hungry, but Father Grande, who lives among us, and sleeps in our humble houses, and works with us in the fields, and teaches us to think, and teaches us that we should try to improve our lives here on Earth, and teaches us that we are as loved by God as a rich person, him the government calls a Communist and a subversive."

The first time in Raimundo's young life that he went to San Salvador was for Father Grande's funeral mass. It was the only mass celebrated that Sunday in all of El Salvador.

Raimundo and his family were among the 100,000 people who crowded into the plaza outside the packed cathedral where Archbishop Romero gave the mass. During the mass Raimundo could not stop the tears that coursed down his cheeks. He was sad that they had murdered Father Grande, and at the same time he was proud to be there in the capital, in the plaza, with so many people. He felt that he was taking part in a historic event and that his small presence in some small way added to the significance of the event, almost as if the event would not have occurred if he weren't standing in the crowd, craning to catch a glimpse of the cathedral over the sea of shoulders and heads. The proud feeling that his participation was a necessary ingredient to history was perhaps a natural feeling, one that he would lose through the years.

During the dry season with so many stars in the sky, so many old friends, Raimundo found peace as he sat on the hillside and remembered. But when the stars were blotted out by black clouds, he could not lose himself in pleasant memories of his childhood, of his gentle father, his hardworking, proud mother, his brothers and sisters, and all the people in the village.

Dark, starless nights did not distract him from the unwanted memories. He remembered that hot, sunny day when he was in the field behind the house and shots rang out. He and his brothers hid for many hours until long after the shooting stopped. When they finally returned to the house, they found their father's body, but their mother and three sisters had disappeared. There were many dead and disappeared in the village. The fat body of Tío Panzón lay in the doorway of his house beside the chair in which he often napped. La Flaca had disappeared. Many of the women in the village had disappeared, never to be seen again. Several people in the village who had hidden themselves witnessed what had happened. The army had come, they told the other survivors, in many trucks. They searched all the houses. They shot many men and carried off women and children in the trucks. Raimundo and all the survivors were stunned and terrified. Why, they asked themselves, had the army done this? Father Grande had taught them to ask why, and later that summer they learned that the army had invaded many villages and killed many people. The army called it Operation Rutilio Grande. They killed not only lay preachers but even people whose only crime was to have a photograph of Father Grande on the walls of their houses. That summer flyers circulated through El Salvador that said, "BE A PATRIOT! KILL A PRIEST!"

Raimundo tried not to think of those things as he sat on the hillside through the long night. But it was impossible to shut out all the memories. Sometimes on starless nights they slipped through his defenses. Sometimes he felt like an old man although he was only twenty-five years old. The years had been long because they had been filled with fear and death and war. There had been three brief years of love, ecstatic years, but his compañera had been killed in battle. There had been many deaths. Of his large family, Raimundo was the only one left. After Operation Rutilio Grande, Raimundo and his brothers had fled to the mountains. They joined the guerrillas. Raimundo was fourteen at the time. He became a messenger for the guerrillas. His older brothers were trained as fighters. Raimundo had been proud to be a guerrilla fighting to avenge his father, his mother, his sisters, Father Grande, Archbishop Romero, and everyone in the village. He felt that his presence and the presence of his brothers meant that the guerrillas could not lose. So many times he had thought that the war would soon be over. So many times he had been disappointed. So many people had died. One by one his brothers had been killed, some horribly, some quickly. Since his compañera's death Raimundo had not stopped thinking about death. He felt old and wasted and did not think he could withstand more pain. There was no more pride left, only mourning.

Once upon a time so long ago that he could barely remember it, in a village so far away that he no longer even dreamed of going back, a boy named Raimundo had a happy childhood. He had lived without fear. Life had been an endless summer day. Oropéndolas sang and yellow butterflies danced in the breeze. The rains cooled the hot afternoons and the children splashed in the pools. At night the fireflies rose from the earth to mingle with the stars. Raimundo knew that he could never recapture that en - chanted childhood for himself, but he wanted his daughter to have it. Ever since he had stolen into Aguilares to see her on her second birthday he had thought about taking her away from the war and the death. The guerrillas no longer trusted him. He had been an officer and had led men and women in many battles. He had been liked and admired by everyone. Since his wife died and that awful black cloud sur - rounded him, no one liked him, no one trusted him. He was alone. He was on a government death list and the guerrillas were watching him. He had been in combat for eleven years, and now all he did was sit on the hillside at night. Perhaps they thought that guard duty would restore him, give him back the belief that his presence meant something. But it didn't. There was too much time to think, too much time to remember.

Once upon a night on a faraway starlit hill, Raimundo de - cided to desert the guerrillas. He would ask permission to see his daughter, and he would take her north where she could have an enchanted childhood.

Timoteo

TIMOTEO'S FATHER, LUIS EMILIO, was a union man. That may not seem like such an important fact in late twentieth-century North America, but it was of life-shattering importance in feudal Guatemala.

Luis Emilio was not always a union man. He had grown up a poor Cakchiquel Indian from the mountains above Lake Atitlán. As a young man he moved to Guatemala City and landed a series of jobs in various factories. Each job was an improvement over the last one until he fulfilled his ambition and became a machine operator. His first experience with a union was at a factory that made car batteries. The supervisor and owner of that plant warned Luis Emilio that there was a union and if he joined it they would fire him. But if he didn't join, he would receive benefits that the union workers didn't, such as four paid holidays a year. Only about half the workers at that factory were union members, and they had the most poorly paid jobs.

Luis Emilio worked at the factory two years before he decided to join the union. He did not want to join or even listen to the union organizers at first because he thought that unions, while not quite evil, were bad. They had something to do with communism, about which he had a hazy notion, and, most importantly, they got workers into trouble. Luis didn't want trouble. All he wanted was to work in order to support his wife and small son, Timoteo.

Luis was young and strong and perhaps more than a little cocky as only the young and the strong can be. An excellent worker, he was confident that he could do any job in the factory, and, if the union let him alone and the bosses let him work, he could earn enough to support himself and his family. Life was that simple.

The union members talked to Luis. They gave him flyers. They invited him to meetings. Luis didn't listen, didn't read the flyers, and didn't attend even one meeting. He resisted the union organizers for two years and was rewarded by several small pay raises, which the union workers did not enjoy. Luis knew that there were problems in the country, but he, a poor, uneducated man, could do nothing about that. And even though there were problems there was still opportunity if a man was willing to work hard. Luis worked hard, hoping that life would be better for Timoteo. For two years Luis did not waver from his philosophy of rugged individualism, not until an accident occurred on the night shift.

There were only two shifts in the factory, each twelve hours long. Luis did not like to work the night shift, but like everyone in the factory, he had to work it in three-month cycles. One night at about three in the morning, through carelessness or inattention or exhaustion, one of the workers lost a hand in one of the machines. No one knew what to do. There was no doctor or nurse at the factory. There wasn't even a first-aid kit. Some of the workers searched the neighborhood for a doctor, and when they found one he refused to go to the factory at that hour. The workers had to take the injured man to the doctor.

The immediate consequences of that accident were that all the workers were docked half a night's pay because of lost production time and the one-handed man found himself without a job. The long-term consequence for Luis was that he opened his eyes. He realized that due to one second's inattention in a long twelve-hour shift, he could easily become an unemployed, one-handed man. That realization made him look at the working conditions. What he saw both frightened and shocked him. Luis noted that many of the more experienced machine operators were hard of hearing, and young, strong, fearless Luis bought himself a pair of earplugs on the advice of the union members. He saw that middle-aged men who had worked in the factory for a long time looked like very old men. Their skin was gray. Their teeth had fallen out. Their bones were brittle. Their internal organs functioned as if they were 100 years old. Union members informed him that those were the results of lead poisoning. Luis noted that many of the welders had vision impairment. Union members said that the company only provided the welders with cheap sunglasses to use when they should have provided safety goggles. Luis noted that when a man was injured or became so ill that he could no longer work, he was fired. There were no benefits, no compensation, no sick pay. The man was simply fired. The retirement plan was simple. Each worker had to set aside money for his own early retirement. All retirements were early because nobody lasted more than thirty years at the factory because of lead poisoning. And it was nearly impossible to set aside money on a maximum salary of $150 a month.

The union wanted the workers to organize so they could demand that the lead pollution be cleaned up, that the company buy ear plugs and safety goggles, that the work shift be cut to ten hours, and that the workers be given paid holidays and medical care for job-related illnesses or injuries. As Luis didn't see how the national security would be endangered if those goals were met, he talked it over with his wife and decided to become a union man.

A few nights after he told the union officers that he would join, he accepted a ride home with the secretary and the treasurer of the union. Luis's newfound solidarity made him feel good about the future. Soon, he thought, they would all get raises, and he would be able to buy an old car like the secretary's. As they drove down a dark street a car passed them and cut them off, forcing them to a halt on the sidewalk. Four big men in guayabera shirts and sunglasses got out of the Chevy Blazer that had cut them off. They had Uzi machine guns. They made Luis and his companions lean against their car while they searched them. They took their identity documents as well as their wallets. Fortunately for Luis, the union, like most unions in Guatemala, knew better than to issue membership cards for people to carry. Unfortunately for the secretary and the treasurer, they had participated in negotiations, and their names had made it onto a death list. Since the men in the guayaberas and sunglasses weren't certain that Luis was a union man, they merely beat him with their fists and only hit him once with the barrel of a gun. They asked him if he was a union member. He said no. They hit him some more and asked him if he were sure. He said, "No. I mean, yes, I'm sure. I'm not a union member." When they were finally satisfied they turned their attention to the union officers, whom they beat savagely. Luis watched from his position on the ground, his arms over his head. The force of some of the blows made Luis wince. The sickening sounds, the fear, and his own sore stomach made him throw up. Finally the men forced the union members into their car and, kicking Luis once in the ribs to be sure they had his attention, they told him that they were going to investigate, and if they found out that he had anything to do with the union they would come after him. They told him that if he said anything to anybody about the incident they would kill him.

Luis was too terrified to tell anyone. When his wife asked him what had happened, why the right side of his face and his right ear were swollen, his lip split, his nose smashed, his forehead gashed, and his ribs bruised, he told her not to ask questions. At work he told people that he had gotten into a fight in a bar. As the days went by and the missing union members didn't appear, he grieved for their families, but he still said nothing. He avoided his co-workers. The only time he associated with them was at quitting time when he always made certain that he was in the center of a group of men when they walked to the bus stop. Two weeks after the incident, when the bodies of the missing men were found by homeless children who scavenged at the municipal garbage dump, Luis began looking for another job. He felt as if he had escaped from a concentration camp when he landed a job at a flour mill, a subsidiary of Gold Medal Flour.

Luis worked at the mill a number of years. His son Timoteo grew. The country seemed to be changing. The first civilian in anyone's memory was elected president. The new president, keeping one of his campaign promises, disbanded the DIT, the secret police, whom Luis thought responsible for his beating and the disappearance and murder of his co-workers. Although Luis still had nightmares about the incident, in his waking moments he began to feel safer. And when the new president stated that he would do everything in his power to stop the repression and even went so far as to state that workers had the right to organize and form unions, Luis believed him. He joined the union at the flour mill.

He joined the union because, although conditions were better at the flour mill than at the battery factory, there were still problems. When the union organizers talked to Luis, they were not pouring soup into an empty pot. All along he had wanted to join the union, but he had been afraid. He was still afraid but he joined anyway.

The union members were threatened and there were a few beatings, but no one was seriously hurt, and no one was disappeared or murdered. There were some difficult negotiations and a strike. Tens of thousands of workers paraded on May Day, International Workers Day. It was an impressive display. The strike was settled, and Luis's union, along with a few others in the capital, won some of their demands. Luis thought unions were the wave of the future. Everyone seemed content except for a few factory owners who shut down their factories, locking out union and nonunion workers alike, and moved their operations to Indonesia where the government knew how to handle unions. Still, things were looking up, no doubt about it. To the working stiff it appeared that Guatemala was taking its first tentative steps into the twentieth century.

Luis began to feel secure as a union man. The union demanded better ventilation so the workers wouldn't die young of lung disease caused by all the flour and chaff in the air, and they won. They demanded a well-stocked first-aid kit and they got one. They demanded certain safety features on the machinery and got some of them. As the union improved working conditions in the flour mill, Luis became a committed activist. He saw that individually or in small groups the workers were powerless, but together they were strong. It was like the Cakchiquel saying he had heard in his youth but had paid little attention to: many small sticks make an unbreakable bundle. With the zeal of a recent convert he repeated that amusing little phrase until everyone was sick of it. Despite the fact that many workers wanted to try breaking a bundle of sticks over Luis's head, they nominated and elected him secretary of the union. His duties included keeping membership lists—the members still didn't feel safe enough to carry cards—recording complaints, and being a member of the negotiating committee.

Negotiations on the new contract that year were acrimonious. When the secretary general of the union was run over and killed while walking home late one night, everyone became nervous. Although the car was never found, and there were no witnesses, the union members suspected a death squad. When Luis found a death threat slipped under his door, he moved his family to another apartment. He did not go out at night. He did not go out alone during the day. He made Timoteo go straight home after school and would not permit him to go out to play. A month later when the new contract had been signed and Luis began to relax, he received another death threat at his new apartment. Then the assistant secretary general and a rank-and-file union member, on their way home from a bar, were shot and killed in the street.

Luis left his job and fled the city. He moved his family to Cakchiquel country. He rented a small plot of land, where he grew corn, beans, and potatoes. Young Timoteo, then thirteen years old, worked beside Luis in the fields. Father and son had never been closer. They made a game of work. When they were weeding, they raced to see who would finish their row first. When they worked on a nearby plantation for extra money, Timoteo earned as much as his father, who allowed him to keep some of his earnings to spend on himself. Luis, who had grown up in the country, was happy to be back working the land. As they worked alongside each other in the fields Luis told Timoteo many things. He explained to his young son that although factory work pays better, it is not a good life, shut up inside a dirty, noisy building, doing the same thing minute after minute, hundreds of times an hour, thousands of times a day, millions of times a year until suddenly one dies young from the contamination and the monotony. Or one looses a hand or grows blind or deaf. It is not right to be a slave to a factory owner. It is stupid to be loyal to the owners, who, when a worker is no longer useful, will not hesitate to throw him away like trash. No, it is better to work on the land, to be outside where one can see the progress of the sun and the plants.

Luis told Timoteo about the time the worker lost his hand and the factory owner fired him. He told him about the death squad that beat him up and killed the two union officers, tossing their bodies in the municipal garbage dump. He told him about the small changes in Guatemalan society and his history at the flour mill. Talking of these things made Luis sad because he felt that he had deserted a cause he believed in. He felt that he had failed. But he was afraid. Because the death squad took his identity document that time they beat him up and because he became a union officer at the flour mill, they would think that he was a lifelong union activist. They had killed two union officials at the flour mill. They would surely have killed him had he stayed. Although things seemed to have improved in Guatemala, there was still great danger, and he did not want to die young. He wanted to live to watch his son grow up, and his daughter, he added, for his wife was seven months pregnant with, he hoped, a girl.

39

Late one night after the family had gone to bed, some-one knocked on the door. Although he had awakened from a deep sleep, Luis knew immediately that they had come for him. He told his wife to do nothing. He crept to a shuttered window and looked out through a crack. He saw several dark figures waiting outside the door and, parked down the dusty dirt road, a four-wheel-drive wagon, a death squad car. The family didn't answer the repeated knock on the door. They didn't make a sound. They didn't turn on a light. They hoped that the men would think they were not at home. They knocked louder. Dogs began barking at neigh-bors' houses. Lights were lit. Finally, the men went away.

Luis did not sleep that night. After that night he stopped sleeping at home. He slept at a neighbor's house, hoping against hope that the men would give up after a while. He told his wife that if the men came back she was not to open the door, but was to tell the men that he had fled, that he had left the country.

Luis's plan was to flee the country after the harvest was in and after his wife gave birth. He needed the money he would make selling his crops for the journey north. More importantly, he could not leave until he knew that his wife and new daughter were healthy and sound.

A month later the men came again. When Timoteo's mother told the men that Luis had fled, they forced the door open and searched the house. They slapped her and yelled at her. She was eight months pregnant and her bal-ance was not very good. She nearly fell when they slapped her. Timoteo ran to his mother to hold her, to protect her. One of the men punched him, nearly knocking him out. They told her she had better tell them where Luis was. If she told them they would leave her alone. She told them that she didn't know. They dragged her outside. Timoteo lay on the cold floor, listening to the angry shouts of the men, to his mother's cries. He cried uncontrollably. He felt sorry for his mother, felt sorry for himself, felt ashamed of himself, a thirteen-year-old who couldn't defend his own mother.

When at last he heard the car doors slam and the car drive away, he ran outside to his mother. She had been badly beaten but was still conscious. She told Timoteo to run and get Luis.

Luis, Timoteo, and a neighbor took the hemorrhaging woman to the hospital. Early in the morning she and the baby died.

Luis no longer wanted to live. He didn't care if the death squads grabbed him. He felt weighed down by an enormous burden of guilt. He should have stayed at the factory, fighting for what was right. He should have continued to sleep at home. He should have let the death squad find him. They would have taken him and let his wife alone. She would still be alive and would have given birth to a healthy daughter. He should have died instead of them. It was his fault that they died. Everything was his fault. He merely went through the motions of living for Timoteo's sake. He moved back into the house in the hope that they would come for him.

Soon the crops began to ripen and he and Timoteo began their sad harvest. Late one night the death squad came for him. He didn't struggle as they dragged him outside the house and shot him.

Timoteo finished the harvest and sold the crops. He was cheated because he was young and an orphan, but with the little money he had he started north. He had just turned fourteen when he started. The journey to the U.S. frontier took three years as he had to work along the way. He celebrated his seventeenth birthday in ECI, the INS detention center for minors. He is a sad boy who works and studies hard to make a life for himself. His eyes only spark with excitement when someone tells him some anecdote about their own mother or father.

Faustino

FAUSTINO WAS A DRIVER by profession. He worked very hard and soon owned his own cab and then another, and then he branched out into buses, eventually owning three tired, old Chevy Blue Birds. Life was good to Faustino. He expanded his transportation empire as well as his waistline, and his children were little images of him. What more could he ask in life? If he had any regrets, it was that he was no longer the muscular, hard-as-nails young man he was when he had been drafted into the army and risen to the rank of sergeant. That had been many years ago, but Faustino remembered those days with warmth and pride. To help maintain the illusion that he was still the same man, he ran his household and his business along military lines, and he stayed in touch with some of his old pals who were still on active duty.

One Saturday night before they got drunk those old pals told him that Guatemala and the army needed him, that there was a shortage of good drivers, that if he, Faustino, helped them out once or twice a month his beloved country would be grateful. And, perhaps, if the opportunity arose, which it sometimes did in regards to licenses or routes or protection, his patriotism would be rewarded. Of course Faustino accepted. To celebrate, the beers were on him. Faustino was deliriously happy that night, and even in the morning, despite the hangover, he was glad. He was glad to be of service for he truly loved his country, and, truly, it couldn't hurt to help out your friends in high places.

Thus Faustino became a military commissioner. He would go to meetings with other military commissioners and about once a month he drove for the army. Several days before the army needed him, they would send a jeep with two soldiers to his house to tell him when and where to report.

Sometimes, usually on Sundays, he went on recruiting missions. Recruiting meant that Faustino would drive a truck with a few soldiers through a village, and when they spotted a likely young man, Faustino would stop the truck, and the soldiers would chase the future recruit. Faustino excelled at those missions as he began to develop a sixth sense for finding the soccer fields in unknown villages, which proved to be the best hunting grounds. Grabbing young men off the street did not bother Faustino's conscience. After all, he had served in the military and it hadn't hurt him. On the contrary, it had made a man out of him. Looking back wistfully on those days, which Faustino often did, he thought that they were the best days of his life.

Sometimes Faustino drove soldiers on training exercises. That was often boring unless there was target practice and they gave Faustino a rifle to shoot. He enjoyed that. The recruits were often terrible shots, and he would show them what a man could do.

After a few years of being a military commissioner, Faustino went on his first combat mission. Well, not exactly combat for Faustino. He drove a truckload of soldiers on a mission to look for guerrillas. He parked the truck on a lonely dirt road a few kilometers outside a small town. The soldiers went off to look for guerrillas, and he remained in the truck. He was a little nervous, he had to admit to himself. After all they were looking for guerrillas, and what if the guerrillas found him? But they didn't, and he went on a few more of those missions. Sometimes there were other truck drivers, and they would have a smoke together while they waited for the soldiers to return. Sometimes he was by himself as the other drivers parked on other roads leading into the town. Sometimes there was a battle.

That type of mission didn't bother Faustino's conscience either, but it made him think and thinking bothered him because, although he had many bad habits, he had never acquired that particular one.

He thought it strange that the battles took place in small towns. He had assumed that the guerrillas had camps in the mountains. Stranger still was the fact that within an hour of hearing the gunfire the soldiers would appear, double-timing in formation, retreating back to the truck. The first few times that happened he was contemptuous of the soldiers. He thought they were cowards or poorly trained young boys who ran at the first sign of a battle. That's why they couldn't defeat the guerrillas. In his day they wouldn't have run as soon as they heard shots. They would have fought it out to the last man. Why, none of these young boys was even wounded. The officers who rode in the front of the truck with Faustino were uncommunicative, even surly. At first Faustino attributed their moodiness to the fact that their troops hadn't performed well. Then he noticed a certain smugness in the officers. They were surly, sure, but they seemed pleased with the operation. How could that be if all the soldiers ran back toward the trucks as soon as the battle broke out?

Thinking was definitely bad for Faustino, and he had too much time to think on those missions while he waited for the soldiers. Why did the soldiers always retreat toward the trucks and then back to the base? Maybe they were cowards and poorly trained, little more than boys with rifles, but that didn't explain why they didn't call for reinforcements once they had fallen back to the trucks. It was an age of radios and helicopters, wasn't it? And why were the officers so pleased when they should have been outraged at the shameful conduct of their troops? Or was it that the soldiers had won the battles? But if that were so, they wouldn't come hightailing it back to the trucks. They would chase the enemy. Or there would be prisoners or at least bodies. And why didn't they call in the reporters and photographers to gloat a little? Show them the prisoners and the bodies? It was an age when battles were fought in the newspapers and television as well as on the ground, wasn't it? Faustino would have liked to be interviewed. His sons could then appreciate what a hero their father was.

And Faustino couldn't get over the fact that the guerrillas always seemed to be in some small, isolated village. That was strange.

These things bothered Faustino, but there was no one he could talk to about them. He was afraid to ask questions or express doubts. His fear surprised him and made him think even more. Thinking about it, he discovered that he was afraid because he had heard rumors about other military commissioners who, for some reason or other, became suspect, whose loyalty was doubted. They had disappeared, their bodies appearing shortly afterwards, dumped by the side of a road, often showing signs of torture. Faustino was afraid that if he asked questions he would become suspect, his loyalty doubted, and he might end up like those others. The safest course was to do what a good soldier was trained to do—obey orders and keep his mouth shut. He kept his mouth shut, but he continued to think.

Thinking about it unsettled Faustino. He began to doubt his most fundamental beliefs. He was on the army's side. He supported them. He worked for them. They were the good guys. Right? Why then was he afraid of them? Good guys don't go out and grab innocent people, torture them, murder them, mutilate their bodies, and dump them beside a public road as a warning to the people. Those who ended up tossed beside the road, they must have done something to deserve their fate, whereas he, Faustino, was innocent. He was loyal. He did what his country asked of him. Nothing like that would happen to him. He had nothing to fear. Still, he was afraid.

The mission to El Plátano was like other missions, per-haps bigger. Faustino and several other drivers dropped their truckloads of soldiers off on a dirt road about two kilometers outside the sleepy town. Faustino had never heard of El Plátano before and soon had reason to wish he had never heard of it at all. The soldiers went off to battle guerrillas. There was gunfire, a great deal of it, for fifteen minutes, and soon the soldiers appeared double-timing it back to the trucks. The officers ordered the drivers to re-turn to the base.

What was different about that mission was that it was re-ported in the press. The day after the mission, the first news leaked out. There were stories about a massacre in El Plátano and rumors of a mass burial in a clandestine grave. At first government and military spokespersons denied that there was a massacre. Even a man from the United States Department of State said that there had not been a mas-sacre. He added with great indignation that the rumors were part of a Communist guerrilla campaign to upset rela-tions between the United States and Guatemala. That seemed to settle it for most people until the surviving citi-zens of El Plátano dug up their dead from the mass grave and gave them proper burials in the town cemetery. The in-ternational press attended the funeral ceremonies. Soon the papers were full of photographs of the victims and in-terviews with relatives and neighbors. Government spokes-persons still denied that there had been a massacre but added that if there had been one, the guerrillas had done it. A military spokesperson cleared matters up considerably when he said that the victims were guerrillas who had been killed in battle. The guerrillas had ambushed an army unit which, against all odds, prevailed against the Communist aggressors, thus writing another chapter in the glorious his-tory of the Guatemalan armed forces. Later both sources admitted that there might have been a massacre in the town of El Plátano, but they had reliable information that proved conclusively that guerrilla forces, disguising themselves in uniforms of the Guatemalan army, had committed the mas-sacre to smear the honor of the armed forces. The honorable armed forces swore that they would not rest until they had brought to justice the perpetrators of that alleged atrocity.

Faustino was not a stupid man. He knew that he couldn't believe everything he read in the papers. But he studied the photos of the El Plátano victims and read the interviews. And he thought. While his native cynicism and mistrust of the news media prevented him from being 100 percent certain that a massacre had occurred, his new habit of thinking made him certain of one thing—if a massacre had occurred, he had seen the people who had done it double-timing back to the trucks afterward. Perhaps the sullen lieutenant who had ridden beside him in the truck had given the orders to round up the people, take them out of town, make them dig their own mass grave, and shoot them. Perhaps the men in the back of the truck had fired the shots. And he, Faustino, had taken them to the massacre and, afterwards, back to the barracks.

"Until the next mission," the grinning sergeant had told Faustino as he left the barracks to drink a beer with his buddies. Faustino always drank at least one beer after a mission. Faustino rightly felt that his patriotic service entitled him to a little celebration. Until the next mission.

The next mission would be the same. All the missions were the same. There hadn't been any battle with guerrillas. The soldiers had gone into the little towns and rounded up the men whose names were on a list and shot them. And not just men. Sometimes whole families. The newspapers said that women had been killed at El Plátano. Grandmothers. Little children. Perhaps the women had collaborated with the guerrillas. Maybe they deserved to die. But children?

Faustino thought about those children a great deal. Not that he felt sorry for them. They were abstractions, pieces of a puzzle, clues in his search for truth. And the truth was that Faustino began to feel so sorry for himself that he had little pity left over for the victims. He was too worried about his own part in what had happened and what would happen next to feel sorry for the dead.

Faustino was sorry that he had ever been in the army, that he had friends in the army, that he worked for the army. Why had he ever agreed to work for the army? He didn't need the money. It didn't pay that much. It wasn't worth the worry. He was reluctant to admit that one of the reasons he had agreed to work for the army was because he thought that it might help him, that there might come a day when his growing business empire would need the right contacts. He regretted his decision.

But he was afraid to quit. He was afraid of what would happen next.

Next came a report that the family in charge of the El Plátano cemetery had been forced to flee. They had received death threats because they had permitted the victims to be buried in the cemetery. Next, the body of the reporter who wrote the story about the family who ran the cemetery was found in the municipal trash dump. Suddenly the news about El Plátano disappeared from the newspapers. Nothing about it was heard on the radio nor seen on the television. The president of the United States was happy to report to Congress that the human rights situation was improving in Guatemala, particularly in regards to freedom of the press. There was no censorship in Guatemala. Everything returned to normal.

Faustino, however, did not return to normal. He could not stop thinking. His world had been turned upside down. Things were not as he had thought, but he could not quite figure out how they really were. He thought about the missions he had carried troops on. He thought about the people who had been killed. He thought about his part in it all, his guilt. He had long arguments with himself about his guilt and in the end succeeded in denying that he was the least bit guilty. He was completely innocent. He was innocent because he hadn't known. He had believed that the army was fighting guerrillas, guerrillas who wanted to destroy his beloved country. He had believed in their cause. He had believed that the army was the good guys. They always were the good guys. Sure, there had been some things he hadn't liked when he had served in the army, now that he thought about it. The corporals and sergeants used to beat up the weaker recruits. But that was to make men out of them. The weaker and slower recruits were Indians, and the officers had to beat them up. It was difficult with Indians because they wanted to stick to their old ways, and the officers had to use force to mold them into soldiers for the good of the country. Faustino remembered the time that one kid died. The corporal said that the kid must have had a weak chest, because he hadn't hit him that hard with the butt of his M-14 rifle. But the corporal had hit him a lot. And the mutilated bodies that appeared in the trash dumps or the ravines or beside the roads. He had heard rumors that the death squads were composed of soldiers who went out at night in civilian clothes. The government always said that the mutilated corpses were of criminals killed by other criminals, or innocent people tortured and killed by the guerrillas, or former guerrilla sympathizers who tried to escape from the guerrillas.

Faustino no longer believed his own government. Had he ever? He searched himself deeply and decided, or rather admitted, that a part of him had always believed that his beloved army, his beloved government, had committed many of those atrocities. That was why he was afraid to ask questions about the mission. That was why he was afraid to talk politics. He had always said that he was bored by politics, but afraid was the correct word. That was why he had been afraid to criticize the soldiers when he thought they were cowards running at the first sign of a battle. That was why he was afraid to let his children join student organizations run by hippie agitators. That was why he was afraid to let his wife go to neighborhood meetings organized by some damn social worker. He was afraid.

He was afraid that if he or his family did anything that the armed forces or the government didn't like, he would end up on one of those death lists he had always claimed didn't exist. He was afraid. He had always been afraid. How could he have fooled himself? Of course he had believed death lists existed. Why else had he, a big, strong, aggressive—all right, arrogant—man, a man's man, a man who had risen from the ranks in a tough army, a man who had worked hard and built his own company, a leader of men, why else had he been afraid to ask questions of the sullen officers who sat beside him in his truck? He was afraid to step out of line.

These thoughts shocked Faustino. They shocked him profoundly. But what shocked him most of all was the inevitable conclusion of his new thinking. For once he began thinking, once he found the precise explanation for so many previously blurred events, once he turned the kaleidoscope of his world view and saw all the pieces fall into place, his newly awakened brain could not stop thinking until he arrived at a conclusion. That logical, stunning conclusion was that he could excuse himself of any wrongdoing. He could deny any guilt. He could claim that he was completely innocent. He could limp along on that old reliable crutch—ignorance. He could say he hadn't known. He hadn't realized. Perhaps deep down he had suspected, but he hadn't really known. Not really. If he was guilty of anything, it was blindness. Okay, perhaps arrogance too. He was guilty of being smug about everything, of being a know-it-all, when, really, he had been a fool. But all that was in the past. Now that he was thinking clearly for the first time in his life, he thought about the future. That was the shocker. That was where the awful conclusion lay. Now he knew. And knowing, if he went on another mission, if he took soldiers to another so-called battle, he would no longer be innocent. If he drove soldiers on a mission knowing that they were capable of killing infants, children, grandmothers, then he would be as guilty as if he had given the order to line them up and shoot them, as if he had pulled the trigger.

Well, maybe not quite that guilty. Perhaps he was exaggerating. Still, he would be guilty.

And—he had to light a cigarette and pour another glass of rum with trembling hands before he could finish this thought—he couldn't tell them no. If he told them he didn't want to go on any more missions, they would suspect him of . . . of what? Being a traitor? Or someone who had changed his mind? Someone who knew too much? He knew how they

51

thought. They wouldn't let him quit. Anybody who quit was the enemy. If they ever had reason to believe that they could no longer trust him, that he might talk, they wouldn't hesitate to kill him. Those other civilians who worked for the army and were killed, perhaps they had simply wanted to quit. How could he quit? How could he stop going on missions? How could he stop participating in massacres? Maybe if he had an accident? Maybe if he broke a leg so that he couldn't drive? That might get him off for a while, but broken legs heal in a few months. Then what? He could move to a different part of the country, but they would find him. They knew what he looked like. All those meetings with the other military commissioners. They didn't do anything at those meetings except socialize. The only purpose of those meetings was for the commissioners to get to know each other. They got to know what each other looked like so that they could recognize any commissioner who tried to run away.

They would find him. It was the age of computers, wasn't it? They had his cédula number, his age, height, weight. They knew how many were in his family, their names and ages. They knew all about him. And what about his business? He had worked so hard to build up his business. What about his nice house he had bought on a quiet, dead-end street? If he ran away he would lose everything.

Faustino felt that his whole life was slipping away, that whatever control he had thought he had over events was completely gone. He was on the edge of a great, dark abyss and he couldn't retreat. He was afraid to go forward. He wanted to stay where he was, not move, not do anything.

He stopped reading the newspapers. He stopped watching TV. He stopped yelling at his employees. He stopped giving orders to his wife. He stopped overindulging his fat little boys. He had no appetite. He couldn't sleep at night. When he did sleep, he had horrible nightmares. Sometimes he dreamed that his mother and children lay dead in front of him, their bodies riddled with bullet holes. They were in a little clearing in the forest. The forest was dark and frightening, the clearing brightly lit. Angrily he looked around to see who had committed that horrible crime. He started to accuse some peasants who stood at the edge of the forest, but they disappeared. He heard laughter and turned around. On the other side of the clearing stood a group of soldiers. They laughed and pointed at him. Their laughter shamed him. He couldn't meet their gaze. He looked down, and as he looked down he discovered that he was holding an Uzi. It was smoking. The barrel was hot. His ears were ringing from the shots. He was the one. He had killed his own family.

Other times he dreamed that he was driving, endlessly driving, the first taxi he had owned. He was on a winding mountain road. He couldn't stop because the brakes didn't work. He didn't want to stop because the taxi was full of soldiers who would kill him if he stopped. The road was full of sharp curves and wound steeply down into a bottomless ravine. He sweated as he jerked the steering wheel from side to side, trying to keep the skidding taxi on the narrow, gravel road. The meter clicked steadily, adding on the quetzales with each dangerous curve. The soldiers owed him a fortune, but he knew they would never pay. He would not live to collect.

Faustino awoke from his dreams sweating, his heart pounding furiously, a foul taste in his mouth. He prowled the house, chain-smoking, refusing to sleep, constantly checking the doors to make sure they were locked, peering out the windows, looking for he-didn't-know-what. He stopped going to work. He went days without bathing, without shaving, without leaving the house. He didn't talk to his wife and children. How could he tell them what was wrong? His sons looked up to him, thought he was a tough guy. How could he tell them he was afraid, terrified? How could he tell them he had participated in massacres?

How could he talk to his wife? He wasn't used to talking to her about anything other than the children, the house, the rising cost of food, or the problems with the Indian cleaning woman. What would she think if she found out what he had been doing, what he had to keep doing to protect his family and himself? She was a religious woman. She took the boys to mass every Sunday. She no longer asked him to go to church. She knew that he had other things to do. Sometimes he was just too tired because he had worked hard all week. Other times he had duties to perform for the military. What would she think of him if she knew what some of those duties involved? What did she think of him anyway? She knew he was a sinner. She knew that he sometimes did things he shouldn't when he was out with the boys on a Saturday night. She forgave him for those sins. What about this? Would she forgive him this sin?

What did she think of him? He hadn't cared for a long time. Now, suddenly, it was important to him. It was important what he thought of himself.

Faustino decided—not that he would refuse to report—that he would try to get out of having to report. He would resort to the tried untruths that had worked so well when he had been a boy in school and hadn't prepared his lesson. He told his wife that the next time the soldiers came to the house she was to tell them that he wasn't home and wouldn't be back for several days, that he had gone away on business.

Soon the soldiers came to give Faustino his orders for the next mission. The dutiful wife stood in the doorway and told them that he was away on business, and she didn't expect him back for some time. She was a nervous liar, and when they pressed her about when her husband was due back, she swore by all that was holy that she didn't know and told them that if her husband did by some chance return in time she would have him report. Faustino, who was hiding behind the door, began to sweat bullets.

The second time the soldiers came, the nervous spouse told them that Faustino was sick. Faustino had told her to say that he had the flu but, face to face with the rigid soldiers, she decided that the flu wasn't serious enough and opted for pneumonia. She added that the doctor was quite worried about him.

That was the last time the beleaguered wife had to lie to the soldiers. Several nights later the sleepless Faustino saw a Ford Bronco with darkened windows drive slowly past his house. As his was a dead-end street, the Bronco soon returned. Faustino, his heart beating wildly, sweating profusely although he was chilled, remained glued to the window. He was dying for a cigarette but did not dare light one for fear of being seen. The seconds and minutes passed slowly, and just as he decided that the Bronco had turned up his street by mistake, he saw it pass slowly, oh so slowly, in front of his house once again.

Flor del Cañón

FOR THE FIRST FOURTEEN YEARS OF HER LIFE, Flor struggled to survive in the rural poverty of Morazán. She was a sickly, skinny girl with a belly swollen by parasites. Since she was the only female in a house of men, she was neglected until she was old enough to work. Her exhausted mother had died giving birth to her eleventh child, Daniel, when Flor was not quite three. Four of Flor's older brothers had died in childbirth or in infancy, leaving a little family of seven children to be raised by Flor's father, Abraham. They crowded together in a small, one-room house built of sticks and grass on a plot of land that didn't belong to them. Flor's father, Abraham, a poor farm worker, let her and Daniel grow wild in the country while he and his oldest sons worked on the large plantations nearby. When she was very young, Flor took charge of the household as well as the care of Daniel.

Every day, when she was nine and Daniel six, they walked hand in hand into Cantón Balacera where Flor earned a little loose change selling watermelon slices to bus passengers, while Daniel went to school. Daniel went to school because he was everyone's favorite, especially Flor's.

When Abraham was given a job at the ice plant by one of his drinking buddies, the little family moved to a two-room adobe house in the sleepy little town, and Flor went to school in the mornings, partly because there wasn't much demand for watermelon slices until the hot afternoons. The five older brothers worked at whatever came their way. They cut cane or picked coffee at harvest time, sold lottery tickets, newspapers, or chewing gum. The oldest ingratiated himself with the soldiers at the small detachment in town and became their regular errand boy. Daniel shined shoes in the plaza in the evenings and on weekends. Their many minuscule earnings resulted in a combined income that was still quite small. It may be true that many drops of water can wear away a stone, but many centavos sooner result in a pocket that needs mending than a new pair of trousers. Yet the family adapted to town life, and on rare occasions a sophisticated Abraham was heard to make disparaging remarks to his drinking buddies about country folk.

When Flor was eleven, she nearly died of amebic dysentery. One day, while she was rapidly wilting at home, a worried Daniel told his teacher about her illness. When the teacher asked how the family was treating her and Daniel replied that they had stopped giving her liquids in the hopes of ending the diarrhea, the horrified teacher took Flor to the hospital in the city. Flor hovered near death for a week. The good doctor thought the emaciated little girl was too far gone to survive, and although he was a caring man, he would not have mourned her death. After all, there were thousands like her in El Salvador, as many as the slender, unrecognizable shoots in the springtime. If one dies before blossoming, no one misses the flower that was lost.

Flor survived, and she left the hospital healthier than she'd ever been in her life. The doctor had rid her skinny little body of as many parasites as he could find, and he had found plenty. The healthy Flor suddenly did better in school, but she was so far behind that she could never catch up. Besides, according to Abraham, girls only needed to know how to keep house and raise a family. Accordingly he got her a job with the wife of one of his drinking buddies.

Flor worked at a stall in the market, selling skirts, pants, socks, dresses, and nylons made in Taiwan and Korea.

Daniel stayed in school. No one in the family had ever been well lettered except, as family legend had it, the husband of a distant cousin who had attended the university for some months and subsequently landed a job in the post office in the capital, sorting mail. The family had even higher hopes for Daniel. When Abraham was with his drinking buddies, he bragged that Daniel would one day be a wise judge like the one who had let him off that time he was charged with drunkenness and disturbance. When Flor was scrubbing the family laundry on the rocks in the river, she dreamed that Daniel would one day be a fine doctor like the one in the hospital who had saved her life. She talked so convincingly of this that the oldest brother, while waiting for the soldiers to send him on an errand, often dreamed that Doctor Daniel would discover a cure for cancer. On his twentieth birthday that brother decided that a cure for a common social disease would be more useful.

At fourteen Flor blossomed. She became a beautiful girl who was guarded closely by her suddenly protective older brothers. That meant whenever she wasn't selling polyester pants in the market she wasn't permitted to leave the house unless one of the men in the family was free to escort her. They escorted her to the river and from a safe distance watched her scrub their clothes on the rocks. When she went to the market to shop, one of the men went with her and usually flirted disrespectfully with the young girls who sold tomatoes or pupusas. They took turns accompanying her to church, lolling in the plaza until mass was over. To the long-ignored Flor, the protection and even the confinement was a welcome form of attention, and although she often flirted with or sassed the men who bought jockey shorts or white socks at her stand, her unaccustomed beauty made her shy when she was away from work.

In 1980, her oldest brother gave his job as errand boy for the soldiers to the next oldest and left home to fulfill his life's ambition. He joined the army and was killed in a battle two months after basic training. To avenge his brother's death, brother number two decided to enlist after the small military detachment moved out of town, leaving him unemployed. The small military detachment had left town for the safety of the large military base in the city because of the increasing guerrilla activity that a short time later was to lead to the death of brother number two.

When she was fifteen, the guerrillas tried to recruit Flor and her older brothers. The guerrillas reasoned that, since the two deceased brothers had worked for the military and then joined the army, the rest of the family was obliged to join their forces. Flor knew nothing about the guerrillas except that they had killed two of her brothers and that her father and his drinking buddies said that they were thieves and murderers who were too lazy to work for a living. Also it was rumored that the guerrillas had carried off two of the young girls who worked in the market who had refused to join them. Flor wanted nothing to do with the guerrillas. One day when they came to her stall in the market and told her that they wanted her to go with them to the mountains, she ran to the police station. That night they slipped a note under the door of her house threatening to kill her and her brothers because they were traitors to the people.

Because of the threats, Abraham and his three oldest surviving sons moved to the city near the army cuartel. He got a job working for the army, and the sons leased a plot of land nearby, which they farmed. Flor and Daniel moved to San Salvador, where they lived for a short time with the distant cousin and her husband, the letter sorter. Daniel attended school, and Flor attended a kiosk in the market where she made enough selling cheap clothes for her and Daniel to move to a tiny house in one of the new slums full of refugees from the country.

Flor liked being the head of the household. She liked renting the house in her own name, paying the bills, supporting her brother, having her own kiosk in the market in San Salvador. When Daniel played the patriarch at home, the role he had learned from Abraham, Flor tolerated the condescension. Sometimes she didn't notice it because she still believed that the man was master of the house. Sometimes when she was tired she didn't think it was worth arguing over who was in charge of such a poor, mean house. But she never let Daniel get away with the least bit of bossiness nor did she let him flaunt his superior education when he worked at her kiosk. Sometimes when he worked with her in the market he would try to lord it over her because, after all, he was a student and well educated, and she was just a poor salesgirl in an open-air market, which was, if one looked at it in its true light, only one step above working in the street. If she would only listen to him, they could double or triple their sales. Flor fired Daniel a number of times, but she always hired him back. Sometimes, when Daniel was lazy and didn't want to work, he deliberately got himself fired. But they never stopped being friends, mostly because Flor had too much good sense to let them become enemies or even strangers. She knew that they needed each other in that large, sometimes hostile city. Daniel needed her financial support if he wanted to stay in school. He needed her to wash and iron his clothes and to fix the meals and wash the dishes. And Flor found that in her unattached state she needed Daniel if she wanted to go for a walk, go to a movie or a fiesta. She needed him to guard her from the men who would follow her, pinch her, harass her, for she was a beautiful, young girl, and the city men, although chivalrous to nuns, grandmothers, matrons, obviously pregnant women, and even beautiful, young mothers with children, firmly believed that any young woman alone was asking to be followed, pinched, and harassed.

In time Flor and Daniel drifted apart. She went out with boyfriends, and he spent more of his leisure hours with schoolmates. Dutifully they went to visit Abraham and their older brothers but not as often as they might. They had never lived in Abraham's new house, and there was nothing there that attracted them. Dutifully Flor sent Abraham money when he asked for it, which was not infrequent. Dutifully she took charge of his house when she visited. Once Abraham, bursting with cane liquor courage, boasted, as Flor put him to bed, that he was thinking of moving back to their old village because he wasn't afraid of the guerrillas.

Flor didn't for a moment believe that her father would move back, but she began to wonder what the village was like. She romanticized the town she had grown up in, where she had sold watermelons as a little girl, gone to school, where she had first sold clothes in the market, had listened to the gossip of the older women as they washed clothes on the rocks in the river, where she had walked everywhere confidently alone until her budding beauty made her a prisoner of her family. One day she took a bus back to the little village. She didn't know why she went, and she had no conscious expectations but nonetheless she found the journey disappointing. She was the lone passenger to get off the bus, and no little girls surrounded her, tugged at her arms and dress while they shouted to her that she should buy their watermelon or pupusas. The village was practically deserted. The teacher who had taken her to the hospital was gone and the school closed. The market too, was closed. No one washed clothes in the river. The town was a mess. Buildings were crumbling. The guerrillas had written graffiti everywhere. On the three walls left standing of their old house, the guerrillas had written that they were going to kill Abraham and his family for collaborating with the enemy. No one bothered her as she walked the streets alone. Still, she caught the first bus back to the capital, where the war seemed far away.

One of her infrequent visits to her father was sad because she had to attend the funeral services of older brother number three who had joined the army and been killed in a battle. She had never been close to her older brothers, not as she was with Daniel, but that was the third brother killed by the guerrillas. Flor cried for the first time since the last funeral, and her hatred of the guerrillas grew. While Abraham, Flor, and her two surviving older brothers talked about their hatred of the guerrillas, Daniel remained aloof. Abraham got disgustingly drunk, and in his drunkenness he told Flor of the threatening letters the guerrillas slipped under the door from time to time. This was the first Flor had heard of the letters. All the brothers had known, but it had never occurred to them to tell Flor. They all felt that she should be protected from such knowledge. Daniel frowned as they talked about the letters until Abraham passed out. Flor thought that the one brother she loved more than the rest was growing farther apart from the family. As they sat talking in the little house, Daniel was like an outsider, watching them, judging them. And in the capital he spent more and more time away from Flor, away from the house. Perhaps that was why Flor fell in love.

One of her visits to her father was a joyous one. Her father sometimes talked about a widow he knew. He would even wink at Flor in a conspiratorial manner and hint that if he weren't careful the widow was going to trap him one of these days. Flor paid no attention even though Abraham was occasionally sober when he talked about the widow. She thought he was talking nonsense for two reasons: one, he was a typical man and thought all women found him irresistible; two, she couldn't imagine any woman so hard up for a man that she would want her dried-up, repulsive father. She laughed at her irreverent thoughts as she walked to the bus stop to go back to the capital. And she laughed again when she mused that reasons one and two were not so different after all.

Laughing, she met the widow of her father's dreams. Señora Vides sold coconuts and bananas at a little stand near the bus stop. Flor's obvious good humor as she bought a coconut made the Señora ask if she had enjoyed her visit with Abraham. Flor watched the old woman expertly cut a hole in the coconut with a machete. Flor inserted a straw into the coconut and sipped the sweet milk, never taking her appraising, laughing eyes off the robust Señora. The two women chatted while Flor waited for her bus. They found that they had a great deal in common. They were both small-business women. They both worked hard and were independent. They both had to put up with or fend off the passes made by their numerous flirtatious customers—the most persistent flirt at Doña Vides's fruit stand was Abraham. The soldiers at the base sent Abraham to buy coconuts nearly every afternoon because the sergeant was particularly fond of the milk, and he was partial to Doña Vides's coconuts because he had been a friend of her son, Froilán, who was away in the army. The two women laughed good-naturedly when Doña Vides told Flor that her father was a great flirt, and they laughed a bit cruelly when Doña Vides said that she would no doubt break the old man in two if they were married.

Every time Flor visited her father she also visited Doña Vides. Sometimes as Flor sat with her father, or cleaned his house, or ironed his clothes, she would become eager to leave for her visit with Doña Vides. They grew to like and admire each other so much that, when Doña Vides's son finished his military service, she wanted to introduce him to her pretty, young friend, and she was as pleased as ponche when they married several months later.

Froilán earned a decent living growing vegetables on a plot of land he leased. Flor moved her business to be with him even though that city did not have a market every day as did San Salvador. She contented herself with selling only on Thursdays, Saturdays, and saints' days. She made that sacrifice to be with her husband, who was tied to the land. Flor and Froilán soon had a daughter and then a son. They moved into a bigger house, one with four rooms. So that they wouldn't feel lonely in all that space, Abraham moved in with them. Clearly he was doing the young couple a favor because he often grumbled to anyone who would listen that the walk to the military base where he worked was so much longer that he arrived too exhausted to run errands for the soldiers. He never mentioned that he was afraid to live alone in his own house.

Abraham was afraid because of a threat he had received. One afternoon when he had been sunning himself in front of his house, someone he had known in the old days, from the old village, passed by. Abraham, whose memory wasn't the best, had been delighted to recognize someone from the old days, thinking hazily that the man was one of his former drinking buddies. But as the man passed, instead of a friendly nod of recognition, he snarled, "One of these days, old man, you are going to fall into our hands." Abraham was upset by this and discussed it with the men in the family. Flor only heard about it through Froilán, who generously allowed Abraham to move in.

Life was good, if somewhat crowded, for the young family. One of the older brothers also moved in with them, and Froilán employed him on his land. The other brother joined the army. Then, in December of 1989, the threats began. First Froilán's friend told him that he should move out of the house. The friend wouldn't say more, and shortly afterward he disappeared. The young couple thought at first that they had an enemy in the town, someone who wanted to frighten them as an act of revenge. Then the notes began to arrive. They were slipped under the door late at night when the family slept. The notes threatened all the family members by name with the exception of Froilán and the children. A note would say, "Abraham del Cañón, we are going to kill you for being a spy." Another would threaten, "Flor, you must pay a war tax of 10,000 colones by the new year or we will kill you." Sometimes a note would say, "Your family has served the army. Now it is time to serve the people. Flor del Cañón, if you do not join us, we will kill you as a traitor."

In the summer, Flor went to visit Daniel, whom she hadn't seen since Christmas. He had changed his address several times since then, and she searched for his room in an unfamiliar neighborhood. When she saw him sitting alone in his dark room, she was shocked by his appearance. He had lost a great deal of weight, and what little flesh remained on his face was sunken and stretched tight, giving him the appearance of someone long dead. Except for his eyes. His bulging, nervous, darting eyes frightened Flor more than his cadaverous appearance. Flor was afraid that Daniel was seriously ill and wanted to take him to a hospital. Daniel did not want to go, and when Flor insisted he told her that he wasn't ill. He was terrified.

Many years ago, when he was a young student, Daniel had joined the guerrillas. He had been very passionate in those days and had wanted to right the many terrible wrongs in his country. He had attended meetings, posted flyers, written on walls, delivered messages, and finally he had fought in the November offensive. When the government did not fall during the offensive, Daniel decided that the situation was hopeless. After the offensive the repression increased. The army invaded the Jesuit university and killed the priests and their housekeeper and her daughter. Many of Daniel's companions disappeared. Later their bodies were found in trash dumps, beside roads. All the bodies had been mutilated and showed signs of torture. Daniel had become obsessed with the fear that one night his mutilated body would be tossed in the municipal trash dump. The vision he carried in his head of his own agonizing death had paralyzed him. He had quit the guerrillas, but they would not permit him to simply walk away. They had sent a note to his old house, threatening to kill him. That was why he had changed his address several times. He was sure that the only way out for him was to leave the country, but he couldn't act. Terror had incapacitated him. He couldn't turn himself over to a coyote and be sure that the man would take him out of the country and not hand him over to the military or the guerrillas. He couldn't cross the frontier on his own. His legs turned to jelly when he had to go out into the street to buy food.

Flor was shocked. She had grown up hating the guerrillas. She had thought of them as murderers and thieves, and here her brother, her favorite brother, the person she had loved most in the world until she had met her husband, her most intelligent and promising brother, had been a guerrilla. In the years they had shared the same house, he had been a guerrilla. When they went to the movies together or to a fiesta, he had been a guerrilla. When their third brother had been killed by the guerrillas, Daniel had been one of them. He had belonged to the enemy who killed his own brother. When, after the funeral, the angry little family had mourned and talked of their hatred for the guerrillas, Daniel had been quiet because he was one of them. Flor had always thought of the guerrillas as the enemy. For years they had threatened to kill her, her father, and brothers. And yet Daniel, the little boy who had pleaded with his teacher to help them when Flor was dying of dysentery, the determined little boy who had hitchhiked and sneaked onto buses to visit her in the hospital, he had joined the enemy.

Flor thought of all those things on the long bus ride home. She held Daniel's hand as they rode in silence on the bus. She tried to reassure him with her presence. She had persuaded him to go home with her so she could look after him. He will be safe in my home until he is well enough to flee, she thought. But is anyone ever safe in my country?

Long after the house had grown quiet, Flor lay awake, softly talking to her husband. The bright beam of moonlight that lit their bed disturbed her, and she kept her eyes closed as they talked. She was not educated and could not express all the thoughts that whirled in her head. She told her husband of her shock at learning that Daniel had been a guerrilla. She told him that all her life she had believed that the guerrillas were evil. They were the bad guys and the army the good guys, just like in a movie she and Daniel had once seen in the capital. She had been impressed by the big North American actor who looked so macho in his uniform with the charming green cap sitting jauntily on his head. He helped the good Vietnamese defeat the evil Communist guerrillas. She had often wished that he would help the good Salvadoran people defeat their evil Communist guerrillas, who wanted to take away the businesses of hardworking people like her. That the guerrillas tried to force people to join them was proof that they were evil, wasn't it? How could her brother, who was so intelligent, join them?

Froilán hadn't seen the movie, but he had had some experience in war. He had been forcibly recruited by the army. Several trucks had swooped down on the neighborhood soccer game, and the soldiers had jumped out and grabbed any young man or boy they could lay their hands on. Froilán was nineteen when the soldiers grabbed him. They didn't give him a chance to tell his mother. They simply threw him into a truck, and when it was full of new recruits it drove off to the base. The recruits were not able to call their parents for the first week. Froilán's mother, Señora Vides, did not have a phone in the house, so he had called the pharmacy on the corner near her fruit stand, and they had delivered the message. Some recruits wrote letters to their families, but many were illiterate and had no way to tell their parents where they were until they got their first leave after basic training. Froilán said that, as far as recruitment went, there didn't seem to be a great deal of difference between the army and the guerrillas.

Flor sat up and turned to him. She looked at his calm figure in the moonlight. "Then do you too support the guerrillas? Those evil people who have persecuted my family? They slip notes under the door at night. They threaten a harmless old man who suns himself in front of his house."

"Your father may be a harmless old man now, but I am not so sure that he has always been harmless. A friend of mine told me that the guerrillas accuse your father of being an oreja, an ear. They say that when you lived in Cantón Balacera, he reported to the army the names of people he thought were suspicious, people who were later disappeared."

"I do not believe it," Flor said. After a moment's thought she added, "And even if he did, he only did his duty. He only reported the names of guerrillas."

Froilán held both of Flor's angry, trembling hands. He told her that he did not support the guerrillas, but neither did he support the army. He had hated all the officers, and they in turn had had nothing but contempt for the soldiers. The soldiers were abused so that they in turn would abuse others. The officers picked on the weakest. They made one boy live in a tree for a month because he had tried to run away. "We were beaten with rifles and the flat sides of bayonets. We were punched and kicked, and we were ordered to punch and kick those who disobeyed or those who were simply slow. And those who enjoyed beating others, the cruelest, they were sent to be trained by the North Americans, by the big, handsome North Americans like the one in the movie you described. They were the ones who invaded the Jesuit university in the night and lined up the Jesuits and killed them. They are the worst. They are the ones who enjoy killing. I have seen soldiers do many bad things. Perhaps in the wars of other countries one side is all good and the other bad, but that is not the way it is here. The soldiers in the army and the soldiers in the guerrillas are all the same people. Sometimes they are from the same families."

At first Daniel was too afraid to talk or leave the house. Flor fed him and cared for him. He regained his health and with it a little weight so that he no longer looked like a cadaver. He played with the children. He began to shed some of the terror that had wrapped itself around him like a shroud. He ventured out of the house, cautiously at first, like a mouse who has recently seen a hawk's shadow glide over its nest. One day, he and Flor went for a walk in the country. Daniel told her that, for the first time in many years, he felt as if he could lead a normal life again. As they walked and talked they began to feel close again. There in the quiet, green fields they began to feel that they were all alone, just the two of them against the world, the way they had felt when they were children walking hand in hand to town, only parting at Daniel's school. Flor broke that closeness when she asked Daniel if he felt remorse for joining the guerrillas, who had killed three of their brothers. Daniel withdrew from her. He stiffened and told her in a cold voice that poverty had killed four of their brothers before they were born, that the cruel poverty in El Salvador killed many children. It had almost killed Flor with its army of amebas.

That night Flor and Froilán went to a dance. Abraham and the oldest sons each went out with their drinking buddies. Daniel stayed home to care for the children. When they returned from the dance, Flor and Froilán were met by excited neighbors who told them that at 10:30 masked men had dragged Daniel out into the street and shot him. Soon after the funeral, a note was slipped under the door telling Flor that hers was a family of traitors, and if she did not join them in a field outside of town at midnight on the following night, they would come for her. They had already killed one traitor and soon they would get her. Flor was too terrified to sleep at home. She went back to San Salvador and rented her old stall in the market. She saved her money. She ate little. She slept under her table in the stall. She rarely visited her husband and children, who had moved in with Doña Vides. Flor was afraid that if she visited them more often, the masked men would invade that house too.

The day after Froilán traveled to San Salvador to tell Flor that Abraham had been shot outside a bar late at night, she paid a coyote $1,400 to take her to the United States.

The Road North

ONCE UPON A TIME IN A TINY LAND so far away that
most people had forgotten where it was, a young couple,
Inocenta and Ulises, got married. Inocenta was sixteen and
pretty. Ulises, eighteen, was an independent man. He had
worked hard for three years in San Salvador before returning home. In the capital he had been a mechanic's appren-
tice, worked in a factory, and finally and most importantly,
driven a delivery truck. It was easy for all the landless peasants in the area to see that his experiences in the city had
shaped him into a fine, sophisticated man. Sometimes, at
night, he would tell the other men stories about those experiences. As they sat outside in the evenings sharing a
cigarette or an occasional bottle of rum, the other men listened to his stories with the same rapt attention that the
emperor had paid to the wondrous stories of Scheher-
azade. At those times the other men envied Ulises. They
envied him his travels. He had been as far as Guatemala,
while the other men had only ventured as far as Honduras,
a few short miles away. They envied him his fine experiences
for none of them knew how to repair a motor or even drive
a car. They envied him for the many, equally wondrous ex-

periences that he didn't talk about—after all, there are many exciting women in the city, are there not? And he is a man, is he not? Many people would say that poor, uneducated peasants have no imagination, but, in fact, when it comes to certain topics they have as much as any university professor. Those poor, overimaginative peasants envied Ulises the wealth that he had accumulated by working at two and sometimes three jobs at a time in El Salvador. With that wealth, he had been able to rent a bigger plot of land—ten acres—where he grew corn and beans. He had even bought a milk cow. But most of all, the other men envied him his two gleaming upper incisors made of gold. Sometimes when he smiled and the sun glinted on those bright golden teeth, the older men, who had fewer front teeth than nature had started them out with, self-consciously covered their mouths. At odd moments the thought would creep into the minds of the men shortest of teeth but longest on imagination that if they could afford gold teeth they too would be irresistible to the opposite sex and have adventures such as they imagined Ulises had had in the capital. For it was well known that all the women thought Ulises very handsome, especially Inocenta, who, having never watched a television or seen a movie, thought Ulises the most wonderful man in the world.

Relatives and friends of the timid bride and handsome groom rejoiced at the wedding, often repeating that theirs was a union of virtue and strength. As the fiesta wore on, some of the women joked among themselves that the bride, despite her name, would soon experience the pains of a woman, and many of the men joked that perhaps she wasn't as innocent as she seemed. Late at night a man who was blind drunk mistook the groom for a drunken pal. He put his arm around Ulises and tried to say something witty about Inocenta, but all that came out was a slur against her name. Everyone suddenly fell silent. The crowd feared that Ulises, who was undoubtedly a man, would react violently, and perhaps he would even go to his house for his machete. But Ulises was a man made tolerant by his travels, a man who understood his peasant neighbors. He demonstrated

his sophistication by merely laughing and patting the suddenly disconcerted offender on the back.

In the first months following their wedding, Inocenta
seemed shier than ever, while Ulises seemed to grow taller.
She was the vine that could not reach the sunlight without
the support of the sturdy tree that was her husband. Ulises
became a leader in the small community. He was a model
for all, not only because he was happy, but also because he
had become involved in the peasants' cooperative that had
recently formed in his village. Not only through the words
of the priest, who passed through the village every other
Sunday, and the catechists, who were his neighbors, but
also through his experience, he had come to believe in the
power of solidarity, of people helping one another in work,
in building houses, in planting and harvesting, in sharing
when someone in the village didn't have enough. Inocenta
was a lucky woman to have such a man for her husband.

Six months after the wedding, Ulises lay beside Inocenta
under a crooked tree that grew around a great boulder
high on the steep river bank. As the leaning tree and boulder protected them from the strafing airplanes, so he protected the trembling Inocenta with his arms and body. All
afternoon from their shelter they watched their friends and
neighbors try to swim across the swift river that separated
El Salvador from Honduras. They had been among the first
to cross the river and had scrambled up the steep bank on
the Honduran side when the planes first swooped down,
firing their machine guns on the hapless people trying to
cross the river.

That morning the Salvadoran army had bombarded their
village with mortars and artillery while the soldiers who had
positioned themselves around the sleeping village in the
night fired on the houses and fleeing people with machine
guns and rifles. Because Inocenta and Ulises were young
and quick, they had escaped by running toward the river
and the safety of Honduras. However, the planes soon
found them in the river gorge. Many people were trapped.
They tried to hide under rocks or logs. They frantically dug
holes in the mud. Many tried to ford the swift river, holding

onto branches or fallen logs since they could not swim. Many were killed by the planes and many drowned in the river. Later in the day a patrol from the Honduran army took up positions further down the river and fired, not at their enemy the Salvadoran army, but at the refugees trying to cross the river and scramble up the slippery slope. Or perhaps that didn't happen. Maybe it was just the confusion of the moment that made the refugees believe that the rifle fire from the Honduran side came from the Honduran army. Later, many people said that soldiers from the Salvadoran army had crossed into Honduran territory and fired on the refugees. Inocenta and Ulises never discovered the truth of the matter.

Three times during the long day, Ulises dashed down the steep bank to help someone who had made it across the river but was too exhausted to climb out of the water and up the slope. He tried to time his forays, running and sliding down the slippery slope as soon as a plane had passed, but there were several planes, and once he ran back up in a hail of bullets, carrying a child in his left arm and tugging the mother with his right. Inocenta, from her vantage point, was terrified, and Ulises had to comfort her when he reached the shelter.

With the darkness of night the massacre ended. In the gathering gloom the survivors appeared from their hiding places and straggled farther into Honduras. On the weary march other survivors joined them, others asked desperately if anyone had seen their missing daughter, mother, or grandmother. Too often they had to answer with great sorrow in their hearts, "No, we have not seen your María de Guadalupe. Perhaps she is with another group." Too rarely they rejoiced when the missing loved one was within their ranks and there was a tearful reunion.

They built a refugee camp in Honduras. Many churches and international organizations such as the Red Cross and the United Nations High Commission for Refugees helped them. They helped the people work together, to cooperate when they cleared a little land to grow vegetables or to build houses. The churches taught them to make brightly painted crosses, which they sold in the North at surprisingly high prices. The government of Honduras helped them by surrounding their camp with barbed wire and a high fence. Through the years the Honduran military occasionally helped them by entering the camp to search the houses for weapons and subversives. The only weapons they found were hoes and shovels donated by the UNHCR, but they found numerous subversives, for all armies have the ability to see subversives everywhere. They took away some subversives for questioning, others they beat up outside the camp. Once they beat up Ulises, leaving him unconscious in the muddy road. His face was so bloody and swollen that Inocenta didn't recognize her husband when the men carried him back into the camp. She finally recognized him when he smiled to reassure her and she saw his handsome gold teeth.

The massacre and hard times in the camp seemed to bring Inocenta and Ulises even closer together. But as the years passed and they had no children, some of the more mischievous men in the camp thought it humorous to joke about the appropriateness of Inocenta's name and Ulises's apparent lack of manhood. If Ulises heard an occasional tasteless remark, he merely shrugged his broad shoulders and smiled his golden smile.

Finally, after years of negotiations and international pressure, the Salvadoran government allowed the refugees to return, promising them safe conduct and promising to let them live in peace in their new settlement. Many of the refugees didn't trust the government's promises and chose to stay in the camp in Honduras even though many church people and representatives from the United Nations accompanied the first group to be repatriated. Inocenta's timid heart fluttered and skipped from fear when she once again stepped on Salvadoran soil. She clung to Ulises's strong arm, frightened that it was a trap, that the military was going to ambush them once again. Perhaps because Inocenta was afraid, Ulises walked bravely into his country, trying to soothe her fears by his example.

In El Salvador they worked very hard rebuilding their village and planting crops, and, little by little, others from the refugee camp recrossed the river to join the bustling community. As the months went by, as the corn grew tall and heavy with big yellow ears, as the bean vines grew green and heavy with beans, as the houses took shape and were finished with plywood walls, screens, and metal roofs, as the school was completed and the children continued with the education they had begun in the refugee camp, the people grew to believe that they would be allowed to live in peace. The first baby was born in the new village at the end of six months, the first child baptized after eight months. At the end of a year the people became independent. They were able to feed themselves, and with the money they made from surplus crops they bought clothes, kerosene, and a few luxuries. Ulises bought a white dress and white patent leather shoes for Inocenta to wear to church and other special occasions. She was twenty and the prettiest woman in the village when she wore her new dress to the farewell party for the last of the international observers.

Less than a month after the international community left, the army trucks drove through the town's dusty street. They passed through slowly, just before sunset when the men had returned from the fields. There were only two trucks, and they didn't stop, but everyone in the village stopped what they were doing to watch silently. That night one of the neighbors felt the need to get drunk. In that reassuring state he made a loud remark about the childless Inocenta and Ulises. Ulises overheard and for the first time that anyone could remember he lost his temper. He yelled at the old man and pushed him until the old man fell down in the street.

A month later an army truck came to the village and took some of the men to headquarters where they were beaten and questioned. Although the men were released that same day with nothing more than a few bruises, the people were terrified. Some talked about going back to Honduras. They had never been happy in the camp, they admitted—it was too much like a prison—but at least they had felt safe there.

Others wanted to send a delegation to the capital to tell the human rights groups and churches what had happened. They asked Ulises to lead the group since he knew the capital. The little delegation set out before dawn the next day and returned at dusk. In the capital they talked to sympathetic people who wanted to help them, church leaders who promised to send observers out to stand by them, and human rights leaders who tried to get government officials to order the army to stop terrorizing the village. When Ulises returned that night he looked very tired. For the first time Inocenta saw fear on her husband's face. For the first time he did not flash her a golden smile when he returned home at the end of the day. Inocenta was frightened and refused to sleep in their new house that night. She and Ulises went out to the fields to sleep. When they returned to the village in the morning, they learned that the other three men in the delegation had been taken from their homes in the night. The men who took them wore masks and civilian clothes and drove a Jeep Cherokee with darkened windows. Everyone knew they were from a death squad. Inocenta and Ulises continued to sleep in the fields at night until the bodies of the three men were found along the highway.

Ulises stood frozen in the doorway of his house, watching the families of the dead men carry the cadavers into their houses to clean them for burial. Since Ulises could decide nothing, since he could do nothing, since he could not act, it was Inocenta who decided what to do. She decided to go to the United States where life was wonderful and they would be able to live in peace. She packed their few belongings and dug up the coffee can that held their savings. She led her strangely lethargic husband out of the house that afternoon. At Inocenta's urging they paddled across the river, pushing a log on which they had tied their belongings. They crossed the river at the same place they had crossed it four years earlier. Inocenta led her husband by the hand up the same slippery slope they had scrambled up that terrifying day. They passed the same boulder and crooked tree where Ulises had sheltered her from the bullets with his body. They slept in the forest that night, and the next morning

Inocenta led them far around the refugee camp, afraid that the Honduran army might still patrol the area.

Five days passed before they arrived in Mexico. Inocenta had bartered with money changers to buy first Honduran lempiras, then Guatemalan quetzales, and finally Mexican pesos. She flagged down buses that crept along the dirt roads and narrow highways. She struck up conversations with other women on the buses, poor women who gave them food, widows who took them to their little huts to sleep for a night, sympathetic women who told them where to get off the bus to walk around the roadblocks where the soldiers checked identity papers.

On their second day in Mexico, they were arrested by the police. They spent three days and three nights in jail trying to sleep on the cold concrete floor with no blanket, no bedding, no extra clothes. They were deported to Guatemala with only the clothes on their backs. The police kept everything, their money, their belongings, and even Inocenta's white dress and patent leather shoes. As they stood inside Guatemala, Inocenta decided that it would be dangerous to stay there without money or papers. When she told Ulises that they should go to Honduras to look for work in Tegucigalpa to save some money before they again crossed into Mexico, Ulises seemed to snap out of his trancelike state. He flashed a grim golden smile and said that they might as well as they had nothing to lose.

In Tegucigalpa, Inocenta's strength seemed to grow. She took Ulises from place to place until he got a job as a mechanic. Inocenta found herself a job in a factory that made sports clothes for North Americans. In the evenings she worked cleaning offices in the center of the city where the marvelous, tall buildings grew from the pavement. After a month she also got Ulises a night job cleaning the offices. She liked working with her husband, but she liked her job in the factory more. There, although the work was long and tedious and the foremen were always angry and telling them to work faster, she made friends with the other women. How they giggled over the strange words on the labels and wondered what they meant. APRÈS SKI. All American

Sportswear Co., San Francisco, CA. Machine Wash, Cold Water. Do Not Wring. Occasionally she went out to a movie or simply to get an ice cream and walk in the park with one of her girlfriends from work. She was not extravagant—she was careful to put aside a little money each payday in another buried coffee can. For the first time in her life she earned money on her own, and she wanted to spend a small portion of it on herself. Ulises didn't understand why she wanted to go out with her girlfriends, and he became angry when she explained that it was the same as when he went out with the boys on a Saturday night in El Salvador with the money he had earned.

It was not that she loved him any less, especially as he was often the Ulises of old with his golden smile. No, it was just that their experiences had changed them both. Sometimes she loved him differently, especially those times when he withdrew and needed to be mothered, or those times when he became churlish and needed she didn't know what.

After six months, Inocenta decided that it was time to go to the north once again. Some men had begun talking to some of the women in her factory as they left at the end of the day, telling them that their pay was too low, the hours too long, and the conditions too bad and that they should form a union. Inocenta certainly thought that the hours were too long, and she would have liked a higher salary and to be treated better by the bosses. But she was afraid to even speak to those dangerous men outside the factory. As far as she knew she had never in her life met a union man or woman, but she knew that where they went, trouble followed. As they lay in bed that night, Inocenta told Ulises of her fears. He held her in his arms, comforted her, and assured her that in his wide experience in San Salvador he had met union men and they had seemed all right, but, the truth is, they were subversives and terrorists. Everyone said so. "Don't worry," he whispered to Inocenta, "maybe they'll just go away."

"No," Inocenta answered, "it's we who will go away. We've saved enough money for the trip to the North. Let's go. It must be very wonderful there. Everyone has so much food and fine clothes and money that there are no problems. Everyone is treated well. Do you know what one of the union organizers told Lupita?" Inocenta giggled. "He said that the Japanese have bought the factory. Anyone can see that it is a lie because the Americans are so rich. Why would they sell anything to the Japanese?"

They were better prepared for the second attempt to cross Mexico. They had more money, they weren't as naive, and they entered through Belize. They had no trouble in the Yucatán but had to pay a bribe to the police at Villa Hermosa and again at Coatzacoalcos. Inocenta did the negotiating as Ulises grew more passive with each roadblock, more withdrawn with each new bus that took them farther north. Inocenta worried about her husband and hoped that once they were in the United States they would get jobs and he would be his old self again. She often tried to cheer him up with little jokes. "Mexico is a great country, but it must be very hungry because it takes so many bites," she told him after paying another bribe near Tampico.

They were broke when they arrived at the posada in Matamoros run by the good sisters. They were made to feel welcome. They rested for a week and even earned a little money working in town. Some of the townspeople advised them as to the best place to cross the Rio Grande into Texas and what to do when they got there. The one who gave the most advice and seemed to be the most experienced was Emiliano, a teenager from Cárdenas, who was on his way to Houston where his cousin had a job waiting for him. Emiliano liked the pretty Salvadoran woman and felt sorry for the quiet, unsmiling husband, and offered to take them with him. Perhaps his cousin could get Ulises a job.

They waited on the Mexican side of the river until twilight. Inocenta thought it best to wait until dark, but Emiliano was impatient. He was young and handsome but had always been frustrated by poverty, a grinding poverty, a poverty that had made his mother old and wrinkled before her time, a poverty that had killed his father in the poisonous oil fields of Poza Rica, a poverty that he was certain would end as soon as he crossed the river. He stood up, and as if leading his troops in a charge, waved an arm and dashed down the embankment. His reluctant troops, Inocenta and Ulises, followed. As Emiliano was about to enter the river, a hail of gunfire rang out from the North American side. Emiliano fell or dove into the water and Inocenta quickly tugged Ulises back up the embankment to their former positions behind a small rise where Inocenta tried to protect Ulises with her body. After complete darkness had set in, Inocenta made her cautious way down to the river to search for Emiliano. She whispered his name several times, called out to him, then finally shouted his name once, but there was no answer.

The terrified pair decided to retreat to the posada.

In the gloom, the survivors straggled farther back into Mexico. On the weary march they met three armed men who preyed upon people about to cross the border. The men laughed at Inocenta and Ulises for going the wrong way. When Inocenta pleaded with the men, telling them that their friend had just been killed and asking that they be allowed to pass in peace, the men made jokes about Ulises's manhood for letting his woman do the talking. The bandits demanded all their money, and when they saw how little there was, they became angry. They aimed their flashlights at their victims and searched them. They tied Ulises up, stuffing a filthy bandanna into his mouth so that he couldn't yell for help. They raped Inocenta.

When the owner of the filthy bandanna reclaimed his property from Ulises's mouth, he noticed the gold teeth. Inocenta, who had endured her own torture, passed out when she saw the men yank the teeth from her husband's mouth.

For several days at the posada, Ulises stayed in bed with his swollen mouth closed. He neither answered when his wife spoke to him nor opened his mouth to receive the spoonfuls of soup she offered him. When he finally opened his mouth to speak, revealing his bare red upper gum, it was to hurt Inocenta. Despite her own bruises and pain she had gone to work. She had hoped to cheer him by showing him the few dollars she had earned to help them on the rest of their journey north, and he asked, his voice full of cruelty, how she had earned the money.

Inocenta called Sanctuary from the Corralón, or the big corral, the refugees' nickname for the detention center at Los Fresnos, Texas. She and her husband had been caught by the Migra one hour after crossing the border near Brownsville, Texas. Sanctuary got their bond lowered, paid it, and brought them to the San Francisco district. Inocenta has a job sewing in a Taiwanese sweatshop, and Ulises has just quit his job as a dishwasher in a restaurant so that he could be home nights with his wife. He is jealous and suspects that she sees other men when he's not there. He doesn't talk much, and when he does, he self-consciously hides his mouth with his hand. They are both nervous about their upcoming trial, and to Inocenta's dismay Ulises refuses to see a psychologist until they have saved enough money to buy him a porcelain bridge.

The Road to the East Bay

THE JOURNEY FROM THE DETENTION CENTER in Los Fresnos, Texas, to the eastern shore of San Francisco Bay is altogether a mixed bag. It's a journey of boredom due to its wearisome length. It's a journey of hope because someone had listened to the refugee's story, encouraged him or her, paid the bond, and promised help in settling into the new world. It's an intimidating journey because few refugees realize how big this country is, and every mile, every minute on the interminable super highways takes them further from the country they fled, the country they are afraid to live in, the country they are afraid to return to, the country they grew up in, the country that is familiar to them, the country they call home. Immigration officials board the bus at several stops along the way. They may carry off some unfortunate person without papers, and each time the refugee worries that perhaps his or her new papers aren't in order, or that they have decided to rescind the papers. It's a journey deeper and deeper into the unknown. Everything is new to the refugees—the vast desert panoramas, the harsh language, the bus station chili or hamburgers, the money, the customs. The refugee is carried along, a passive stranger in an aggressive land. It's a two-day journey, often made longer when the refugee changes to the wrong bus in Los Angeles and learns that local in English means that the bus will avoid the superhighway as much as possible, often choosing instead the scenic little roads that pass through all the marvelous towns in the Central Valley—Bakersfield, Fresno, Madera, and Merced, to name but a few.

I've never seen the L.A. station, but I imagine it as big and bustling and confusing. Every time a refugee kindly calls from L.A. to keep me up to date on his or her progress, that image is reinforced by the noise in the background, the roar of conversation, and the blare of loudspeakers, all in English, all unintelligible to the timid traveler. Sometimes I think I hear, mixed in with the human noise, the roar of the great diesel engines, the blare of horns, the beep beep beep of buses backing out of the echoing garage. But that may be my romantic imagination.

The refugee says he is calling to keep me informed of his progress, but I suspect it's for reassurance.

For the journey Sanctuary equips the refugee with a few dollars for food, instructions to get off at the Oakland terminal, and a list of phone numbers to call until someone answers. We always emphasize that they must get off at the Oakland bus station, which is one stop before San Francisco. Very few do. Most call from San Francisco, often at 1:00 A.M., to tell us that because they were asleep they missed the Oakland stop. When the telephone operator wakes me from a pleasant, warm, beckoning sleep at 1:00 A.M. to ask if I'll accept a collect call, I know immediately that a new arrival is in San Francisco. So far I've always accepted the calls.

At 1:00 A.M. traffic jams on the Bay Bridge are rare and the drive to the San Francisco bus station takes twenty minutes, only fifteen minutes longer than the drive to the Oakland bus station. In those lonely hours of the night the importance of those fifteen minutes is exaggerated by the knowledge that in a few hours I'll have to climb out of my cozy bed and go to the office. I stop begrudging the refugee those fifteen minutes each way when he or she is in the car.

After the long journey of boredom, hope, and fear, inter-spersed with numerous naps, the refugee is finally awake, and more than awake, excited, excited about the future, en-chanted by all the sparkling city lights, the maze of super-highways. It must be like stepping into the future, into a dream full of glittering lights. Once away from the sodium lights near the bus station, the night is kind to the cities of the Bay. As we cross the long expanse of the Bay Bridge even rusted freighters glimmer like palaces floating on the smooth pool of ink that separates the sparkling cities. It seems as if everyone has a wonderful house and a car. The young men especially are enchanted by the sight of so many cars even though traffic is light at that hour, and, no doubt, much to the delight of the auto makers' chief executive offi-cers, they begin to fantasize about the day when they'll have their own cantankerous, unreliable, polluting, life-threaten-ing dream car. I listen to the hope-filled refugee and the curmudgeon in me retreats. I do not begrudge him his dream of a car. I see only the beauty of the lights and the cars and the highways. I see the cities surrounding the Bay with new eyes, eyes that will be reluctant to open at 6:00 A.M.

One refugee, Bonifacio, who slept through to San Francisco, out of a combination of politeness and guilt did not call. He inquired at the ticket agent's office and was told that the next bus to Oakland would depart at 7:00 A.M. He decided to wait for that bus. He sat up all night in the wooden bench seat deliberately designed to be uncomfort-able so that people wouldn't be lured in off the streets to spend the night. He kept one eye on the cardboard box that contained his worldly goods and another on the weird people doomed to haunt bus stations in the wee hours as punishment for some grave transportation crime they had committed in a previous life. Possibly they had robbed a stagecoach, murdering the passengers and drivers, or, worse, had designed the uncomfortable bench seats that plague bus stations and airports.

The bus to Oakland departed at 7:00 A.M. as advertised, and when it arrived in Oakland twenty minutes later, Bonifacio began to regret his consideration of my sleep. Having had only the vaguest notion of the geography of California, as have most New Yorkers, he had thought that Oakland was hundreds of miles and several hours from San Francisco. He explained his error with a likable, self-deprecating humor to the volunteer who answered his call and picked him up at the Oakland bus station. Well rested by an uninterrupted night's sleep, I was already out of the house when he called.

No refugee has been lost on the long journey from the Corralón in Los Fresnos, Texas, but we came close once, that is, we left one in limbo for a weekend.

When we bond refugees out of the Corralón in Texas, we tell them to go to one of the two places of refuge in Harlingen, Casa Romero, or Posada San Benito, while we make arrangements for their bus tickets. Once they are out of detention we are not in as much of a hurry for the refugees to land on the eastern shore of San Francisco Bay as are the people who run the always overcrowded houses of refuge in Harlingen. Sometimes, due to lack of space at our end, we don't get around to sending the bus tickets for a week or more. Sometimes, due to lack of patience, the refugee nags us into action. Sometimes, due to lack of space at the Texas end, although never lack of patience, the good people who run the Casa or the Posada take the initiative.

One fine morning the coordinator of one of the houses in Texas called and left a message on La Hermana's answering machine to warn her that she was about to put Rosa on the bus, which she promptly did.

Sleepy Rosa arrived in San Francisco one Friday morning at 1:00 A.M., armed only with La Hermana's home phone number, which she promptly called. Rosa had had no experience with answering machines, but she had been warned that they infested the country. When it became clear that the voice on the other end of the line was a taped message, her pulse raced at the thought that her voice was about to be recorded. She waited for the tone, as the machine instructed her, gathered her forces, and then blurted out a breathless message. Afterward Rosa settled in at the bus station, waiting for something to happen. When nothing happened by sunrise, she called again and, steeling herself, left a coherent message in the care of the selfish machine. She sat again and waited some more, trying not to fidget in the uncomfortable bench seats. She had been in worse situations. At least she wasn't in danger, she told herself, although some of the characters who had passed through the bus station during the night had frightened her. One motley man had awakened her from a fitful sleep when, in the center of the large, dim waiting room, he began screaming at some invisible being. She had been ready to retreat but as no one else ran or paid him the slightest attention, she settled back onto the tortuous bench.

All the ghosts disappeared with the dawn, and the bus station's reawakened bustle instilled her with a different kind of fear, the fear of standing out in a crowd. She was a shabbily dressed Central American who clearly didn't belong in that elegant bus station, and she was afraid of being evicted. As the morning wore on and still nothing happened, she looked for someone who looked like her, someone who spoke Spanish. She found a Nicaraguan couple and told them her story. They took Rosa home with them, called once again to leave another futile message, and gave her breakfast while they waited for the return call promised by La Hermana's disembodied voice. After the breakfast dishes, when the rush hour traffic had cleared, they drove Rosa to the East Bay and, when they couldn't find the Sanctuary, dropped her at a shelter in Berkeley.

The volunteer who manned the shelter that day, a woman named Karen, spoke a little Spanish, enough to understand the basics of Rosa's plight. Karen helped the nouveau street person make several more calls to La Hermana's infernal machine, and, as the day wore on and no one came to pick Rosa up, Karen also began to worry. Rosa seemed so trusting and defenseless that Karen was afraid to leave her in the shelter overnight. When her tour of duty ended, Karen took decisive action. She took Rosa home with her. Karen told herself that at the worst it was just for a night, and if no one came for her that evening, they would surely come in the morning.

At home Karen added another candle to her menorah and shared some matzo with Rosa. Karen made another call to the unresponsive machine then called a friend of hers, one of the public health nurses in Berkeley. The friend told her that she knew the East Bay Sanctuary well as she often helped them with their health care program. When Karen got another number to call, my home number, she thought she had a bingo. She dialed with great expectations but found that instead of a bingo she merely had another number covered by an answering machine. Because Karen didn't want to appear to be in a hurry to get rid of sweet, young Rosa, and because she assumed that I knew all about the misplaced refugee, the message she left on my machine was puzzling. Something about a refugee who had gotten lost, but not to worry because a woman named Karen who worked in a shelter had taken her home and everything was all right, so really don't worry, and they had left a message with La Hermana, and the only thing was that the woman had to leave town on Monday. Karen left her number and repeated it.

Karen pondered what to do about Rosa now that she had led her out of the wilderness. Her experience in entertaining strangers from El Salvador was limited, and it was obvious that the stranger politely perched on the very edge of the sofa was equally inexperienced in being entertained by strange North Americans. For want of a better idea, Karen invited her new friend to take a hot tub at her club. Rosa, while carefully munching minute bits of the dry cracker and surreptitiously picking crumbs off her breasts and lap, pondered the meaning of the menorah and the matzo. She thought the gold candleholder and white candles pretty, but she was surprised that Karen didn't have enough candles for all nine places in the menorah. It was the first sign of poverty she had noted in Karen's flat and that sign of poverty make her feel more at home. The matzo, however, left something to be desired. It was all new to Rosa, a Catholic peasant who had met as many Jews in her life as she had taken hot tubs. She accepted the invitation with the same animation that she accepted another matzo. As she dutifully bit off yet another tiny piece, she wondered if she would have to go to confession all on account of the dry cracker.

As I had been out of the office for a few days, I knew nothing about Rosa. When I got home that evening, I listened to the message. It is possible to give one's every waking moment as well as the better part of the sleeping ones to refugees, if one is so inclined. In my struggle against that possibility I sometimes decide that anything short of a crisis can wait. As I didn't know Karen or Rosa, as there didn't seem to be any rush because Monday was several days away, and as the emphasis was on not to worry, I didn't. I sensibly got dinner to the slow simmering stage, poured a glass of richly deserved cheap red wine, and called La Hermana to ask her uncommunicative machine if a refugee was missing. Then I called Karen. Naturally, by the time I called, they had gone to Karen's club to exercise and take a tub. I left a message on Karen's machine and, my plan having worked to perfection, enjoyed my wine and dinner.

Rosa didn't enjoy the hot tub. All her life she had bathed in cold water. Hot water was for cooking, and she was afraid that that was what the water in the enormous tub would do to her. She endured the torture for a few minutes before politely excusing herself. Once out of the soup kettle she began to worry about Karen who seemed to be unaware of the danger and who stewed in the 103-degree water for thirty minutes. But strangest of all to Rosa, that healthy young woman who at the age of six had begun working on the plot of land her parents rented, that strong young woman who had planted and weeded and harvested, that muscular woman who had ground corn by hand, who had carried heavy loads of firewood on her back, heavy jars of water on her head, strangest of all the strange things she had seen since fleeing her home was watching all the men and women in the club religiously perform their exercises. They huffed and puffed around the gym. They pedaled furiously on bicycles that went nowhere. They rowed steadily in make-believe boats that would sink in any river she had ever seen. They grunted and groaned as they kept lifting and lowering heavy weights. Rosa was fascinated by all the curious activity that seemed to accomplish nothing and was content to do nothing for a change.

The next day, Saturday, Karen and I played phone tag, and that night Karen took Rosa to the races. Karen's father had been a race fan, and, as it was the anniversary of his death, Karen made her annual pilgrimage to Golden Gate Fields. Rosa was intimidated by the crowd, and the strangeness of the situation made her shy. She hadn't seen so many people in one place since the funeral of Monseñor Romero. She had never gambled. Although a country girl, she had never even seen a horse before. She thought the sleek animals wonderful and was enchanted by their names as Karen tried to translate them. Karen gave Rosa two dollars, and they each bet on long shots. Watching the beautiful horses gallop around the track while the crowd cheered gave Rosa goose bumps. The thought that she had two dollars riding on the most beautiful horse frightened her. Her late father and disappeared brothers used to pick coffee on a large plantation for a dollar and twenty-five cents a day. The idea that she had risked two dollars just like that and might win sixty dollars in a matter of minutes without having to work excited her. As shy as she was, she found herself rising and cheering with the rest of the crowd when the horses galloped into the stretch. Rosa's horse, Blind Justice, came in next to last, half a length in front of Karen's hope, Tonite's The Nite. FrndsNHghPlcs won by a length.

To console themselves the gamblers went out for Italian food. Rosa wasn't completely unworldly. She had eaten spaghetti before. Twice to be exact. Once in the Corralón and the second time in the Casa Romero on the night she got out of detention. However, she had never eaten linguini con frutti di mare, which for some inexplicable reason she ordered. Neither had she eaten clams, mussels, or shrimp before, their being too expensive for institutional menus. She didn't like her pasta much but put a good face on it and managed to clean her plate, leaving only a few clams and mussels hidden in their shells. An excess of food was not one of the problems her family had had to overcome, and not once in her life had Rosa's mother told her, "Eat! People are starving in China!" The wine was the worst part of the meal. Rosa toyed with her Chablis. She thought it tasted like rotten grape juice and, when Karen asked her if she liked it, merely murmured that it was okay and that she had never drunk alcohol before. She didn't fool Karen, who asked if she'd rather have a soda. Rosa's face brightened as much as the waiter's soured when halfway through the meal he was required to bring her a cola to go with the linguine con frutti di mare. The zabaglione tasted nothing like her idea of dessert. Although it was sweet, at the same time it reminded her of the sour taste of the wine. And even four spoonfuls of sugar didn't make her cappuccino sweet enough, but she was too timid to add still more to the vile fluid.

In fact, from a culinary standpoint, the meal was a failure. Rosa didn't like the food at all and would much rather have gone to a truck stop for a chili burger and a decent cup of java. Still, being in that Italian restaurant, sitting across from her new friend, was one of the high points of her life. The food didn't matter in the least because the atmosphere and the experience were awe inspiring. In her luxurious bed in her own private bedroom, Rosa lay awake a long time re-membering the magical evening, the excitement of the horse race, the elegant restaurant, and the enormous tip that Karen left the waiter. Rosa told me that she had had such a wonderful time that she couldn't sleep for a long time that night. I think it was the cappuccino.

Sunday they went out for bagels and coffee. Rosa, after the first bite, sheepishly picked the lox off her bagel. Then, as it was a fine day, they went for a walk in Golden Gate Park. On Sundays cars are banned from the eastern half of the park and the roads are filled with bicyclists and roller skaters. At a large intersection the crème de la crème of the roller skate community shows off for each other and the crowd that gathers. Rosa was captivated by the skaters. She had never seen anything like them before. They were like dancers and acrobats on wheels. And they were performing there in the park where anyone could watch for free. And the park! It was green and lovely and as large as a coffee plantation.

Rosa saw many amazing things that day. They shopped in Chinatown. They had coffee in a punk cafe. From the windy cliffs above Ocean Beach they watched multicolored hang gliders take off and soar with the drab sea gulls. When I arrived at Karen's house that evening, Rosa was worn out. She was reluctant to leave Karen, yet ready to get on with her life. It was time to stop being a tourist, time to get to work.

Rosa shares a house in a poor neighborhood with other refugees, a house filled with the smell of fried meat, boiled tripe, beans, and tortillas. She works as a house cleaner. Although she gets a decent hourly rate, more than most refugee men, she doesn't make much money because it's difficult to fill up her week with work. She works half days for some of her señoras and every other week for others. She spends long hours on buses traveling from house to house. Most houses are hard to get to, the bus service is poor, and the county is cutting back because of the budget crisis. In the winter, when it's dark early, she is afraid to walk home from the bus stop. But she is independent. She has enough to get by. Every now and then she and Karen meet for lunch or dinner. Every now and then Rosa treats. On the anniversary of the death of Karen's father, they go to the races and lose two dollars and then to the Italian restaurant where Rosa has linguini con frutti di mare and a cola. Tradition is important to immigrants.

Declaration of Carmen Grande in Support of Her Petition for Asylum

I, Carmen Grande, declare the following:

1. I was born February 13, 1970, in the city of San Vicente, El Salvador. My family lived in Guernica, a small village one hour by bus from the city. My father rented a small plot of land where he grew corn and beans. My mother was a housewife.

2. Although I have no brothers, I have three younger sisters and a large extended family. Because many of my cousins and uncles participated in protests in the late 1970s or supported the guerrillas, they were disappeared or killed by government security forces or death squads, or they were forced to flee for their lives. Some of the disappearances or murders were of more distant relatives or happened in other villages and didn't affect me very much. It was if they had happened to strangers in distant countries. Some of my most vivid and frightening memories are of incidents that happened close to home.

3. My cousins Oscar and Camilo Torres supported the FMLN (Faribundo Martí National Liberation Front), which is the name of the guerrillas in El Salvador. I think they supported the FMLN because of what had happened to their father. They lived across the street from us in Guernica. We grew up together and sometimes played together although they were boys and were older. Late one night in May of 1980, we heard screams from their house, but we were too terrified to go outside to see what was happening. The screams did not stop for a long time. It was horrible to hear. I did not get out of bed the whole time. It was like having a nightmare, only I was awake. I put a pillow and a blanket over my head, but the screams did not go away. The next day we found out that a death squad had burst into my cousins' house in the middle of the night to take them away. Their mother, my Aunt Areceli, screamed and screamed, trying to stop the men. She screamed for help, but we were all too frightened to even leave our houses to see what was happening. She begged the men not to take her sons. One of the death squad men laughed at her. "Don't worry. We'll return them to you," he taunted her. When they weren't returned the next day, Aunt Areceli went to the police station and the National Guard base in San Vicente, but the authorities denied that they knew anything about her sons. Aunt Areceli went every day to ask about her sons until an officer at the National Guard base told her that if she kept bothering them, the same thing would happen to her.

4. Two weeks after they were taken, my cousins' bodies were found. They had been brutally tortured, killed, and their bodies tossed beside the road to San Vicente. Aunt Areceli took the bodies of her sons to her house to have a wake. A neighbor warned her not to have a wake but to bury her sons quickly. We later learned that the neighbor was a member of ORDEN, a paramilitary group that spied on people and had ties

to the death squads. My aunt buried her sons quickly and went to live in San Vicente. My cousin Oscar was seventeen when he was killed. Camilo was fifteen.

5. My uncle Jacobo Torres was a member of FECCAS, the peasant union that worked for land reform and better treatment of the farm workers. One day he did not come home from working in the fields. That was in the summer of 1979. A few days later his body was found in a field. His head had been cut off and was on a post beside the body. The authorities did that. In those days they killed many people, mutilated their bodies, and left them in public places to frighten the people. Everyone was terrified by those tactics. Some like me became more timid; many, like my cousins, joined the guerrillas.

6. The two events that I have described affected me very much, more than many of the other atrocities in my family. Although I did not see my uncle Jacobo's body, I heard my family talking about it and was able to pic - ture the scene as clearly as if I had seen it. In a way that may have frightened me even more than if I had seen it. I was nine years old at the time. In my nightmares I still see that picture that I imagined when I heard my parents talking about it. I was ten when the death squad took my cousins from their house. Today, I do not like the silence. I always keep the radio or televi- sion on because in the silence I can still hear Aunt Areceli's screams. Sometimes I have nightmares that men are invading the house where I am sleeping.

7. I think that the reason my aunt Areceli became so frightened when the National Guard officer told her to stop bothering them or else was because of what had happened to my aunt Marta about a year earlier, shortly before my Uncle Jacobo's death. She was grabbed by the military and taken to the base where she was beaten and repeatedly raped. Later she was released but she was never the same again. She disap-

peared one night. She lived in another village, Cantón La Paz, so we weren't certain about what had happened to her. We heard that she had left her house one afternoon and nobody ever saw her again. The reason the military did those awful things to her was because they had picked up her husband and she would go to the police station and the army base to ask where he was. She even went to Mariona Prison. She went to the courts and the archbishop's office. My Aunt Marta was a fighter. She was an older woman. Her sons had moved away. Later they all joined the guerrillas.

8. A cousin of mine who lived in the city, Tomás Duruti Grande, was a student. He went to a secondary school to study for his bachillerato in law. He joined the student organization MERS (Movimiento Estudiantil Revolucionario Salvadoreño, or Salvadoran Revolutionary Student Movement). MERS was not a political organization. Its goals were to try to improve education in El Salvador, to get better pay for teachers, and to get better teachers. I know from my own experience that many of the teachers in the poor schools in the rural districts were themselves backward and poorly educated. For instance, when I was seven and was learning to write, my teacher thought it was a sin or a work of the devil that I tried to write with my left hand. She forced me to write with my right hand. She hit me and threatened me. She often humiliated me in front of the other students. This caused me to do badly and I fell behind in school. My cousin Tomás, on the other hand, did well in school. He was very intelligent and a leader of MERS. In November of 1980, National Guard troops entered his school and took him away along with another student who was also a member of MERS. We never saw or heard from them again.

9. Many of my relatives and neighbors in Guernica received threats. Sometimes someone would slip anonymous notes under their doors during the night so that

when the people awoke in the morning they would find the notes. Sometimes the threats were verbal. For instance, someone would tell someone else in the market that Fulano de Tal had better move away or the army would come for him one night. From 1979 to 1982, most of the residents of Guernica were either killed, disappeared, or moved away. Guernica became nearly deserted. The school closed in 1981. I was glad of that even though I had quit school a year earlier because I had so many problems.

10. When I left school I helped my father in the fields. To earn extra money we would work on a large coffee plantation nearby, Finca Tío Rico de Miami. I worked there three years until 1984 when we were forced to quit. One day some of the muchachos, as the guerrillas were called, came up to us in the fields and ordered us to stop working. They told us that we should not work for the rich. I was too frightened to speak, but my father told them that what they said was true but the poor could not afford to pay us. The muchachos laughed, but still they ordered us to leave the finca. They said, "Let the rich pick their own coffee." Since they had weapons, we had to obey them. Since we could no longer work, we finally left Guernica. We went to live in San Vicente in 1984. We hoped we would be safer there.

11. Because of all of the violence I was a timid and frightened girl. Because of all the problems I had at school, I and everyone else thought that I was stupid if not retarded. That's partly why, when we moved to San Vicente where there was a school, I did not continue my education. Also, we were very poor. I had to work. I began an apprenticeship as a seamstress in a small shop. I worked there for several years.

12. In 1986, when I was sixteen, I went back to school at night to finish my primary education. The night school teacher was not as backward as the teacher I had had

in Guernica, and I had no trouble because I was left-handed. The teacher did not humiliate me or anybody in front of the rest of the class. For the first time I liked school. The only trouble was with the student organizations. The student activists wanted everybody to join. They often held meetings at the school and handed out flyers. I did not join. I was terrified about getting involved because of what had happened to my cousin Tomás Duruti. And I was afraid to tell the other students to leave me alone because I was afraid of them, afraid that they would make fun of me or pressure me, and I was afraid that an oreja (spy) would report me. I went to a meeting once because the students dragged me in, but I could not stop crying. I cried so much that they kicked me out for disturbing the meeting. I cried because I was terrified that the death squads would find out that I had attended a meeting.

13. Sometimes the student activists gave out flyers as students left the classrooms. When they gave out flyers you had to take one, and you couldn't just throw it away because they watched you. Once a girl who was in my history class threw a flyer in the nearest trash can. The activists saw that and scolded her for throwing it away. When they handed out flyers, you had to keep them for a little while and throw them away when no one was looking. One time I forgot that I had a flyer in my bag. I took the bus home that night. The National Guard stopped the bus and searched everyone. They found the flyer in my bag. I explained that I hadn't known it was there. I told them that another student must have slipped it into my bag. I swore that I wasn't a member of any student group and that I had nothing to do with politics. They ordered me to get off the bus. I was certain that they were going to arrest me and would torture me and kill me. I was so terrified that my muscles would not work and I couldn't get up from my seat. The soldiers thought that I was resisting them and began to get angry. But then another passenger

on the bus who was a neighbor spoke up for me. He said that he knew me, that I was a good girl, and that I worked to help my parents during the day and went to school at night. He told them that I wasn't involved in anything. The soldiers let me go then. But first they studied my identity papers carefully before returning them. They did that to frighten me even more. They told me that they knew where I lived and if they found out that I was involved with any terrorist groups they would come for me. When the soldiers left the bus, I was so frightened and upset that I didn't even thank the man who saved me. I didn't sleep at all that night, and the next day my eyes were so red and swollen from crying and lack of sleep that I was clumsy at work and was scolded for it. The woman who owned the shop thought that I had problems with a boyfriend. I tried to explain that I didn't have a boyfriend, that I had never had a boyfriend because I was too shy and afraid, but I couldn't tell her the real reason why I had stayed awake crying all night because I was afraid that she would fire me for getting mixed up in those kinds of things.

14. When I was eighteen, I finished my primary school education, and I got a job at a factory in San Vicente. The factory was owned by a Turk. We made sports clothes, which were sold in stores in El Salvador. I worked at a sewing machine for ten hours a day, six days a week. I worked there for a little over a year, long enough to get one raise. When that job ended, I was earning the equivalent of $18 a week. The job ended when the owner closed the factory. He said that he had to close it because he was bankrupt. The factory soon reopened with some other Turk as the owner. He refused to hire any of the old workers back. He paid all the new workers less.

15. In 1990, I moved to San Salvador and got a job working at a factory in the free trade zone named Ropa Diana, S.A. We made sports clothes. The factory was owned

by a North American, and the clothes we made were for export to the United States. I earned $3.50 a day for working ten hours a day, six days a week. The reason I earned so much was because there was a union at the factory and the owner paid us high salaries so that we would not join the union. When I was hired, the supervisor, a German, told me that if I joined the union I would get into trouble with the army. I promised that I wouldn't join the union.

16. I worked at Ropa Diana for three years. I didn't join the union. None of the girls who worked at the sewing machines, as far as I knew, were union members. The men who ran the heavy equipment and machinery were nearly all union members.

17. There was heavy security at the plant in case of problems with the union, I think. There were guards at all the doors. The guards wore camouflage uniforms and carried machine guns. I think that they were there to scare us. I know that they scared me. Also, outside every factory in the zona franca, there were often soldiers who threatened us as we left work.

18. Although at least half of the workers were not union members, we sometimes had to collaborate with the union. In 1991, there was a strike and we could not enter the shop because the union members would not let us. In 1992, there was a work stoppage. Both the strike and work stoppage forced the owners to give us small raises and ten-minute breaks in the mornings and afternoons.

19. On April 15, 1993, there was another work stoppage. All of us girls sat at our machines, but we could not work because the union engineers had cut off the power. The supervisor came to where we sat and yelled at us for not working. We tried to tell him that we couldn't because there was no electricity, but he wouldn't listen. He wrote all of our names down on a list. After that we were afraid. We thought that the su-

pervisor would call the army. We wanted to leave the factory but the union members wouldn't let us. They told us to stay in our places until our shift was over.

20. The supervisor called the army. That's the way it is in the free trade zone. Whenever there is a problem, the supervisors or owners call the army, and the soldiers come right away. It is as if the army worked for the factory owners. The soldiers invaded the factory, shouting and shooting their guns in the air and hitting people with the butts of their rifles. One of them hit me in the chest with his rifle and broke my collarbone. They kicked us out of the factory by force. They broke the arm of my friend Juana, who worked at the sewing machine next to mine. We had to go to the hospital. At the hospital they gave us some aspirin and put Juana's arm in a sling and sent us home. They told me that they couldn't do anything for my broken collarbone, but they put my arm in a sling too. Today, I have a large lump where the bone knit improperly.

21. The next morning, although I was in great pain, I returned to the factory. I was afraid that I would lose my job if I didn't, and I needed to work. I was more afraid because the supervisor had put my name on a list. I wanted to explain to him that I was not a member of the union and that I did not want to collaborate with the work stoppage, but the union members had cut off the power and forced us to remain at our machines. When I arrived at the factory, there were many union members milling around out in front. They were very angry. There had been a fire at the factory during the night and part of the factory had been destroyed. The factory was closed until further notice. The union members blamed the owners. They said that the owners had deliberately burned the factory to get rid of the union. Juana and I and some of the other girls went inside the factory to see how much damage had been done. When we saw the supervisor, we tried to talk to him, but he would not listen. He told us that we

were Communist subversives, and if we did not leave at once, he would call the army again and have us removed by force and arrested. When we all started shouting at once, begging him to listen to us, he called the security guards, and they surrounded us, pointing their machine guns at us. We were afraid that they would shoot us so we left.

22. Once we were outside the plant, we did not know what to do so we milled around with the union members. They were very angry and wanted to invade the factory. Finally the supervisor, surrounded by security guards with machine guns, came to the big door and talked to the men. He assured them that the fire was an accident, that it had been caused by a short circuit, and that once the damage was repaired the factory would reopen and everyone would get their jobs back.

23. Since Juana and I were in great pain we went home. My shoulder and chest hurt so much that I hardly went outside the next few days. I stayed in bed and worried and cried a great deal. When a neighbor came one morning to tell me that some men had taken Juana from her house the night before and shot and killed her in the street, I became terrified. Juana had been active in her neighborhood. She organized the people and petitioned the mayor's office to get running water and electricity and paved roads for her neighborhood. I thought that maybe that was why they killed her, but at the same time I was terrified that they killed her because of the strike, because the supervisor had taken our names down and accused us of being Communist subversives. That day I fled to my parents' house in San Vicente. My parents were afraid for me and advised me to flee the country until things quieted down.

24. On May 1, 1993, I fled El Salvador. I stayed in Mexico for several weeks. I received a letter from my mother (see exhibit C) telling me that soldiers had come to the house to ask for me. Among many other things I am

charged with arson, with burning the factory down. When I read my mother's letter I cried. I cried for days because I was sad and felt alone and afraid. I was sad because I knew that things would not quiet down, and I could not return to my home. If I did, they would arrest me and perhaps torture me and kill me. I was afraid because I had never been outside of El Salvador before, and I did not know what to do or where to go. My mother told me that my Aunt Areceli had fled to the United States. She advised me to go there and live with her. The United States seemed very far away and frightening, but I was afraid that the Mexican authorities would catch me and deport me to El Salvador and then the army would grab me. On June 14, 1993, I crossed the frontier near San Ysidro, CA.

For these reasons I am petitioning for asylum in the United States.

I, Carmen Grande, swear under penalty of perjury that the preceding statement is true and correct to the best of my knowledge and belief.

Carmen Grande   Date

I, Tenyr Midden, attest that I am competent to translate from English to Spanish, and I certify that I read the preceding statement in Spanish to the declarant and that she understood the contents thereof before she signed it.

Tenyr Midden   Date

Declaration of Diego Francisco Juan
in Support of His Petition
for Political Asylum

I, Diego Francisco Juan, declare the following:

1. I was born March 15, 1971, in the village of Xiscá in the township of Ixtapán, in the Department of Huehuetenango, Guatemala. My mother and father are Chuj Indians. They spoke Chuj in our home. Chuj is my first language, Spanish my second. I did not learn Spanish until I went to school. Although the school teacher was also Chuj, he taught in Spanish. I only went to school for four years, and I am not fluent in Spanish. I make many mistakes and sometimes have trouble understanding it.

2. Xiscá is a small village of about 200 houses. Everyone who lived there was Chuj. There was a school and a church and several small stores. Most of the people were farmers who owned small plots of land on the sides of the mountains, where they grew corn and beans. A few had land in the valley. The land on the mountains was not very good, and the people could

not grow enough to support themselves. They had to go to the hot country to work, to the cardamom and coffee plantations in the lowlands to the north, or to the cotton and sugar plantations on the south coast. My father and my older brother would often go for two or three months at a time. The first time that I went with them to the hot country to pick coffee, I was eight years old.

3. I attended school in our village. I learned to read and write. I am very glad that I had the opportunity to learn to read and write. My father and mother do not know how, nor do many people in Xiscá. I entered school late, at the age of ten. I did not graduate. I stopped going to school when I was fourteen because the school closed. The military commissioner accused the teacher of being a subversive. He accused him because of the way he taught, and because he did not participate in the Patrulla de Autodefensa Civil [hereinafter called civil patrol]. He was the only teacher we had. Two days after the school was closed he disappeared.

4. In 1980, the guerrillas began passing through Xiscá. They would go from house to house to talk to all the people. They wanted people to support them, and they wanted the men to go with them to fight the army. They told everybody that they should not go to work on the large plantations because the pay was too low. In those days my father earned one quetzal a day on the coffee plantations and 1.25 quetzales on the cotton plantations. That was when the quetzal was equal to one dollar. The guerrillas told us that if we united, the owners would have to pay us better wages, perhaps three or four quetzales a day. That would have been a lot of money. My father wanted to earn more money, of course, just as all the men in the village would have liked to earn more money, but the guerrillas wanted everyone to go on strike. Some of the men said that the army would come and punish us if they went on

strike. The guerrillas said that they would protect us, but they were the first to run when the soldiers came.

5. The guerrillas asked for food. We gave them a little food, and as far as I know nearly everyone in the village gave them food. They were very thin and hungry. God wants us to give food to anyone who is hungry, so we did not refuse them. The guerrillas said that they wanted to help us, but in reality we helped them. Some of them spoke Chuj and they seemed like good people, but others carried rifles and threatened those who refused to feed them or said that they didn't have enough. When the priest came to town, he would warn us against joining the guerrillas. He told us that violence and fighting would not solve our problems. One or two men from Xiscá joined the guerrillas, but the rest were afraid to go with them. Everybody said that they just wanted to be left in peace to work as they had always done. The guerrillas painted words on the walls of the houses. They painted things such as LONG LIVE E. P. G. (Ejército Guerrillero de los Pobres, the Guerrilla Army of the Poor) and DOWN WITH THE ARMY. They would often post flyers on the trees by the road. A few times we would read the posters, but most times we didn't because we were afraid.

6. In 1981, the army came to Xiscá. They came early in the morning when the people were eating breakfast and had not yet left for their fields. They were very angry. They killed many people and animals and burned many houses. As soon as the soldiers entered the village they began shooting. When we heard the shots we went outside to see what was happening. We saw the smoke from the burning houses and were frightened. Many people ran by. They shouted for us to run too. They told us that the soldiers were killing everybody. Because we lived on the opposite side of town from where the army entered, we had time to flee. The soldiers went from house to house. If people were inside, they asked them where the guerrillas were. If they did

not like the answers or if there were words painted on the house by the guerrillas, the soldiers would kill the people. Then they would burn the house. Sometimes they put people in a house and then shot into it with their machine guns and rifles. Then they would burn the house. Most people fled. Some hid in the church; some ran away to the mountains. They thought that everyone who ran away was a guerrilla and shot at them.

7. The soldiers surrounded the church. They ordered the women and children to come out. The people thought that the army would let the women and children go unharmed so they told them to leave the church, but the army killed them with machetes. They raped many women first. While they were doing that, the soldiers left a back window of the church unguarded. When some of the men inside the church saw what the soldiers were doing to the women and children, they realized that the soldiers would kill them next, so they went out the window and ran to the mountains. The old men who could not climb out the window were killed. I did not see the massacre of the people who had hidden in the church because I had escaped with my family to the mountains, but one of my uncles, Pascual Francisco, told us what happened. He lived in the center of town. When the soldiers came, he fled to the church with his family. When he saw that the army was killing everyone, he climbed out the window and ran away to the mountains. He was very sad that the soldiers had killed his wife and son, who was only six months old. Months later, because he was so sad, my uncle killed himself.

8. My family fled to the mountains. We remained hiding there for six days. We were very sad and frightened in the mountains. Many people cried. It was cold and it rained and we were hungry, but we were afraid to return to our village while the army was still there. Some of the men sneaked back into the village at night to get

food from their houses. When they came back, they told us that the army was still there, and they had robbed all the houses. Many houses had been burned and many bodies and pieces of bodies were in the streets. The stories those men told when they came back from the village made me even more afraid, and when the army finally left, I still did not want to return.

9. The army left after six days, and on the seventh day we returned to our village. We found that our house had been burned with all our things in it. The chicken house and the building where we kept our pigs had also been burned with the animals inside. The army also burned our crops. We cried when we saw the destruction. We did not know what to do. We walked through the village and talked to many of our neighbors. It was frightening and sad to see what the soldiers had done to our village. Most of the houses as well as the church had been burned. Everyone was crying and mourning their dead. There were bodies everywhere. Many were children. Many women lay dead with their skirts raised above their waists. All had been mutilated. My Uncle Pascual's wife, Angelica, and their baby had been killed. My grandparents, Felipe and Josefina Juan, who had been too old to run, had been burned inside their house. I did not help my father and mother and my older brother gather the bodies for burial because I was too afraid to touch them. Instead, I helped dig graves in the cemetery. I do not know how many people had been killed, but there were a great many dead. At that time I was ten years old.

10. Everyone was afraid the army would return. Some were too afraid to remain in the village and fled across the border into Mexico. The men who stayed talked among themselves. They asked Bernal Díaz to go to the army headquarters near the city and ask them what we had done wrong and what could we do so that they would not be angry with us again. Mr. Díaz was Chuj

like everyone else, but he spoke Spanish well. He was a businessman and owned a little land and a truck. He or a driver who worked for him would carry workers to the coffee and cardamom plantations to the north in his truck. Sometimes he carried cattle to market. Sometimes people and cattle were carried in the truck at the same time. The army did not rob him of his truck because it was in Huehuetenango delivering cattle at the time of the massacre. Even though he had served in the army, he too was frightened when the soldiers came, and he had fled to the mountains with all the rest of us. He was an important man in the village because he had a little land that was in the valley, a truck, and a rifle and pistol.

11. Though the soldiers were very angry and had killed many people not only in our village but in other villages too, Mr. Díaz went to the base in Huehuetenango to talk to them. We were afraid that the soldiers would kill him and he would not come back. We thought that he was very brave to go and talk to the soldiers when they were so angry. When Mr. Díaz returned, he told us that the army was angry with us because we had allowed the guerrillas to pass through town and had given them food. Mr. Díaz had explained to the soldiers that the guerrillas carried weapons and there was nothing we could do. The soldiers told him that they would kill anyone who collaborated with the guerrillas or gave them food. They said that we had to protect ourselves from the guerrillas. They made Mr. Díaz the military commissioner, and he organized the civil patrol in the village. He didn't want to, but the soldiers told him that he had to do it.

12. All the men between the ages of eighteen and fifty were forced to patrol. But since there weren't enough men, they also took fifteen- and sixteen-year-old boys. Mr. Díaz told another lie when he said that patrolling was voluntary. Everyone was forced to patrol. Mr. Díaz was supposed to report to the army the names of any-

one who missed his turn for patrol duty or who was suspicious or collaborated with the guerrillas. He did not do this, at least not at first, because he knew that the army would kill the person. If someone did not report for patrol duty, the patrol would go to his house and take him to the patrol headquarters where he would be locked up in a room without food or water for two days. That was better than killing the man. My father and older brother had to patrol from the beginning.

13. Everyone was divided into groups of about twelve, and each group had to patrol about every fifteen days. Ten patrollers walked through the streets of the village and around the outskirts while two men stayed at patrol headquarters in the center of town. At first only the two patrol members who stayed at patrol headquarters were given weapons. They were given carbines, and the ones who had to walk around the village carried only sticks and machetes. No one was given training in how to use the carbines. Mr. Díaz had his own rifle and pistol, and he knew how to fire them. He explained to the men how the rifles were loaded and fired, but no one was permitted to practice. After he was made military commissioner, Mr. Díaz always wore his pistol.

14. Absence from patrol duty was not permitted for any reason. If someone was sick, he had to pay a neighbor or friend five quetzales to patrol in his place. If someone wanted to go to the hot country to work for a month, he had to pay someone to take his place for the turns that they would miss. That was a hardship because paying someone for two turns while you were working for a month could amount to nearly half of that month's salary. My older brother Francisco and my father made arrangements with some relatives, and they took turns patrolling for each other when one of them was working in the hot country. This worked out better, but then a few years later Mr. Díaz himself be-

gan to charge everyone ten quetzales to be gone for a month. You had to get permission from him to leave, and he chose the replacement.

15. We lived in a shelter with a roof of sheet plastic and walls of brush for about a year before we finished building a new house. We had lost everything when the soldiers burned our old house, and we had very little money so we could not buy materials right away to build a new house. The new house was much smaller and not as nice as our old one. The same was true with many other people in Xiscá. It took several years to rebuild the town, and it was not as nice as it had been.

16. In March 1982, I think, Ríos Montt became president in a golpe de estado (coup d'état). General Ríos Montt was an Evangelical Christian. There had been a few Evangelicals in Xiscá before that time, but after General Ríos Montt took over, many more converted, including Mr. Díaz. That year the Evangelical preacher began coming to town about three times a week to hold assembly. I wanted to go to assembly because many of my friends attended, and they told me that they had a good time. There was much music and singing, and sometimes when the Holy Spirit entered someone, they would do strange things like roll on the floor or talk in a language that was neither Chuj nor Spanish and that no one understood. Perhaps it was English. My father would not let me join the Evangelicals. He said that our family had always been Catholic no matter who was president. However, the Catholic church had been destroyed the previous year by the army. There had been plans to repair it and some work had been done. The doors had been replaced and the windows boarded over to prevent animals from entering, which would have been a sin, but the roof was never replaced and many birds built their nests in there. No more work was ever done on the church after Mr. Díaz converted. I don't know if it was because he would not allow the church to be rebuilt.

Now I think that it was because the people were afraid that he would not allow it, and maybe no one asked him. Or maybe people were afraid that the army would be angry.

17. Mr. Díaz was, at first, a good man, I think, and he tried to help people meet their obligations, and the punishments he ordered were fair. Then, in about 1985, he became angrier and less just and the punishments became more severe, and sometimes he turned people in to the army.

18. After 1985, when someone missed patrol duty, he would be taken to the central plaza. All the people in the town were ordered to go to the plaza to watch. There the man was tied up and the other patrol members on duty that day were ordered to whip the man on the back two times each with a rubber hose. The first time this happened the prisoner was Hermenigildo Coj. He was then about sixteen years old, and although he was usually a good boy, he was also somewhat rebellious. My brother, Francisco, was on patrol duty that day and was ordered, along with all the others on duty, to beat Hermenigildo. Francisco refused. My brother was a catechist and had become the lay preacher after the church was burned and the priest stopped coming to the village. He did not believe in violence. He did not want to beat Hermenigildo and told everyone that it was wrong to beat him. Mr. Díaz then ordered that my brother be tied up beside Hermenigildo and that he be whipped too. My brother said that he would rather be whipped than whip someone else against the wishes of God. Many people in the plaza supported my brother and began talking. But when Francisco was tied up and whipped with Hermenigildo, they became afraid and did not say anything. Francisco's back was very sore for a long time.

19. That same year or maybe the year before, Mr. Díaz took over the lands of the people who had been killed by the military or who had fled to Mexico. No one had worked the lands or tried to take them over, not even family members, because we were all afraid. Those lands had remained idle since 1981 when the army killed all those people. Mr. Díaz took over those lands, and he became very rich. Then, to punish someone in the patrol for being late or for falling asleep on duty, he would order them to work on his lands. We were not paid for this service just as we were not paid for patrolling.

20. Also in 1985, in assembly, in front of all the Evangelical Christians in the village, Mr. Díaz accused Maestro Jesús of being a subversive and a guerrilla collaborator. He said that because of the way he taught he must be a subversive, and because he did not participate in the civil patrol, he must be a guerrilla collaborator. Maestro Jesús was not obligated to participate because teachers were exempt from patrol duty, but still Mr. Díaz accused him. I did not see this. I only heard about it later. But all the Evangelicals were there at assembly and they saw it. When I heard about this, I asked my father once again if I could go to assembly and see all these things, but he refused. I don't know what Mr. Díaz meant about the manner in which Maestro Jesús taught school. I thought he was a good teacher. The son of Mr. Díaz was very stupid and arrogant and did not do well in school. Perhaps that is why Mr. Díaz accused the teacher. Whatever the reason, it was a very serious matter because several days later the teacher disappeared. Mr. Díaz said that proved that he was with the guerrillas. He then warned us not to have anything to do with the guerrillas. We didn't know how they could have done this without anyone seeing them, but the teacher lived with his parents in a house that was apart from the rest of the village. Ten days later his body was found by the road near a neighboring vil-

lage. When the parents went to bring the body back for burial, they were shocked at how mutilated it was. I didn't see it myself, but the father said that his son had been tortured. Mr. Díaz said that the guerrillas had killed him and mutilated the body because they were afraid that he was about to betray them. The teacher's family said that someone had told them that two patrol members who were friends of Mr. Díaz had carried Maestro Jesús away in the truck. The teacher's family disappeared the following night. Mr. Díaz said that the guerrillas must have come to kidnap them during the night and would probably kill them too. He ordered the patrol members who had been on duty that night to work on his lands as punishment for allowing the guerrillas to enter the village and kidnap innocent people. We found out later that the family had fled to Mexico.

21. I missed the teacher. He was a good person. I also missed school very much. I was going to graduate that year but I didn't. The school closed, and we never got another teacher. Mr. Díaz took over the land that belonged to the teacher's family. It was good land in the valley.

22. Also in 1985, the army sent an order to all the military commissioners in Xiscá and the nearby villages to pick five men from each village to go with the soldiers into the mountains to look for guerrillas. Those men were to march in front of the soldiers to protect them from guerrilla bullets. They were not given arms to carry, only sticks and machetes. They would be the first ones killed if there were a battle. They were to be cannon fodder. My brother, Francisco, was the first chosen from our village because Mr. Díaz was still angry with him for refusing to beat Hermenigildo. Francisco refused to go with the soldiers and fled to Mexico.

23. Because my brother had fled, Mr. Díaz forced me to join the civil patrol even though I was only fourteen

years old. I did not want to patrol because I was afraid, but I was also afraid not to. I had seen them beat Hermenigildo Coj and my brother, and I did not want to be beaten. Neither did I want to be accused of being a guerrilla collaborator. I patrolled about every two weeks. Also at that time I had to work even harder on the family land because with my brother gone it was necessary to help support my family. Not only did I miss a whole day every two weeks by patrolling, but the day after patrol duty I was too tired to work and had to rest. Patrol duty was very hard. I had to march all night in cold weather, in the rain, even when I was sick. It was very hard and I was often miserable. It was like being a slave.

24. When Lauriano Diego paid for permission and then left to go to work in the cotton fields on the coast for two months, Mr. Díaz raped his wife, Dominga, and then forced her to live with him. She did not want to do it, but she had to just as the men had to patrol and work on the lands of Mr. Díaz. When Lauriano came back, he was angry but he was also afraid and he did nothing. He only talked to some of the people in the village. One night the soldiers came to take him away. They released him a week later. Lauriano told his father, who told my father, that the soldiers had beat him with the butts of their rifles and tortured him. They tied his hands behind his back so tightly that they hurt. They told him he should get on his knees and pray because they were going to kill him. One of them put a pistol to his head and very slowly pulled the trigger. When the gun went click but did not fire, the soldiers laughed at the scare they had given him. They did that often, each time telling him that this time there was a bullet in the gun. Once they tied his hands and feet and blindfolded him and carried him to a helicopter. They told him that they were going to fly very high and throw him out when they were over the mountain. After a few minutes in the helicopter the

soldiers threw him out. Lauriano was terrified and was certain that he was going to die. He hit the ground very hard but the fall was only a few feet because the helicopter had not taken off. They did all this to make him tell where the guerrillas were, but because he didn't know, he couldn't tell them. When they released Lauriano, they warned him that they were going to come for him again. As soon as he was well enough, he fled to Mexico.

25. In 1987 or 1988 all patrol members were given rifles when on duty. We were given M-16 rifles, made in the United States. We did not know how to use them. I have never fired a weapon in my life. The only training I ever had was when Mr. Díaz showed us how to load our rifles and told us how to fire them. The soldiers who brought the rifles spoke to us in Spanish, and Mr. Díaz translated their words into Chuj. They told everyone that we had to fight the guerrillas and not run away if we saw them. They told us that if we lost our rifles and were still alive they would know that we had given our rifles to the guerrillas and they, the soldiers, would kill us as collaborators. Having to carry a rifle made me even more afraid of the guerrillas.

26. We knew there were guerrillas in the area although we never saw them. When we were on patrol duty and heard the dogs bark on one side of town, we always went to the other side to hide. Sometimes they would enter Xiscá late at night and slip notes under the doors telling people to stop patrolling and not to support the army. Many people in Xiscá were angry with Mr. Díaz for taking the wife of Lauriano Diego and telling the army to kill the teacher and for many other bad things. Some people let the guerrillas enter their houses late at night. Some gave them food. Others went with them.

27. My country became a democracy in 1987 when Vinicio Cerezo was elected president. These things didn't

seem to matter in Xiscá where I lived. The patrols continued. Mr. Díaz grew angrier and more violent. Some
said it was because the guerrillas were becoming more
active and the soldiers had begun to threaten him.
Some said that he had grown so rich that some of the
officers in the military wanted to take his lands from
him, and they were looking for a reason to have him
arrested. Whatever the reason for the change that
took place in Mr. Díaz, he began to think of many
severe punishments. When Juan Tomás was caught
sleeping when he was on duty guarding the patrol
headquarters, Mr. Díaz had him dig a deep pit and fill
it half full of water. Juan Tomás had to spend a day
and a night in the pit and it was very cold. He was sick
for a long time after that and missed several turns of
patrol duty. That made Mr. Díaz even angrier. Once
I dropped my rifle, and he made me hop ten times
around the plaza like a rabbit. That made my legs hurt
very much. Once Raúl Pakal lost some bullets, and Mr.
Díaz made him live in a tree for three days. He could
only come down to relieve himself once a day. His family had to lift food and water and a hammock up to him
by rope. He had to sleep in the tree. Mr. Díaz said that
the next time anyone lost bullets he would be reported
to the army.

28. Beginning in 1987, shortly after Raúl was forced to stay
in the tree, two patrol members were detailed to guard
the road leading into town. We were told to stop all
vehicles and ask the people for their papers. If the
people from Xiscá wanted to travel, they had to pay
five quetzales (one dollar in 1987) to the patrol members, who had to give the money to Mr. Díaz. This job
was not as hard as patrolling in the streets, but Mr.
Díaz often came out to inspect the guards on the road
to make sure that we were awake. Because I could
read, I was usually assigned to this job when it was my
turn to patrol. I did not think that it was right. And

sometimes people said bad things to me when I took their money. But I had to do it.

29. In August 1988, I was on guard duty on the road outside of town. Late at night the guerrillas surrounded Juan Andrés and me. Juan was my cousin and a year younger than I was. I don't know how many of the guerrillas there were because it was dark, but some of them had rifles that they pointed at us. They ordered us to give them our rifles and we did. We did not want to fight. The guerrillas talked to us and asked us to join them but we were afraid. The guerrillas warned us that if we did not go with them, the soldiers would accuse us of being guerrillas anyway and kill us. We believed them but still we did not want to go with them. The guerrillas tied us up and left us on the road. We got loose and ran to our homes to hide. We were frightened. At dawn some men came to my house and pounded on the door. Mr. Díaz and four members of the patrol came into the house to look for me. We had an old well in the patio behind the house. I had hidden in there as soon as the men knocked. They searched the house but didn't find me. My father told them that I had come home and then left for Mexico right away. Mr. Díaz was very angry and said that he hoped the army would catch me.

30. I hid in the house for a week. Every time someone came to the door I hid in the old well. My parents told me what was happening in the village. They told me that Mr. Díaz and some men found my cousin Juan hiding in his house and took him away. His parents went to Mr. Díaz to beg for mercy, but Mr. Díaz said that it was too late, that he had already taken Juan to the army. They went to the army barracks, but the commander said that they had no record of Juan Andrés. Five days later Juan's body was found in a field. It had been horribly mutilated. Mr. Díaz told everyone that the guerrillas must have kidnapped Juan

and me and that when Juan tried to escape they killed him. All this made my parents even more afraid, and they urged me to run away to Mexico. But I didn't want to. The truth is that I was afraid to run away by myself. I had never been away from home in my life. I suppose that I hoped that after a while Mr. Díaz would forget about me, and I would be able to lead a normal life.

31. One night at about midnight I heard the dogs barking. I quickly slipped out of the house to hide in the well. I waited there a long time in the dark, until my parents came to tell me that it was safe to come out. They told me that four strange men dressed in civilian clothes came to the house and asked for me. They were very big and spoke only Spanish. They were very angry when my parents told them that I had fled to Mexico. They searched the house. They told my parents that they would return for me. Our village is remote and strangers rarely passed through, and that was the first time that strangers had ever come to our house. My family and I thought that those men must have been from a death squad sent by the army.

32. On that same night I said good-bye to my parents and started walking toward Mexico. I left Guatemala on August 24, 1988. I was seventeen years old.

For these reasons I am petitioning for political asylum in the United States.

I, Diego Francisco Juan, swear under penalty of perjury that the above declaration is true and correct to the best of my knowledge and belief.

Diego Francisco Juan   Date

I, Tenyr Midden, state that I am competent to translate from English to Spanish and that I read the above declaration to Diego Francisco Juan before he signed it.

_____   _____

Tenyr Midden   Date

Declaration of Zoila Calderón in Support of Her Petition for Asylum

I, Zoila Calderón, declare the following:

1. I was born November 23, 1965, in San Pedro Sula, Honduras. At that time my father was a day laborer. Later he worked regularly in construction. My mother did not work outside the house. As there were seven of us, and my father did not earn much money, we were poor and we lived in a poor neighborhood where there was neither running water nor electricity. It was a new neighborhood on the edge of the city, and many of the houses were makeshift, made of whatever people could find—cardboard, old sheets of metal, wood, or sticks. We lived in a small house made of sticks with a thatched roof and a dirt floor.

2. Because we were poor, I did not go to school as a child. Instead, when I was nine years old, my parents sent me to work in the house of a rich lady on the other side of the city. I lived with the other servants in that big house and visited my parents on my one day off a week. Every fifteen days I received my salary,

which I gave to my parents, who then gave me a small allowance for bus fare. Although the rich family did not beat me and gave me rice, beans, and tortillas to eat, and the other servants tried to help me, I was very lonely and frightened and cried myself to sleep the first few weeks. I eventually stopped crying myself to sleep and accepted my situation, but I never liked that job. Living with that family taught me that the rich do not live in the same world as the poor. For instance, they never went into the barrio where my parents lived. I doubt that they even knew that it existed. Also, the children of the house all went to school. They had nice clothes and ate meat every day. They did not have to work and never washed or ironed their own clothes. They had a daughter who was two years older than me. She treated me, at times, as if I were a doll, and at other times as if I were her personal slave. She often laughed at me and said that I was stupid. When she complained to her mother about me, her mother would say, "Well, what can you expect from her class of people?" They often talked about me in my presence as if I didn't exist.

3. I grew to believe that rich people were better than I was and that I was only a poor, illiterate servant girl, worth less than the daughter's fancy doll.

4. I worked for that family for seven years. During that time, they raised my salary twice. I had to ask for each raise, and they complained each time I asked. When I asked, they made a big fuss, as if my salary would bankrupt them. Only during my last year of working for them did they pay me the equivalent of about a dollar a day.

5. When I was sixteen, I got a job with another family. I did not have to live with them, which meant that my hours were shorter, and still the salary was nearly double my old salary. When I told my former employers that I was leaving, they accused me of treachery and

disloyalty. They asked how I could do that to them after all they had done for me. However, I am sure that they soon found another young girl from a poor, large family to work for them for practically nothing. When I started my new job, I was able to live with my parents. By that time four of my older brothers had married and moved out of the house. Also, my father had steady work in construction. In those days we had more money than ever.

6. When I was sixteen, I met my husband, Medaba Liento. We began living together in 1982, when I was seventeen years old and he was twenty-one. We married in 1984. Medaba was a baker. He and his family baked bread and delivered it to the small stores in the neighborhood. Medaba's father had a small pickup truck, which they used to deliver the bread. To Medaba, that truck was a symbol of who he was, someone who was a success. He was always cleaning and waxing it.

7. Medaba encouraged me to go to night school to learn to read and write. He was the first person to tell me that I was not stupid and that I was smart. It was just that I had not had the opportunity to go to school, he would tell me. I liked going to school, and the teacher also encouraged me by telling me that I was smart and I learned quickly. Just going to school was an education. All the other students were adults who were poor like me and had grown up illiterate and ashamed and thinking that they were stupid. I made many friends in school. I began helping my father-in-law and husband with their accounts and orders in the bakery. For the first time in my life, I began to think that I was worth more than a rich girl's doll, that maybe even I was as good as a rich girl.

8. On August 15, 1985, Medaba was forcibly recruited by the Honduran army. The soldiers grabbed him one morning when he was making his deliveries. When he

didn't return home, we looked for him and learned that the army had taken him along with other young men to the military base. My father-in-law and I went to the base to try to get him released. Under Honduran law, married men aren't supposed to be drafted. But the officers at the base refused to release him. We went to the base many times, but the officers only got angry with us. Finally my father-in-law hired an attorney to secure his release. The attorney took our money but didn't do anything. He kept saying that those things took time and we should be patient.

9. Medaba didn't have much time. After basic training he was transferred to Battalion 316 as a truck driver. Battalion 316 is famous in Honduras because they run death squads, and they kill people accused of crimes. Everyone in Honduras is afraid of Battalion 316.

10. The first few weeks in Battalion 316 Medaba was not permitted to leave the base. His duties were to repair trucks. Then one Saturday he was ordered to drive a truck with two officers and two soldiers to a small town. When they arrived, they went to the jail. There they found four men who had been accused of stopping a bus and robbing the passengers. They took the four men from the jail and ordered Medaba to drive to an isolated spot in the country. Medaba was ordered to stay in the truck while the others got out. The four prisoners had their hands tied behind their backs and their feet tied together. The officers ordered the two soldiers to beat the prisoners with their rifle butts. When the prisoners were on the ground, the officers ordered the soldiers to cut them with their bayonets. The soldiers tortured the prisoners slowly, cutting them deeply in their arms and legs. It made Medaba sick to see what those poor men were suffering. After what seemed like a long time, the soldiers shot the men in the head. They left the bodies there in the field for the people to find, as a warning to others.

11. The soldiers got back into the truck and ordered Medaba to drive to the nearest town. There they stopped at a cantina. While Medaba stayed in the truck, the soldiers and the officers sat at different tables and drank beer.

12. Medaba was frightened by what he had seen and realized that they would never permit him to leave the battalion alive. He was afraid that one day they would make him do those things. He knew that if he wanted to escape he had to do it right away. He asked the officers permission to use the bathroom in the cantina. They gave him permission, and he entered the bathroom and climbed out the back window. He ran as far and as fast as he could. He got a taxi to take him to the next town. There he got a ride back to San Pedro and home.

13. He came home late that night tired and frightened. The moment that I opened the door and saw his face I knew that he was in trouble. He told me what had happened and that he had to change his clothes and run away. He had to flee the country as soon as possible because they would soon come for him.

14. Within hours of my husband's return, several cars stopped in the street in front of our house. They were big four-wheel-drive American wagons with dark windows. We knew immediately they were from Battalion 316. Medaba fled out the back door. I heard shouts and many shots, and then for a long time everything was quiet. After what seemed like a long time I heard the car doors slam and the engines start. The cars drove away. Then nothing. I waited and waited. I did not sleep that night. I did not leave the house that day. I did not eat. I only waited for some word from my husband. Or worse, I was afraid that a neighbor would come and tell me that my husband's body was in the street. But no word and no neighbor came, not that day, nor the next. I prayed that he had escaped.

15. Six days after my husband fled, a neighbor came to tell me that his body had been found tossed by the road at the edge of the city. It was awful to see his body. He was black and blue from the beating, and there were many cuts and burns all over.

16. I was shocked by my husband's death. I was frightened. I moved back in with my parents so I wouldn't be alone. I was also very angry. I wanted to avenge his murder. The only way I knew to punish the murderers was to report what had happened to the police, to the newspapers, and to CODEH (Comité de Derechos Humanos, the Committee for Human Rights). I realized that it was dangerous for me, but I didn't care. I was angry and I wanted revenge. As I expected, the police didn't do anything, and the newspaper reporters wouldn't even talk to me, a poor woman from a poor barrio. But the people at CODEH wrote down my story. They asked me many questions. They wanted to know where the four prisoners were tortured and killed. I told them as much as I could. They said they would investigate.

17. While I continued with my complaint, I went back to night school. I was sad and angry, and at the same time I needed to fill up the lonely hours. Medaba had often told me that the only way to get ahead in life was to become educated. I thought that the rich used Battalion 316 and the death squads to terrorize the poor, to keep them from getting ahead in life. I was determined that I would not be terrorized, and I was determined to educate myself.

18. On March 14, 1986, while I was at night school, three men in civilian clothes came to my parents' house to look for me. My father asked them who they were, and they refused to tell him. They became angry when my father told them that I wasn't home. They pushed their way into the house and searched it to see if I was hiding. They even looked under the beds. They demanded

126

to know where I was. My father was very frightened, but he told the men that he didn't know, that I hadn't been home for two days. They said that I was probably with my guerrilla friends, but it didn't matter because sooner or later they would find me.

19. That visit frightened me. I was sure that the men were from Battalion 316 or a death squad, and they had accused me of being with the guerrillas because they were going to kill me. Some of my friends told me that there were rumors going around in the streets that I was with the guerrillas. That's what the death squads do, they spread rumors that someone is with the guerrillas, then they kill her. Their visit made me realize that I wasn't as brave as I thought I was. I was terrified that they would torture me, that they would do to me what they had done to my husband. I ran away. I went to live with my aunt in the country, in Olancho Province.

20. At my aunt's house I didn't do anything for a long time. I was very depressed and frightened. I slept a great deal, often day and night, sometimes only waking to eat the meals my aunt prepared for me. Often I had nightmares in which I saw my husband's mutilated body. I dreamed that they were coming after me and I had nowhere to hide. When I awoke, I cried. I cried over many little things that made me think of my husband and what they had done to him. Sometimes I wished that they would find me and kill me. My poor aunt did her best to help me but nothing cheered me up. She bought me a beautiful Chinese silk scarf for my twenty-first birthday. It was so lovely and I knew that Medaba would have liked to have seen me wearing it—I cried when I put it on.

21. Little by little I became more animated. I began to sleep less. I began to help my aunt with the cooking and the cleaning. Although it was difficult for me to force myself to leave the house because I was terrified,

I began to accompany my aunt to the market. I went with her to the river to wash the clothes. Little by little I began to take an interest in life again. I began to talk to the other women at the market and especially at the river. The women treated me with sympathy, as my aunt had told people that my husband had recently passed away. She didn't tell them how or that the death squads were looking for me. As I became active again, I wanted to go back to school, but my aunt lived in a small village. The nearest large town where there might have been a night school was forty minutes away by bus, and there was no return bus at night. I needed something to do to occupy myself.

22. An older woman named Constancia Campos befriended me. She made a special effort to talk to me whenever I washed the clothes on the rocks on the river. She told me many stories to make me laugh. When she laughed, her whole body quivered, and her smile was quite funny as her front teeth were missing. She knew that she was fat and her smile was ugly, but she was able to laugh at herself and her troubles. She had never been to school and was quite impressed when I told her that I had learned to read and write as an adult. She was even more impressed to learn that some of the other students at the night school I had attended were grandparents. She laughed at me when I showed my surprise the day she invited me to her wedding. She knew that I was surprised, not because she had invited me, but because I would never have imagined that she would marry, that any man would want to marry her. All my life I had thought of myself as unattractive except when I was with my husband, but I don't think that I ever considered myself as ugly as Constancia. She laughed at her plainness as I was never able to do. She surprised me even more when she told me that she had been married three times before. Two husbands had died and one had disappeared. She had eight children. Although she looked

old and ugly, she told me she was only forty-two years old and she still liked men.

23. It was Constancia who got me interested in joining the National Peasants Union (Unión Nacional de Campesinos, or UNC). She explained that under the agrarian reform legislation landless peasants could acquire land that was not being used. The problem was that the peasants first had to file papers with the government to get title to the land and the government usually worked for the rich and not the poor. As soon as peasants filed for unused land, the government either informed the absentee landowner or another rich man who might be interested. Because of that, landless peasants in many parts of Honduras resorted to land invasions. A land invasion occurs when a group of peasants actually moves onto the land before they have a title.

24. Constancia told me that a group of peasants from the village was considering invading fifty acres of land nearby that belonged to a North American company. The land was not being used, and by law the peasants could claim it. If I joined the UNC, I could move onto the land with them and become a landowner. She told me that the group needed someone bright like me who could read and write.

25. At Constancia's wedding, I met many of her friends who were also in the UNC and who were planning to participate in the land invasion. Until that time I had kept to myself in the village, but at the wedding I met many people, and, for the first time since my husband was killed, I enjoyed myself. I wore the beautiful Chinese scarf that my aunt had given me. I danced with many of the men. I was very popular and having a good time until I began to feel guilty. I began to feel that I was shameless. My husband had been murdered only six months ago, and there I was carrying on like a woman of the street. I left the party when no one was

looking, like a thief who sneaks out of the house he has robbed.

26. The next day Constancia came to my house to ask why I had left the party so early. Many of the men asked where I had gone, she told me and laughed. I could not help blushing. I apologized for my rudeness and told her what had happened to my husband. I was certain that she would see how disgracefully I had behaved when I told her. But she didn't see it that way at all. She sat on my bed and comforted me. She told me what had happened to her husbands. The first one had simply run away because, she thought, they could not seem to stop having children. The second had been a leader in the regional UNC. FUSEP (Honduran Security Forces) took him and other union officers away. Later, their bodies were found beside a road. They had been tortured before they were shot in the mouth. Her third husband had been killed by the Nicaraguan contras who stole food from the peasants. They killed him because he had complained. "I loved all my husbands," Constancia told me, "and after I lost each of them, I thought that I would never love another man. I thought that I would mourn for the rest of my life. But the men and I could not seem to leave each other alone. At first I would feel guilty when I took up with a new man. But just a little guilty. And soon I forgot the guilt. Now that I look back on my life, I think that I was right to remarry each time. For some women life is not complete if they do not have a man to love. Perhaps for you it is not the same. But you are young and you have not been a widow long. If it is right for you to find a new man, when the time comes, you will know it. You tell me that your husband encouraged you to go to school. He encouraged you to better yourself. I think he would have encouraged you to continue with your life. If that means you should take another man someday, so be it. Your husband is with God now. He cannot be jealous or stingy. You betray

him only if you stop living. Always remember, Flaquita, it is fine to feel guilty; that shows a noble spirit. But it is finer still to feel loved."

27. Constancia consoled me and gave me good advice. She also helped to educate me politically. She told me, "You must continue to live, and since you are poor, that means that you must continue to struggle. The strongest weapon the poor have is the will to continue. The rich fear that most of all because they know that we will never be satisfied with a few centavos or a few rags or a few pieces of dried tortilla. The fifty acres we are about to invade, that is nothing to the rich. They could easily give it to us and not miss it. After all, no one is using that tiny piece of land. And it is not that the rich are completely stingy, although they are very stingy. No, it is that they know that we will not simply take our fifty acres and that will be the end of it. They know better than we do that once we have the land we will demand more. Next we will demand electricity and schools and doctors. We will continue living and demanding until we are equal. That is why the rich cannot permit us to take the first small step. That is why they will fight us at every step. And that is why, Flaquita, you must continue with your life. Who knows, perhaps, someday you will take pity on some poor man and take him for your husband as I have done. It can only be out of pity that we accept them. They are such miserable creatures!"

28. I joined the UNC. I was made secretary of our group because of my education. I helped organize the cooperative of seventy members. We called ourselves Tierra Fértil. My duties were to keep a record of the members and the hours they worked. When we invaded the land and began earning money, I would keep a record of sales, payments, and purchases. It was very exciting. We met with members of the national union. They taught us how to file the papers for the land we wanted. I helped fill out the papers and went to the city

with a delegation to file for the land. I felt useful. Because I had learned to read and write I became an officer of Tierra Fértil. It made me realize how powerful a weapon education was.

29. After some months of planning and preparation, we filed the papers to claim ownership of the land. The next day we invaded the land. All seventy members of our cooperative, including women and children, moved onto the land. We took all of our belongings with us—clothes, pots and pans, furniture, lumber, and tools to build houses. We quickly built the houses and began to clear the land for planting. We planted corn, beans, tomatoes, squash, and lettuce. It was hard work but very exciting. I think that we were excited because we felt strong, because we worked together. We felt powerful because we had taken control.

30. Without telling anyone, without even saying anything to him because I was still in mourning, I secretly admired one of the workers, Epifanio Castrejón. He drove the tractor that pulled the wagon loads of lumber for the houses. He cleared the ground and tilled it so we could plant. He was very handsome and dedicated. He was indefatigable. The day we invaded the land, he worked without rest from before dawn to long after the sun had set. The next morning he was out before dawn, clearing the fields and tilling the soil. I remembered that he had seemed to like me when we danced together at Constancia's wedding.

31. When we filed our papers with the National Agrarian Institute (INA) in accordance with the laws of Honduras, the institute gave us permission to plant our crops and told us that, if the papers were in order, we would soon receive title to our land. I was certain that the papers were in order because I had worked very hard on them.

32. About a month after we took over the land, Mr. Abarizio, a local cattle owner, who was very rich and

owned large tracts of land and many head of cattle, let his cattle loose on our land, where our crops were just beginning to grow. Mr. Abarizio had also hired a gang of men who carried weapons to protect his cattle and to prevent us from driving them off our land.

33. The officers of the cooperative went to the INA. We found out that Mr. Abarizio had recently been given title to our land. The clerk at the office, who was sympathetic, said that there was nothing we could do. He told us that Mr. Abarizio had paid bribes to INA officials. Although members of the national union had told us that such things happened, we were shocked at such blatant corruption.

34. With the help of the UNC we hired an attorney to fight the case, to prove that we had applied for the title to the land before Mr. Abarizio, and that the title was illegally given to him.

35. On October 24, 1986, FUSEP surrounded our cooperative. They destroyed our houses and belongings and evicted everyone. The next day we reinvaded the land and began rebuilding our houses. About a month later FUSEP came again to Tierra Fértil. They forced many of the men into their trucks to take them away. We were afraid that they would beat up the men or even kill them if they took them away. We were frantic. Constancia and I organized the women and children. We surrounded the trucks and refused to move while they held our men. It was a very tense situation because for a while we thought they would run us over. We forced FUSEP to release the men. The soldiers were very angry when they left.

36. About a week later the officers of the cooperative, two men and I, attended a meeting in town with our lawyer and members from the national union. After we left the meeting, we, the officers of Tierra Fértil, were grabbed by a group of men who blindfolded us and took us somewhere. We think it was the city because

of the traffic noises. Although the men wore civilian clothes, I was certain that they were from FUSEP. They put us in two small cells, the men in one and me in another. It must have been a clandestine prison because we didn't see or hear any other prisoners. We were held against our will for three days. We were not allowed to call anyone. We were not taken before a judge. We were not charged with a crime. My hands were handcuffed behind my back, my feet tied together, and I was blindfolded the entire time I was in jail. They did not give us any food, but they gave me water twice a day. I was not beaten, but I was interrogated. They wanted to know who I was, why we took the land, if we had any money, and whether we were Communists. They threatened to kill me if I did not leave the cooperative and the union.

37. After three days, they put us into a truck and took us out to the country where they released us. When they released me, they threatened me. They said that they knew that I was a Communist and that it would be worse for me the next time they caught me. They released us on a dirt road surrounded by forest. We didn't know where we were. It was very difficult for me to walk because my legs were stiff and sore from being tied up for three days. One of the men could not walk at all because the torturers had broken his leg by hitting him with their rifle butts. The other man also had difficulty walking. They had both been severely beaten. We hitchhiked back to Tierra Fértil. It took us all day.

38. When we arrived back at the cooperative, I went straight back to my ramada to rest. My house had been destroyed when FUSEP evicted us about five weeks earlier so I only had a ramada to protect me from the sun and rain. Soon after I returned, Constancia came to visit me. She was relieved to learn that I hadn't been tortured or raped. I told her that at last I had found an advantage to being ugly—not even the soldiers wanted to rape me. At first she was shocked. She began to tell

me that I wasn't ugly, but then she saw that I was joking. We laughed, and then I noticed that my beautiful
scarf had gotten very dirty in jail, and I began to cry. I
cried from all the pent-up fear and exhaustion. It is
good that women can cry. It is like sleep after work. It
makes us stronger to continue the struggle. Men who
refuse to cry cannot rest. The man who had been arrested with me and could still walk left the cooperative
that night.

39. I believed the FUSEP men when they told me that the
next time it would be worse for me. I believed that they
were capable of torturing and killing me. At the very
least they would beat me. I was even more afraid that
they would investigate and discover that Battalion 316
was looking for me. Then they would certainly accuse
me of being a Communist and an enemy of the state. I
was terrified of Battalion 316 because I had seen what
they had done to my husband. I was truly terrified that
they would do the same to me. Still, I stayed on, partly
because I didn't know what else to do and partly because I was very stubborn.

40. Because we stayed on the land and fought the case in
the courts, Mr. Abarizio resorted to violence. The private army of thugs he had hired had, until that time,
merely guarded the cattle and threatened the men in
the cooperative. Suddenly they attacked a group of
men who were working in the fields. The thugs were
on horseback, and they charged the men. They attacked with machetes. They cut off Eusebio's right
hand. They cut off Epifanio Castrejón's right arm. This
is a tactic that the cattle barons use in Honduras.
When they want to take over some land that poor
people are living on, they send their army of thugs to
intimidate them. If the people refuse to go, the thugs
cut off the hands of the men to prevent them from
working.

41. We took the two men to the hospital and then we went to the police. We knew that the police would not do anything, but we reported the crime anyway. They said that they would investigate, but not once did they come out to the cooperative or visit the men in the hospital. The police never investigate or arrest the rich, only the poor.

42. People in the cooperative were frightened. Several families had already left. Constancia came to my hut the evening after we returned from the police. She was very sad. She came to tell me that she and her husband were leaving the cooperative. They were going to move to another part of the country or maybe even to Mexico. They thought it was too dangerous for them in Olancho Province. Now that Eusebio had lost his hand, he was marked as someone who had participated in a land invasion. They even thought about going to the United States where everyone was happy and able to work and live without fear. She apologized to me for leaving. I tried to comfort her as she had so often comforted me. I told her that she and Eusebio had made the right decision. I told her that the cooperative was falling apart and that I, too, was thinking of leaving. I hadn't really thought of leaving. I only said that to make her feel better. Before she left I gave her the most precious thing I had—my lovely silk scarf. She didn't want to take it because she knew that I loved that scarf. I told her to take it to remember me by. I reminded her that I had still not given her a wedding present, and I wanted her to have it. She accepted it, she said, because it would always remind her of me.

43. The next day Constancia came to say good-bye. She was wearing my scarf. She seemed very happy. She was her old self, laughing and joking. She said that it was due to the scarf. She felt like an attractive young woman again because of the scarf. She told me that she was going to leave her children at her mother's in the village, and then, who knows? She might go to the

hospital to pick up her husband or she might look for another man, a younger man, someone who had two hands to hold her with, the way a young woman like her needed to be held. She laughed so wickedly that I had to laugh too. She promised to send me a letter to let me know the name of the man she had run off with. I cried when she left. We were all sad to see her go. Her laughter and love of life represented the spirit we all had when we founded Tierra Fértil.

44. During the next few days it seemed that the violence had stopped. It was as if there were a cease-fire. The men in the cooperative did not work in the fields, and the thugs who worked for Mr. Abarizio did not attack anyone. FUSEP did not come to destroy our homes and evict us. We began to think that the authorities and Mr. Abarizio were nervous because they had cut off the men's hands and still we did not give up. We thought that perhaps going to the local police had helped after all. We began to think that we might win. Two men from the national union came to tell us that there was great hope that we would win the case in the courts because it was obvious that we had applied for title to the land before Mr. Abarizio.

45. Eusebio came to visit us the next day. He was very nervous. He was afraid that the cooperative would be raided while he was there. He didn't want to stay long. The stump where his right hand used to be was swathed in white bandages. One of the teenagers asked him if it hurt a lot, and he explained that he felt pain in the hand that was no longer attached. He was afraid that something bad was happening to the hand, and he asked the men if they had buried it. They assured him that they had. I thought the only reason he had come was because he was worried about the missing hand, but he took me aside and asked me if I knew where Constancia was. She hadn't gone to the hospital to meet him as they had planned. I remembered her joke about picking up another man, and I thought that

maybe it wasn't a joke after all. I didn't tell Eusebio about it. How could I? I didn't want to believe that my good friend would leave her husband that way, but she herself had talked about it. I was very sorry for Eusebio.

46. A few days later my aunt came to look for me. She was very excited and nervous. I wasn't in my ramada when she arrived but one of the neighbors told me, and I went to meet her. When I entered the ramada, she burst into tears and threw her arms around my neck, hugging me as hard as she could. I didn't know what was going on. Finally, when she was able to stop crying, she explained that she had been worried about me. She thought that I had been killed. People in the village had told her that my body had been dumped by the road that leads to the city. They knew it was me because the head was covered by the Chinese scarf I always wore.

47. I was certain that the government security forces wanted to kill me. I was certain that when they killed my friend Constancia they thought they had killed me. I was afraid that they would soon discover that they had killed the wrong person and would look for me. I fled Honduras on December 22, 1986, and entered the United States on January 24, 1987.

48. I am afraid that if I were to return to Honduras, FUSEP or Battalion 316 would capture me. They would accuse me of being a Communist to justify torturing and killing me. It is well known that the authorities have lists with the names of people who are active in unions and land invasions. They would have my name on their lists because of my membership in the UNC and because I was an officer of the Tierra Fértil Cooperative. Battalion 316 was already looking for me because I had filed a complaint against them.

For these reasons I am petitioning for asylum in the United States.

I, Zoila Calderón, swear under penalty of perjury that the preceding statement is true and correct to the best of my knowledge and belief.

_____   _____

Zoila Calderón   Date

I, Tenyr Midden, attest that I am competent to translate from English to Spanish and I certify that I read the preceding statement in Spanish to the declarant and that she understood the contents thereof before she signed it.

_____   _____

Tenyr Midden   Date

The Interview

CHICO CORDERO sat in the asylum unit waiting room with all the confidence of a lifelong loser even though he was finally on a winning streak. He had escaped Honduras, crossed Mexico, and entered the United States without getting caught. He had made friends who helped him learn the ropes that undocumented immigrants have to unknot. One gave him a place to stay; others helped him land a few odd jobs; many advised him to apply for asylum. But he had been afraid to take that final step. Applying for asylum was, in effect, turning himself in to the dreaded Migra, something he had been very reluctant to do. He had managed to survive for a year without documents but like most mojados, or wetbacks, he had merely been treading water. He hadn't earned enough to bring his wife to El Norte and he couldn't go back. After the nominee for attorney general of the United States had to withdraw because she had employed undocumented workers, Chico found it more difficult than ever to support himself without that all-important work permit, el permiso.

Early one morning his friend, Tomás, proudly took him to the Sanctuary. At the Sanctuary they seemed to know what they were doing, at least as far as Chico could tell. But then he was barely literate. He had, however, gone to night school as an adult—one year in Honduras and two years in Mexico. His wife had encouraged him to go to school, and he was proud that he had learned to read and write. Still, he had no patience with paperwork and had been only too glad to leave everything in the hands of the Sanctuary. They had filed his application for asylum and had supplied him with an attorney and an interpreter for the interview. He was on a hot streak even though he had missed his first interview appointment because he had gotten a little too cocky. He hadn't listened when his attorney told him that the asylum unit offices were not in the immigration building and carefully explained where to go. Since he knew where the immigration building was, he had thought that he didn't have to listen. Naturally, when he found he had gone to the wrong building, he panicked and got lost in San Francisco.

Still, as with so many things, that was in the past. His attorney saw to it that he got another interview as well as a firm lecture on the importance of paying attention. One Sunday, a month after the missed interview, he had made a practice run to the asylum offices, and the following Wednesday, the day of his interview, he had shown up at 6:00 A.M. for his 10:00 A.M. appointment. The main difference between Chico Cordero and the homeless people on the sidewalk at that hour was that he paced up and down the block with a good deal of energy. At 9:30 A.M. he was seated in the waiting room between his interpreter and his attorney.

His wife, as she had done since their marriage, still came through for him, though she was thousands of miles away. Just yesterday, he had received another letter from her. She told him that things were looking up for him and that soon he would win asylum and they could be together again. She told him not to get nervous or bite his nails during the interview. His attorney and interpreter also encouraged him. They told him not to worry, that the worst that could happen was that they would get a tough asylum officer who would deny his own grandmother asylum, but regardless, he would get his work permit and be able to look for steady work while he waited to go before an immigration judge. All he had to do was tell the truth. Answer the questions calmly, and if he didn't understand a question or was confused, he should say so. Chico Cordero paid attention to that advice. He nodded his head abruptly to show that he had heard it. He even repeated some of his attorney's words. But the longer he waited, the more he became fixated on his hands. How dirty and swollen they looked. His nails were short and jagged and each tiny protuberance cried out to be gnawed on. He sat on them, but that interfered with the ritual knocking of his knees. He ran them through his hair, but to do that, he had to stop the rocking motion of his body. In the end he placed them on his lap and slowly and compulsively rubbed his wrists and hands.

Chico's ravaged hair, his wild, sweaty face, and his constant hand washing reminded the attorney of Lady Macbeth, a character she would rather not have the asylum officer call to mind when listening to Chico's case. She suggested that he go to the bathroom to splash cool water on his face and comb his hair.

Of the sixteen asylum officers in San Francisco, several are excellent, many are reasonable, a few are moody, and one, Mr. Whittly, executes his duties with a rigid consistency that crushes all foolish hobgoblins. That is, he executes his duty as he sees it. The other officers, in varying degrees, think that their job is to assist refugees with decent asylum claims and to deny the petition for those with weak claims. Mr. Whittly knows with certainty that his job is to assist the border patrol in turning away the invading hordes who would overrun our country were it not for the vigilant few.

The morning of the interview Mr. Whittly reread Chico Cordero's application and supporting documentation. He referred to the State Department Guide to Country Conditions. He smiled a satisfied smile when he found nothing to rebut the alien's request for asylum.

Mr. Whittly was in a reflective mood that morning. It was time for the interview with Chico Cordero, but he was in no rush. He basked in the inner glow of a job well done. He wanted to concentrate on it, think about it, make it last. It was one of his few pleasures in life, and he wanted to cherish it. He reflected on his peculiar suitability for his job. He liked interviewing people almost as much as he disliked people. He liked picking over an alien's story, pouncing on inconsistencies, not unlike Perry Mason pouncing on a contradiction in a witness's testimony.

The comparison to Perry Mason was an apt one, Mr. Whittly thought, except that Perry got the glory and fame, while he labored in the shadows. Maybe if he went to law school. It wasn't too late. People often went to law school at forty. He could become a famous attorney. Not a defense attorney like Perry Mason. Perry's clients were all good guys, but that was just television fantasy. In the real world defendants were lowlifes, and if they weren't guilty of the crimes they were charged with, they were guilty of others equally as heinous. No, Mr. Whittly would be a prosecuting attorney. He would be the Perry Mason of the people, people meaning the government, not ordinary, everyday people.

However, Mr. Whittly would not go to law school. Not that he was lazy or unable to do well on the LSAT. Some of his colleagues were attorneys, and he was certainly smarter than they were. He was practically a lawyer as it was. He wrote briefs, citing the relevant laws and applying them to the facts of the case, every time he denied a petition for asylum, which was frequent. No, it was just that Mr. Whittly did not like lawyers. He had to deal with them all the time. Some of his more objectionable colleagues were lawyers, and smart-alec lawyers came into his office all the time, representing idiot clients. They argued with him. They quoted the law to him. Worse, they sent rebuttals to his denials in which they had the gall to tell him that his reasoning was faulty or he had applied the law incorrectly, or misunderstood the regulations. Lawyers! They're as bad as the low-lifes they represent.

All that Perry Mason-noble-lawyer-and-innocent-client drivel was TV fantasy. Although Mr. Whittly was thoroughly grounded in reality, he found it fun to watch someone like

Perry, who was able to think on his feet. That's what I do on my job, thought Mr. Whittly, as he leaned back in his chair.

As proud as he was of his ability to think on his feet, Mr. Whittly was equally proud of his ability to research a case. He had spent his most contented hours perusing the asylum unit library to find ammunition for the battle against cheats. He sometimes spent long hours at home, working above and beyond the call of duty, searching in his personal library. He had stayed up late the night before, agonizing over the case of a Christian minister from an African country who claimed persecution by the Moslems. He had been about to despair, fearing that he might have to grant the alien asylum, when well after midnight he leafed through the Bible he had picked up in a motel room when he was on temporary duty in Florida denying Haitian cases. In the Bible he found inspiration. He immediately knelt before his beloved computer and began composing the Notice of Intent to Deny. He quoted Luke 9:23, in which Christ said, "If anyone wants to be a follower of mine, let him renounce himself and take up the cross every day and follow me. Anyone who wants to save his life will lose it, but anyone who loses his life for my sake, will save it." From that holy high ground it was child's play to show that the Christian minister had not acted according to the tenets of a true Christian when he had fled for his life. And if he wasn't going to follow the tenets of his religion, he might as well have stayed in his own country and stopped preaching, as the Moslems had warned him to do.

That very night Mr. Whittly made himself a note to pick up a Koran for his personal library in case a Moslem ever claimed persecution on account of his religion. Mr. Whittly was certain that somewhere in that holy book he would be able to find an appropriate citation to use in denying the case.

As Mr. Whittly scurried down the hallway toward the waiting room, staying close to one wall, he rubbed his hands together, not unlike the way Chico Cordero had been rubbing his. Mr. Whittly was looking forward to the next interview.

Mr. Whittly turned from the hallway into the waiting room without losing wall contact. His nose quivered as he examined the waiting crowd. He could tell the attorneys by their clothes and their arrogant appearance. He could almost smell the aliens. He called out Chico Cordero's name, and two neatly dressed North American women rose from their seats and approached him. The one with the briefcase was obviously the lawyer. The other must be the interpreter. Mr. Whittly was disappointed to see that the alien had skipped out, thus denying him the pleasure of the interview. But the lawyer told him that her client had just gone to the bathroom and would return in a moment. At that moment Chico Cordero emerged from the bathroom.

As the INS does its best to save trees, there were no paper towels in the bathroom, and Chico Cordero emerged rather wet. He wiped his face on the sleeve of his shirt and his hands on his pants. His wavy black hair was slicked back, his black mustache plastered to his lip. Chico was dark-skinned, and his suddenly slick appearance made Mr. Whittly think of the Argentinean tango dancer he had recently seen on one of the Perry Mason shows. The tango dancer hadn't done it, but he might as well have, since he was a gigolo.

As the attorney introduced Chico, Mr. Whittly couldn't help but grimace. Chico mistook the grimace for a smile and thought that his hot streak was holding, that he had gotten one of the nicer asylum officers.

Few monks' cells were as austere as Mr. Whittly's office. The white walls were as bare of artwork, photographs, certificates, or comic strips clipped from the newspapers as the desk was bare of even a stray paper or misplaced pencil. The room was clean, almost sterile. He sat rather crookedly in his chair as he swore in the interpreter and had her sign a form. Then, through the interpreter, he swore in Chico, noting his slick, dark appearance, his nervousness despite his cocky manner.

Chico was not at home in the white room with industrial gray carpets, gunmetal gray furniture, and white acoustic tiles on the walls and ceilings. As Chico was not an observant man, he couldn't say why the room seemed vaguely like another room he knew so well, or why he was suddenly nervous and ill at ease. Still, he was determined to be brave as his wife had encouraged him to be. He answered too loudly the preliminary questions—name, address, date, and place of birth.

Mr. Whittly asked him if he had a California ID and Chico handed him his plastic card. Mr. Whittly carefully checked the data on the card with page one of the alien's petition for asylum. Almost as an aside he asked, "When did you enter the United States?"

"June 14, 1991," Chico belted out with an air of certainty. The interview was a piece of cake, and Chico had grown more confident with each question he was able to answer.

The triumphant Mr. Whittly smiled as he asked, "Then how do you account for the fact that your ID was issued on June 2, 1991?"

Not being particularly concerned about such minor things as dates, Chico did not understand what the prob-lem was.

Mr. Whittly was disappointed in the alien's reaction, or lack of it, and had to patiently explain that it was impossible for him to have gotten an ID twelve days before entering the United States. His patience was tried when the alien attempted to pass it off as a matter of no importance. He pressed the alien on the matter, but Chico Cordero could not account for the discrepancy in dates. He was certain that he had entered on June 14, 1991. He had arrived in Oakland the next day. People had told him about the casual labor pick-up at 22nd and Foothill, and while there, waiting for a job, he had met Tomás. The sophisticated Tomás, a Poptí Maya, who, in his sixteen months in the United States, had learned to use the telephone and take the computer-ized trains, enjoyed showing the naive newcomer the ropes. He had shared his apartment with Chico and had taken him to the Department of Motor Vehicles to get his ID. That had been about a week after arriving. If he had arrived on June 14th, then the ID should be dated the 21st—Chico had done well in his math classes in night school. Perhaps they had made an error on his ID.

The crooked smile of Mr. Whittly was more affecting than his grimace. "I hardly think that's likely."

"Well, then, I dunno?"

"When did you enter?"

"I dunno. I thought I entered on June 14."

"Then how could you have gotten an ID at an earlier date?"

"I dunno. I don't see how that could be. I guess I must have entered earlier. But I always thought it was June 14."

"Why did you think it was the 14th?"

"I dunno."

"Well, when do you now think you entered?"

Where the white acoustic tiles and the close, sterile atmosphere of the room had, at first, only subliminally affected Chico, the repetitious interrogation, the rapid nagging about a detail consciously reminded him of a similar interrogation in a similar room. The black, dilated pupils of his wide eyes began to dart from side to side as if he were looking for a way out. He began to gnaw on his fingernails, then quickly removed his hand from his mouth with his other hand. The tip of his tongue slid across his dry lips. He squirmed in his chair as if it hurt him to sit. He could no longer make eye contact with Mr. Whittly as his attorney had advised him to do. When not looking for the emergency exits or at his tempting fingernails, his eyes strayed to the light fixture on the ceiling.

As if closing in for the kill, Mr. Whittly leaned even closer to the distasteful alien on the other side of the desk. "Well, how do you account for the discrepancy in the dates?"

"Even if my client had entered the U.S. a few weeks or months earlier, it's a nonrelevant issue. Couldn't we just move on to the essential details of his petition for asylum?" the lawyer had the temerity to interject.

"I consider this an essential issue. As far as I know, he may have entered three years earlier, before his claimed persecution took place. So can we please let him answer the question, Ms. Uhmmm . . . ?" Mr. Whittly knew the attorney's name. He had a very good memory for names. He pretended not to know it to put her in her place.

Chico Cordero did not answer the question. Although clearly flustered, he dug his heels in and repeated over and over, "I dunno. I dunno. There must be some mistake." He refused to think about the question or how the mistake had happened. He refused to cast his mind back to the time of his entry into the United States to try to work the problem out. He knew he was in trouble, and he instinctively resorted to the tactic that had saved him last time. He denied any knowledge of the murder. He denied any knowledge of the guerrillas. He refused to confess. He knew that if he confessed he would be killed. He was weak. He was in pain. He was completely powerless. He would do anything they wanted him to do, but he would not confess. If he confessed, they would kill him, and he would never see his wife again. He thought of her. He tried to think only of her while he answered the questions, "I dunno. I dunno. I dunno." She was the only good thing that had ever happened to him. He had been a loser until he met her. She encouraged him to make something of himself, to work hard at his crummy part-time job in construction and go to night school. It was difficult for him. He was embarrassed. He was exhausted. He wanted to quit so many times, but his wife gave him the strength to go on. He concentrated with all his might on her.

"I don't see that this line of questioning is getting us anywhere, and it only seems to be upsetting my client," the attorney said. She was concerned because Chico was doing the same things he had done in the waiting room, rocking back and forth, rubbing his hands, running them through his hair. "If we could move on to the events that made him flee Honduras perhaps you'll understand why hostile interrogation—"

"I am not hostile," Mr. Whittly insisted through clenched teeth. "I am merely trying to ascertain when Mr. Cordero entered the United States, Ms. Uhmmm . . ."

"He has already stated a number of times that he doesn't know how he confused the date, but that he arrived about a week before applying for his ID. Can't we accept that he arrived in the latter part of May and move on?"

Mr. Whittly twitched his lips into a smile. He was not upset with the pushy, obnoxious female attorney who thought she could waltz into his office and tell him how to conduct the interview. Oh no, he wasn't upset. He moved on.

As Chico Cordero told his story, Mr. Whittly, that humanitarian asylum officer, did not feel it necessary to pay complete attention. He had the written declaration in front of him. He could follow along, occasionally checking a detail, always looking for contradictions, prompting with abrupt questions, while he began rehearsing a few well-chosen lines he would use at the end of the interview.

Chico, licking his cracked lips and rocking and rubbing, related in short, choppy sentences through the translator how the DNI, the dreaded Honduran secret police, had arrested him for the murder of one of their agents. Someone had heard the murder take place outside his house. He had also heard the name, Cordero. The man had not gone outside his house to see what had happened until daylight. He had been afraid. When he saw the body, he called the police.

The agent had been murdered with a machete at 3:00 A.M. The murder was reported to the police at 6:00 A.M. The DNI wasted no time in discovering that a Cordero lived in the neighborhood. They searched his empty house and found a machete. The blade was clean. They questioned the neighbors. By noon they arrested Chico Cordero at the construction site where he had recently been promoted to foreman. They did not take him to the regular prison but to a special building. They put him in a cell with other prisoners who told him that the men who interrogated and tortured prisoners usually wore masks. That way if the prisoners ever got free, they would not be able to identify their torturers. If the torturers did not wear masks, it was because they knew that the prisoner would never leave alive. The agents who came for Chico did not wear masks.

Chico was interrogated and tortured for ten days. The room was small and very clean. The walls and ceilings had white acoustic tiles so that screams could not be heard in other parts of the building in case a human rights agency visited. The torturers wanted him to confess that he was a terrorist and had killed their agent. When he refused to sign the prepared confession, they would handcuff his wrists tightly and hang him by the handcuffs from an overhead beam. That hurt. After a few minutes his wrists and hands would begin to swell, which made the handcuffs hurt even more. While he hung from the beam they would beat him with La Chinona. La Chinona was a four-by-four piece of lumber with a tapered end for a handle. It was painted white and the name La Chinona was painted on it in big black letters. During interrogations the agents enjoyed taunting their victims, telling them to confess or they would give them a taste of La Chinona. A taste meant hitting the victims on the buttocks and back of the thighs. Although they tried not to break bones with La Chinona, the torturers were only human and sometimes made mistakes. Chico Cordero was not sure that they hadn't broken something in his left leg, because it still hurt him, and he walked with a limp. He described it as having air in his leg.

Sometimes, when they took Chico down from the beam, they would take him to another room where there was a large tub of water. They would stand Chico in the tub, the water coming up to his chest, and put two electrical wires into the water to give him a jolt of 110 volts.

That description got Mr. Whittly's full attention. He asked the attorney, "A hundred and ten volts! Wouldn't that kill someone?" He was suddenly sorry he had asked her. It had just slipped out in the momentary enthusiasm of thinking he had caught the alien in another lie.

"I know nothing about electricity. I can only suppose that it's not always fatal as my client is here to tell us about it. Also, I think we should keep in mind that when he says it was 110 volts, he is merely repeating what the torturers told him."

Mr. Whittly did not want to admit that that was a good point. Instead he questioned Chico Cordero closely on the matter, ready to pounce upon some detail that he could use to trip up the alien. He asked, "What were the wires hooked up to?"

Chico lifted his eyes to the fluorescent light fixture in the white ceiling and said that they were hooked up to a light just like that one.

Mr. Whittly made a mental note to research the subject of Honduran electrical systems and how many volts would kill a man. He sensed that here was another weak point in the story, the exact kind of thing Perry Mason would have caught.

The torture sessions lasted about an hour. They only tortured Chico once a day because the DNI specialists had a long waiting list of clients. That's the beauty of a state that routinely violates the human rights of its citizens—they often can't dedicate as much time as they would like to each individual. They have to spread their efforts around democratically.

When they dragged Chico back to his cell, the other prisoners tried to help him. They massaged his wrists and hands to try to bring the swelling down, but he was in so much pain that the only real help they could give him was psychological.

Chico's wife was frantic when she heard that he had been arrested by the DNI. She went every day to the DNI building to ask for him and to leave food for him. The DNI agent on duty at the door always denied that he was being held there. He denied that they held any prisoners there. But he always accepted the food, which he ate for lunch.

Chico's wife knew that her husband was innocent. She knew that, on the night of the murder, he had come home after his classes at 9:30 and hadn't left the house again until the next morning when he went to work at 6:00 as usual. More importantly, she knew that innocence didn't matter to the DNI. Accusation was as good as conviction, followed invariably by execution, unless . . .

Chico's wife was poor, but she was not fatalistic. She knew that direct action was required, and she was the person to take it. The afternoon of her husband's arrest she began visiting the neighbors in the barrio. In one and a half frantic days she got over 300 people to sign a petition stating that they knew Chico Cordero and that he was honest, hardworking, didn't drink or beat his wife, and was not mixed up with the guerrillas. She composed a handwritten declaration swearing that Chico was at home at the time of the crime. On the third day of her husband's arrest, she took the petition to CODEH, the Human Rights Committee, a nongovernmental agency. They examined the petition and declaration and were suitably impressed and said that they would assign an attorney to the case and try to get Chico transferred to the regular prison before it was too late.

On the morning of the eleventh day, a judge ordered that the prisoner Chico Cordero be transferred from DNI custody to the presidio where he was to remain in confinement until his trial. Although the DNI agents were upset with this interference in the process due a terrorist, they did not torture Chico that day. They cleaned him up as best they could and took him to an office with the same interior design as the room where they had beaten him with La Chinona. They told him that he was being transferred to the presidio. They warned him not to get his hopes up, that he would never leave prison alive. And if he told anyone about the torture or the other prisoners held there, his wife would disappear. They made quite sure that he understood that she would suffer even worse treatment than he had.

In his new prison Chico Cordero was allowed to see a doctor for his injuries. The doctor casually examined him, gave him two aspirins for pain, and told him to stay off the painful left leg and keep his sore hands elevated as much as possible. Chico's wife visited him every day. He didn't tell her about the torture, and she didn't ask him, although it was obvious to her that he had had a rough time. It hurt her to see him sit so tenderly on the chair in the visiting room and to see him caress his swollen wrists and hands. Every day she brought him food, which the guards took from her, searched for weapons or files, and, for added spice, inserted a note that said that he would never leave prison alive. Chico began to wish he had never learned to read. The death threats bothered him so much, and his fear that the guards would add poison to the food was so great, that he finally asked his wife to stop bringing him food. He didn't tell her why. He merely mumbled some excuse about it being better to share the communal slop with the other prisoners.

Chico also received visits from his attorney. The CODEH attorney noticed Chico's limp, the swollen and sore wrists, and the tender way he perched on the edge of the chair. He asked Chico how the DNI had treated him. Chico looked at his feet and muttered, "All right." The lawyer asked if he had been tortured or beaten. Chico continued examining his feet as he mumbled, "No." He asked his client how they treated him in the presidio. Chico said, "Okay," not bothering to mention the death threats.

As a rule they did treat Chico okay in the presidio, at least as okay as they treated anyone. There were threats, sure. DNI agents had talked to some of the worst murderers in the prison, offering those with life sentences the possibility of better treatment or even shorter sentences if they killed the terrorist Chico Cordero, making it look like a prison fight. Chico was often threatened in the exercise yard. The other prisoners in his cell protected him by making sure that he was never alone. Other than those minor incidents, Chico was not mistreated, and his body began to heal. Then, about a week before his trial, a guard took him out of his cell and made him clean all the toilets in the block. That was a particularly punitive and disgusting chore, as the guard didn't give him brushes, sponges, or rags to do it with; he had to wipe all the filthy toilets clean with his bare hands. When, after several hours of that repulsive work, he complained, the guard took him to a small room, ordered him to take his shirt off, and beat him with a lamp cord. The thin wire painfully cut the skin on his back. When Chico was on the point of passing out, the guard threw the ragged shirt at him and ordered him to put it on. He warned Chico that if he showed anyone the welts or told anyone about the beating he would kill him. Chico kept his shirt on and his mouth shut.

The trial lasted about an hour. The DNI produced their lone witness, the man who had not seen the crime, but had heard the name Cordero. They also introduced evidence that the deceased agent had been investigating terrorist activity in that barrio, as well as several anonymous statements accusing Chico Cordero of terrorist ties. The CODEH attorney countered with testimony from the defendant and his wife and the petition signed by over 300 people swearing that Chico Cordero was of good moral character and had no terrorist ties. Chico was found innocent. The judge, a moderately brave man, was just able to restrain himself from making certain caustic remarks about DNI investigative procedures.

That night Chico Cordero was welcomed home by many of the neighbors who had signed his wife's petition. He felt like a returning hero.

When he awoke the next morning, he found a note someone had slipped under the door during the night. The note was unsigned. It said, "Chico Cordero, you got out of jail, but you will not get away with your terrorist activities." During the following months the notes appeared often. Some merely said that they hadn't forgotten about him, others that they would come for him soon. Chico began to have trouble sleeping. He lay awake at night, listening, remembering. When he did fall asleep, the slightest noise woke him with a start. He had no appetite. He lost weight. His boss fired him from his job, either because Chico was listless and slow or because he had been warned to get rid of that terrorist. Chico's wife advised him to flee to Mexico until the DNI forgot about him.

Chico lived in Cancún for two years. He got a job in construction and lived in a miserable barrio the rich tourists never saw. Chico's wife wrote him long, chatty letters, telling him about her work, the neighbors, the family. Several times during the first year she mentioned that some men had watched the house, or a neighbor had told her that some men had been asking about Chico. She encouraged him to continue his education, and he enrolled in night school. She advised him to look for another job before quitting his old one when his boss took extra deductions from his paycheck because he didn't have Mexican papers. He took her advice and soon found a better job. Chico wrote short, emotional letters to his wife. He told her that he was lonely and that he felt as if he were nothing without her. He told her that she was the only good thing that had ever happened to him in his life. As his education progressed, his letters got longer, and he told his wife many things about himself, about his father who had been killed in a cave-in in the silver mines near Santa Bárbara, about his mother who took him to live in Tegucigalpa, about his life on the streets, but he never told her about the torture.

After two years in Mexico, he missed his wife so much that he dared to go back to Honduras. His wife hadn't mentioned for some time the strange men who had asked for him or watched the house, and the optimist in him believed that the DNI had forgotten about him. When he got home, the pessimist in him took over, and he lay low. The first week he hardly ventured out of the house, and he slept only fitfully at night. When he slept, he dreamed that the torturers were coming for him or that with painfully swollen fingers he was signing a confession. Little by little he made longer and longer forays from the house. He got a job as a laborer. He went with his wife to the market. His wife took him to dances. He enrolled in night school. Life returned to normal until one morning another note waited for him. It said, "Chico Cordero, did you think we had forgotten about you? We never forget about terrorists. One night when you least expect it, we will come for you."

That afternoon Chico fled Honduras once again. He went to the United States.

As he told his story, the interpreter was moved. She had to pause twice to blow her nose and wipe her eyes. She patted him on the knee several times to reassure him. She wanted to hug him and tell him it was all right, that he was among friends, not only because she felt compassion for him, but also because she wanted him to stop rocking back and forth and rubbing his wrists and hands. She did not see how anyone could not be moved and was certain that Chico would win asylum.

The attorney was proud of Chico. He had rallied from a very bad beginning and had told his story, if not calmly, at least coherently and in great detail. He had answered every question the asylum officer had asked him. His answers had been detailed and consistent with his written declaration.

When Mr. Whittly asked the attorney if she would like to ask her client any questions or add anything, she said, "I think that my client has shown that he has a well-founded fear of persecution by government authorities in Honduras. The persecution is based on his imputed political opinion. The DNI accused him of being a terrorist guerrilla. His belief that he will be persecuted if he were to return to Honduras is based on his past persecution when he was arrested and brutally tortured for ten days. Although not signed, we can logically conclude that the anonymous notes threatening him with death were sent by DNI agents, and they clearly show that the DNI is not willing to conform to the decision of the court. They still consider him a terrorist and will continue to persecute him.

"As further documentation of his case I have included a copy of the court decision in which my client was found innocent of the stated charges and a number of articles from human rights agencies, such as Amnesty International, that accuse the DNI of torturing prisoners without regard to due process of law, executing people suspected of ties to the guerrillas, and of ties to the death squads."

Although she was certain that they had presented a very strong case, the attorney wasn't certain that Mr. Whittly would grant asylum. She had heard of him from other attorneys. But perhaps even he . . .

Mr. Whittly was also pleased. His features dissolved into his crooked smile as he muttered his standard speech, informing client and attorney that they would be notified of his decision in writing within ninety days. He could not help boasting that, where other asylum officers sometimes took six months to a year to write their decision, he was very prompt. He stood up to indicate that the interview was over.

Chico Cordero also stood, relieved that the ordeal was over, ready to bolt out the door. He was disappointed when his attorney delayed his escape. She asked Mr. Whittly to issue her client an arrival/departure record and approve his application for an employment authorization document. Mr. Whittly was even more pleased. He found the arrival/departure record already prepared in Chico Codero's folder, and as he handed it to the alien, he informed the lawyer that he would not approve the request for an employment authorization document. As Mr. Whittly had hoped, the attorney was stunned. She asked why not, and Mr. Whittly, smiling his crooked smile, said that he considered the case to be frivolous.

"Frivolous?" The attorney nearly shouted.

"Yes, frivolous. I think he's lying."

"Lying? Which part do you think he's lying about?"

The smug Mr. Whittly replied, "He lied about the date of his entry into the United States. That shows that he is not credible. I think he lied about everything."

"What about the document from the court? That proves he was charged and found innocent as he said. He clearly wasn't lying about everything, as you say."

"The interview is over," Mr. Whittly informed the attorney. "I don't have time to argue with you. I have other aliens waiting. You'll be able to argue my decision in writing when you receive my notice of intent to deny. Have a nice day."

Bad Jokes

ONE WINTER MORNING when Zacarías came into the office, La Hermana asked him in passing how he was, and he proceeded to tell her. "Bueno, Seester"—he always calls La Hermana Seester—"I had the flu but I'm better now. My stomach isn't precisely correct but I think it's from eating Mexican food last night. And my back hurts me a little because I helped a friend move his furniture. But, bueno, Seester, the only thing that really bothers me is that my feet hurt on these cold days."

Since I found the conversation amusing, I leapt into it in a spirit of high good humor that took a long hard fall. "There's no need to suffer from cold feet in this country. This is the land of plenty. Why don't you buy some electric socks?" I suggested.

Zacarías and I are always trading bad jokes, which is a good deal for him because my bad jokes are generally not as bad as his. He may have a different opinion on the relative merits of our humor, but he'd be wrong. Sometimes he laughs heartily at my jokes, often politely, and then he tells me a joke that I usually do not think funny or, more often, do not understand. Still, I laugh politely. Humor is cultural,

I suppose. For instance, there's a joke that the gringo religious community loved and the refugees didn't seem to understand. "What's the difference between our president and God?" Answer: "God never thinks he's president." The refugee reaction to that one was to laugh politely or stare at me in wonderment. Once when I was trying to amuse some female refugees by telling them that boys were made of sugar and spice and everything nice but girls of worms and snails and puppy dog tails—none of which translated very easily or well—Zacarías commented that if I were a parrot they would all buy me, meaning, I suppose, that no one would buy a parrot who didn't jabber. There must have been some humor in that comment because the refugees laughed uproariously.

Staring in wonderment was Zacarías's reaction to my suggestion about electric socks. Never one to be timid when the opportunity to make a fool of myself knocks, I rushed in to explain that here in the U.S. of A. certain stores sell electric socks, battery powered, to keep your feet warm, etc., etc., and they come in all colors, including shocking pink. Finally, after a lot of hard work on my part, Zacarías chuckled and changed the subject.

That night I woke up in the dark hours, not with a vague feeling of angst or the usual nagging feeling of something left undone. This time it was different. This time it was the sharp pain of knowing that I had hurt Zacarías with my thoughtlessness. He seemed to have taken it well, all things considered, but what was wrong with me that I'd made that awful joke?

In Ireland, according to La Hermana, all lawyers are pronounced liars. When you get into trouble you might need a liar to help you out. That's another joke that doesn't translate well into Spanish. Still, Zacarías, while not understanding it, seemed fond of it. When he called to invite me to his trial, he told me that he'd been practicing all week with his mentirosa. I laughed politely. I looked forward to the trial. Zacarías and his wife, Ester, had an excellent case and an excellent liar and, best of all, a judge who was both excellent and just. I was certain that they would win political asylum and could then petition to bring their children to the United States. Zacarías and Ester looked forward to their trial. It had already been delayed twice. They were anxious about it, anxious to get it over with, anxious to find out if they were going to be permitted to live in the United States, and anxious about their children whom they hadn't seen in two years.

I called Zacarías and Ester the night before the trial. They were all wound up from going over the case with their mentirosa, reliving a time they would rather forget. I don't think I helped them in the least with a bad joke about having to learn the names of all the presidents when it came time for them to apply for citizenship. "And don't forget the present one who thinks he's God," I added. Zacarías made a noise that I supposed was a polite laugh and hung up.

As a compromise La Hermana and I arrived at the immigration building fifteen minutes late. She is normally at least half an hour late, which proves her fluency in Spanish, and I am normally early, proving that I still have a lot to learn. We found a little crowd of people in the hall outside the courtroom and on closer inspection found that Zacarías and Ester were among them. Zacarías was leaning back against the wall and looking glum, while Ester leaned face forward against the opposite wall. From the shudders that coursed through her body and the racking sobs that echoed in the corridor, I figured that she was crying. La Hermana went to comfort Ester and I to Zacarías. We shook hands. His eyes briefly met mine as he thanked me for coming, and then he carefully studied the polished floor while he explained that the trial had been postponed for a year because the judge was out of town. After a few minutes of forced chatter Ester came over to me to apologize for not greeting me. She gave me a teary hug. Their lawyer joined us. She was quietly furious that Immigration would do such a thing to her clients and her without notifying them. She said that the judge had been sent to Florida for a week to hear the cases of some of the Haitian boat people and was certain to be angry when she returned and found out that no one had bothered to notify Zacarías and Ester. We stood in the hallway a long time, doing not much of anything, mostly watching Ester cry and Zacarías study the floor.

Not only did I spend a long sleepless night because I was outraged by the cruel joke the INS had played on Zacarías and Ester, but I didn't see the least humor in it until Zacarías called the following week to tell me that the judge had returned and rescheduled the trial for the coming week. It's difficult to get a hearing rescheduled so quickly but the judge granted their lawyer's request for humanitarian reasons. Zacarías joked about it. "Fíjate, the whatshername, the little Guatemalan girl, she'd think she'd won the lottery if she showed up at court to find that the judge was gone and her trial had been put off for a year. Maybe we made a big mistake asking for a new trial so soon. Maybe we should have been glad to wait another year. That would have been another year that they couldn't deport us."

In the hall outside the courtroom—the hall with the fascinating floor—Zacarías and Ester were leaning against opposite walls, studying the linoleum. Their faces lit up when Seester came into their field of view. Trailing in her wake, even I came in for some of the greetings and hugs. Zacarías soon resumed his position against the wall, and I obstructed his view of the floor by standing in front of him while he informed my feet that he didn't care what happened. "Bueno, they can send me back to El Salvador. I don't care. Bueno, if they don't want me here, I don't want to stay. They say that the only reason I came here was to get rich, to make lots of money. Pues, let the gringos clean their own offices for $4.25 an hour. They think I came here because my goal in life was to be a janitor. Let them send me back. Bueno."

The trial began half an hour late because the judge asked both attorneys to step into her chambers for a conference where they stipulated that Zacarías would not have to testify about being picked up and tortured by the Salvadoran National Guard. His testimony began with the time he was in the hospital. His attorney led him through his story.

An asylum trial is not like a regular trial. The attorneys can sometimes get away with leading questions. And if they don't ask them, the judge sometimes will. Some judges frequently interrupt to question the respondent. (That's what the courts call the refugee, and it's a good deal better than the other term the INS uses for human beings seeking asylum—aliens. Ironically enough, sensitive INS officials take offense at the term La Migra.) In an asylum hearing, refugees have to show that they have well-founded fears that they will be persecuted because of their political opinion, race, religion, or membership in a social group if they are to return to their country of origin.

Zacarías was very nervous as he testified. Torture victims normally exhibit one of two reactions when they testify. They can be calm and seemingly unaffected as if viewing the events from a great distance and as if the events were happening to someone else, or they can be extremely agitated. Zacarías chose the latter. He trembled, his voice wavered and broke, he took many sips of water from a glass nearby, which he frequently filled, his torso rhythmically rocked back and forth, and often his voice trailed off so that we were all on the edge of our seats listening. The interpreter, sitting next to him, often had to ask him to repeat a word or a phrase.

"Bueno, I was in the hospital three months recovering from my wounds."

"And during that time did you contact the International Red Cross?"

"Bueno, I called them and asked them if they could protect me or move me to another hospital. They said they could not move me because the other hospitals were not safe."

"Why did you want them to protect you? Didn't you feel safe in the hospital?"

"No."

Because Zacarías simply answered yes or no to his attorney's next few questions, the judge took over. "Why didn't you feel safe in the hospital? Did you have visitors?"

"Visitors? Bueno, yes?" The question seemed to surprise him. For him the term visitors meant only friendly people.

"Who were these visitors?"

163

"Bueno, Ester came to see me." He could tell that the judge was waiting, but he didn't know what for, so he added, "And my parents."

"Did anyone else come to see you?"

"Some men."

"Who were these men?"

"I don't know their names."

"Were they in uniform?"

"No."

"Did they threaten you?"

"Bueno, I don't know?"

"Were you afraid of them?"

"Pues, yes!"

"Why were you afraid of them? What did they say to you?"

"They asked me how I got my wounds. They asked me if I was a guerrilla and was wounded in battle with the military. Pues, they knew how I got my wounds. The Red Cross told me that they were policemen or military men. The men said they would be back to visit me again."

"Did they come back?"

"Pues, yes! They came back and told me that it was the guerrillas who had captured me and tortured me. They warned me that I had better be careful because the guerrillas knew where I lived, and they would come after me again one night."

Zacarías's attorney took over the questioning again. "When they said that, did you think that what they really meant was that the military might come after you?"

"Pues, yes!"

"Why did you think that?"

"Pues, because of the way they said it. And then they laughed."

"What did you do after this second visit?"

"Bueno, I asked my parents to take me to their house."

"Were your wounds healed at that time?"

"No. I still could not walk, but I was afraid to stay in the hospital."

I hadn't known all the details of Zacarías's story, and I was fascinated, on the edge of my bench and leaning forward to catch his soft, quick Spanish words before the interpreter changed them into impersonal English. I was fascinated by Zacarías's quick eyes, which tried to meet the judge's gaze or the interpreter's but quickly fell to his twisting hands or the floor.

After more than a month in his parents' house, some men approached his father in the street and asked questions about Zacarías. Zacarías decided to flee. He went to Mexico, where he stayed a few months, working when he could find a job, but his feet grew worse. The wounds hadn't completely healed when he had fled, and they reopened. He returned to El Salvador and lived in his grandmother's house, afraid to live in his own or his father's house. He stayed six months in El Salvador, working with his father, after his feet had healed. One evening on the way home from work they were stopped by two men who asked Zacarías where he was living and where he had been all that time. They asked him if he had been with the guerrillas. That night he fled to Mexico once again. For a year he lived in Mexico City, where he apprenticed as an electrician. But he missed his family. He returned once again to El Salvador. This time he stayed only a few weeks, sleeping in different houses, before he and Ester fled to the Land of the Free, where they were arrested upon crossing the border.

Now it was the INS attorney's turn to ask questions. His were the usual questions. Why didn't you stay in Mexico? If you are afraid of returning to El Salvador, why did you return twice? Isn't it really true that you came to the United States for economic reasons, just to get a good job? While I half listened to the familiar litany, my mind wandered. I was still fascinated by Zacarías's lonely, swaying figure in the witness stand. I remembered him as he was that day a year and a half ago when I first met him. Nervous, embarrassed, unable to look me in the eye, he had made me feel very awkward. I tried to put him at ease by telling him a few bad jokes that I wasn't sure he'd heard, let alone understood. I had taken him to a doctor who had volunteered to examine him. As interpreter, I was not part of the usual doctor-patient relationship. I felt that my presence made the examination more uncomfortable for all concerned. The doctor was horrified when she saw his feet and wrote an affidavit stating that his condition was consistent with the symptoms of torture. And she volunteered to help us with other cases.

The next few times that Zacarías and I bumped into each other were times when he had appointments with his psychologist, who used an office next door to our office. Zacarías knew that I knew why he was there and that knowledge embarrassed us both. But gradually we grew used to each other, and eventually he began to stop by my office to visit. He would tell me jokes that didn't seem at all humorous, but I would laugh politely. When he had trouble keeping up with his landscaping job because of his physical problems, I made an appointment for him at a clinic in the county hospital and then stopped by the hospital to explain the situation to the doctor. It was a teaching clinic full of Barca-loungers with medical options, crowded close together so that the patients could examine each other while they waited for the doctor and medical students to migrate their way. I told the doctor that Zacarías wouldn't mind the medical students so much as the curious eyes of the other patients, and he promised to give Zacarías a curtained cubicle. The doctor was great. He too was horrified and became committed to Zacarías's cause. He worked very quickly on the case and got the orthotic pads built and fitted in a matter of days. The pads helped. They helped a great deal.

So many memories of Zacarías and Ester flashed before me as the INS attorney plodded through his questions, trying to trip Zacarías up, trying to make him contradict his testimony. Slowly I grew angry. Why was my government putting Zacarías and Ester through this torture? It was a clear case. Why bother to even try it? Couldn't the INS attorney see what he was doing to Zacarías? How could he live with himself? How did he rationalize to himself what he was doing? Was he only doing his job? Was he was doing it for a greater good, to keep undeserving immigrants out of the U.S.? The men who had attached wires to Zacarías's feet and shocked him night after night, were those men only doing their jobs? As the torture continued and the burns on his feet grew to open wounds and his foot muscles became permanently deformed, did they tell themselves that they were doing it for a greater good, for the national security? They saw that Zacarías had nothing to tell them, that if he had, he would have told them, that he would tell them anything they wanted to hear, if only they would stop.

Finally, the lawyers stopped, and the judge called a recess before rendering her decision. As Zacarías and Ester huddled around the table where their attorney sat—Ester in tears and Zacarías awkwardly crumbling the attorney's notes—the judge walked past them and kindly told them in rapid Spanish that she was going to grant them asylum. Because of Zacarías's anxiety and all the nervous sips of water, he had to go to the bathroom. I waited uncomfortably in the bathroom while Zacarías stood at the urinal. He had drunk a lot of water. Finally, without turning to face me, he sidled over to a sink and splashed cold water on his face to relieve the tension and hide the tears. He finally turned to me, his face wet and red. "Bueno, how do you think it went?" he asked me.

He had been so nervous that he hadn't even heard the judge tell him that she was going to grant them asylum. Before I could answer, he smiled for the first time and said, "That chair, it felt as hot as the electric chair must feel."

I was glad that I had left that bad joke about electrical devices for him to make.

Terror

THERE IS BEAUTY EVERYWHERE in the world if we will only see it. The other day I was brought to a halt when the rain clouds parted, and the slanting rays of the autumn sun lit up the oranges and browns of the neighbor's persimmon tree; in the western sky the sunlight silvered the edges of the dark clouds. I can still see that lovely scene. I can recall many scenes of beauty, a loved one's smile, the joyful shouts of children at the corner playground, the warm smells of my grandmother's kitchen. Fifteen years ago at sunset in the far north I was driving in a convertible. A long freight train rode beside me. The sunset turned from scarlet to violet to deep purple. The rushing wind, the whistle of the train, the rhythmic clackety-clack of the steel wheels on the rails, and the hum of rubber tires on smooth pavement were the orchestra that accompanied that beautiful sunset. At a curve in the road the train and I bent away from each other, and when we were reunited, in the open door of the car beside me, there sat a hobo. He smoked a cigarette and admired the sunset. We traveled together for some minutes, and when we finally went our separate ways, he smiled and waved good-bye. It was an enchanting scene, a scene of beauty and companionship, and I cherish it still.

Music, art, literature, so many things can be beautiful. The human voice. Laughter. Bad jokes can be beautiful even if followed by groans instead of laughter. But can anyone fully enjoy all these things, all that is beautiful, when terror looms over him? Can anyone who knows even a small portion of the terror of Central America read this page without cringing in expectation of some horrible story? Can anyone who lives in a climate of terror enjoy beauty without some small part of their being listening, watching, waiting for the other shoe to drop?

Can we, living here in the United States, imagine what it's like to live in a climate of terror, where even those who try to live normal, uninvolved lives are afraid? And they are afraid. Many will deny it, but if questioned closely, they will admit to some fear, a fear that has become such a part of their lives that they don't realize it's abnormal. They know that terrible things happen, of course. Those terrible things may happen to other people but they instill fear as they are meant to do. And everyone knows about them. A campaign of terror is, by its very nature, public. Those who deny their fear read the newspapers. They watch TV, listen to the radio. They talk in the family, among friends. A distant cousin has disappeared. An acquaintance at work or at school simply doesn't show up one day. A neighbor suddenly flees the country. The mutilated body of a young man has been tossed in the street.

The man who lives in a climate of terror but claims not to be afraid will double back and take a longer route to work to avoid a body dumped in the street. If a coworker tries to tell our unafraid man that the body had been mutilated, our man will quickly change the subject because he doesn't want to know, as if not knowing makes him safer. When first questioned, he would deny that he was terrorized or even afraid. He would simply say that the matter didn't concern him. But such unconcern over a dead, mutilated body in the street is not normal. Curiosity, pity, shock, outrage, fear, those are normal reactions. It's not normal to seek refuge in ignorance. It's not normal to be unconcerned about a brutal civil war raging in one's own country. Such an attitude is the result of terror, of waiting for the other boot to drop.

Can we, living here in the United States, imagine the effect a sudden clap of thunder has on those who live under the storm clouds of a reign of terror? They may not behave rationally; they may not behave as you and I would behave. When the quick lightning explodes in their lives, those who had been sheltered from the storm may stampede, while activists, those who are constantly out under the storm clouds, may exhibit great courage.

A widow and her son came into the office one busy afternoon. They were a pathetic pair and filled people everywhere with pity. Everywhere they went people helped them. With the help of a friend they had fled El Salvador. With the help of strangers they had lived in Mexico for two years. With the help of more strangers they had crossed the border without falling into the hands of La Migra. With the help of still more good Samaritans they had managed to make their way north to the San Francisco Bay Area. On the advice of strangers they came to Sanctuary. At Sanctuary they met two Cakchiquel Indians from Guatemala, themselves refugees, who took them into their home. As the pathetic pair told their story, I made a mental note to buy a box of tissues for the office. It was that kind of story.

They had lived in a small house in a rural neighborhood. They were in bed one night when a violent knocking at the door woke them. Dad hurried to the door and opened it a crack. Six armed men in camouflage uniforms and jungle boots with their faces painted black burst into the house, pushing Dad aside. They threw open the children's bedroom door. The daughters were eighteen and sixteen and the son thirteen. They grabbed the daughters and began to take them away. The daughters kicked and screamed, and the whole family was screaming and crying. Dad pleaded with the men not to take the daughters. They ignored him so he tried to stop them as any father would. They dragged them out into the night. Mom and Son heard Dad and Daughters crying and pleading, begging the men not to kill them. Their voices came from the weed-covered field across the road. The neighbors must have heard, but no one rushed to help. Everyone was terrorized. Shots rang out and suddenly all was horribly, deathly silent.

It all happened in less than five minutes. Mom and Son were terrified. They were afraid that the men would return for them. Mom and Son ran out a side door, across a field behind the house, never looking back. They didn't stop for money, papers, clothes. They simply ran as fast as they could.

After an hour of interviewing the pair together and two hours with the son alone, the only possible motive for that shattering event that I could probe out of their open wounds was that the younger daughter, without telling the family, might have joined a student group or associated with student activists. School was in town half an hour's bus ride away, and Daughter always returned home in the early afternoon when classes ended, except when there was an occasional dance. An earthquake had damaged the school a few years earlier, and because the economy was failing and the government preferred to spend its colones elsewhere, the students had to give dances to raise funds to repair the school. Perhaps some student group that lobbied the government for subversive things such as books or higher wages for teachers or funds to repair the school also participated in the dances. An army building was several doors away from the school, on the other side of the church. Perhaps they kept a close watch on the students.

As tenuous as that was, it was the only possible motive for the tragedy that I could discover. The family was remarkably uninvolved in the civil war. Dad's job was innocent enough, as was Older Daughter's. Neither of the daughters had boyfriends, none that Son knew about anyway. Mom and Dad did not permit them to go out at night.

Widow and Son do not know why their family was persecuted. And if they did know why, there is still the question of whether or not their fear is reasonable.

Any reasonable person listening to Widow and Son tell their story would be moved. Any reasonable person would think that these people are indeed refugees. But whether they will win asylum in the United States is another question. Just a few years ago an asylum officer would have routinely denied them asylum and put them in deportation proceedings. Some would have denied their petition for asylum because they could not show that the persecution was on account of their race, religion, nationality, etc. Some would have denied it on the grounds that Widow and Son were not threatened, that if the men had intended to harm them they would have killed them inside the house with everybody else instead of taking Dad and Daughters outside the house. And some particularly mean-spirited officials would have argued that Widow and Son cannot definitely state that Dad and Daughters had been killed, as they did not stick around to see the bodies.

When I first interviewed them, I was so caught up in their story that it didn't occur to me then that they hadn't seen the bodies. Later when I thought about it, I wondered what I would have done in their place. Would I have hidden in the field behind the house and at dawn, if the men had gone, would I have been brave enough to look for the bodies? To see if perhaps one of the daughters was still alive? To see if I could help? Part of me answered yes, that it would have been the least I could do. But then I don't live in an atmosphere of terror. I don't know how I would react if I lived in that climate. I don't know what it's like to wait constantly for the other shoe to drop, to be afraid that a car will screech to a halt beside me in the middle of the day, that armed men will jump out and throw me into the car and take me away, disappear me. I don't know what it's like to be gnawed by fear when a loved one is late, to be terrified that when my child goes to school she will get involved with a group that the death squads watch.

Death squads sometimes drive slowly, in their four-wheel-drive American wagons with dark windows, through villages or isolated neighborhoods in broad daylight simply to remind the locals of their existence (as if they could forget), to

173

instill terror in case they were in danger of becoming care-free, to keep them obedient in case they were feeling rebel-lious. Intellectually, I know that happens, yet I cannot feel the fear that a Ford Bronco with dark windows can instill by simply driving slowly past my house. If I have any fear at all when I see a four-wheel-drive vehicle cruising my neighbor-hood, it's fear that the occupants will throw beer cans on my lawn. I cannot understand what it's like to be terrified by an unexpected visit by strange men in the middle of the day. I frequently have unexpected visitors, but it has not once crossed my mind that they may be from a death squad. My greatest fear is that they are Jehovah's Witnesses. Nor can I completely understand the terror such visitors can instill just by their presence, just their tone of voice, just the way they look at me. I cannot understand this because I don't live in a land where people are disappeared as a matter of course, where mutilated bodies are dumped in public places to keep the population terrified and obedient.

One of the refugees was recently denied affirmative asy-lum at his interview and is now in deportation proceedings. He had been forcibly recruited by the Guatemalan military. The details of his training are common for Guatemala but shocking to anyone who has never heard them before. However, he survived with only a few scars to his body as well as his psyche, and he managed to maintain a healthy mistrust of the army. Although he was only incompletely in-doctrinated, on occasion, with his boyish machismo leading the attack, he was overrun by male bonding and the warrior persona. He tried to perform his manly jobs well and he even volunteered. He volunteered for parachute training. Because he was big and strong and a paratrooper, because he could read and write and even type a little, he was pro-moted to corporal and then to supply sergeant.

When he had only a few months left to serve, a sergeant from G-2, the intelligence branch, sent a memorandum to all the company commanders on the base saying that G-2 needed a sergeant who was intelligent and could type. Our refugee, Miguel Ángel, even though he had only one month left in the army, was volunteered by his company commander. Miguel Ángel knew nothing about it. Soon G-2 ordered him to report. He became frightened when his commander told him that G-2 wanted to see him, but like a good soldier he reported. They gave him a typing test. The G-2 sergeant told him that he had done okay on the test. He'd made a few mistakes and needed practice, but he had passed. The sergeant then explained that they needed someone like Miguel Ángel. It was a fine career opportunity. Miguel Ángel was deferential to the higher ranking sergeant but firm. He thanked him and told him no. He said that he wanted to leave the army and move back to his hometown where he had been offered a job in a restaurant run by his father. Back at his own company Miguel Ángel's captain tried to talk him into accepting the offer, but he remained firm.

One week later another sergeant from G-2 took Miguel Ángel aside and told him that there were a lot of soldiers taking drugs, and it was a disgrace to the army. They should be rooted out, he said, and he asked Miguel Ángel to help him find out who they were. Miguel Ángel refused. He told the G-2 sergeant that he only had three weeks left in the army, and he didn't want to get involved.

Now you may think, as the asylum officer thought, that Miguel Ángel had nothing to be afraid of and that it was normal for the army to try to talk a valuable soldier into reenlisting. But Miguel Ángel, a paratrooper and a decorated hero of the Guatemalan army, was frightened. He wasn't sure they would let him out of the army. He thought that they might even kill him. Like most Guatemalans Miguel Ángel knew that G-2 had its own death squads. Many Guatemalans would say that its primary function was to run the death squads. Several G-2 deserters have informed human rights groups and the international press — the stories did not appear in the San Francisco papers because at that time they were preoccupied with the football playoffs and a juicy sex scandal—that G-2 keeps computerized death lists, and members dressed as civilians go out at night in four-wheel-drive wagons with dark windows to kidnap people whose names are on the lists. The lucky ones are killed immediately and their bodies sometimes dumped in conspicuous places. The unlucky ones are taken back to G-2 where they are tortured horribly and eventually killed. The lucky families are able to find the remains of Father, Mother, Son, or Daughter and put them to rest. The unluckiest families never find a trace.

Once a soldier is in G-2, he cannot leave until he retires or dies, the latter often occurring before the former. And if, at any time, his loyalty or readiness to obey orders becomes suspect, or if someone higher up thinks that he has become too dangerous because of some compromising knowledge, then he too is likely to be tortured and killed. This system is the same with G-2 of the Salvadoran army and Battalion 316 of Honduras.

Miguel Ángel was right not to get involved when the second sergeant asked him to help identify drug users. He knew what it would mean. Had he agreed to that minor involvement, had he done something as innocuous as turn in the name of one person who smoked marijuana, he would have been trapped. G-2 would have taken Miguel Ángel and the accused to a G-2 torture chamber where Miguel Ángel would have had to watch while G-2 members tortured the accused, ostensibly to learn the names of drug users, subversives, and terrorists, and then killed him. Afterwards they would have made it clear to Miguel Ángel, without actually saying so, that he knew too much about their methods to leave. He would have been forced to join them.

Of course, all this is speculation, but Miguel Ángel was right not to get involved in any way. He is a Guatemalan. He knew the system. He knew the terror.

When the day came for him to leave the army, his captain asked him again if he had changed his mind and told him that he was making a big mistake. Miguel Ángel said that he wanted to be a civilian. Miguel Ángel was afraid that they wouldn't let him out of the army but they did. He and his wife moved to another state in Guatemala where Miguel Ángel worked in his father's restaurant. Two weeks after leaving the army, a sergeant and a private from G-2 in uniform visited Miguel Ángel at the restaurant. They drank beer and asked him if he wasn't sorry that he had refused to join G-2, and how could he like working in a restaurant more than being in the army? Miguel Ángel told them that he liked being a civilian because he was freer, when he left work there was no one to boss him around. The soldiers told him that it wasn't too late. That he could still join G-2, but Miguel Ángel said no, thank you. The soldiers stayed for a few hours drinking beer, then left. The visit frightened Miguel Ángel very much because it showed that they hadn't forgotten about him. They hadn't just let the matter drop.

Two weeks later Miguel Ángel received another visit at work. This time it was from two men in civilian clothes. It quickly became clear that they were from G-2 because of the questions they asked. They told him that they couldn't understand why he hadn't accepted the G-2 offer when he had the opportunity. Although they didn't come right out and threaten him, Miguel Ángel was terrified. He was terrified because they wore civilian clothes when they were obviously there on business. He was terrified because they didn't tell him that it wasn't too late, that there was still time to change his mind. He was terrified because their tone of voice convinced him that they were going to come for him one night. He was terrified. He fled to Antigua while he made preparations to leave the country.

The asylum officer who denied Miguel Ángel's petition for asylum, besides being just plain ignorant about Guatemala—he thought that Antigua was a different country—could not understand why someone who had served honorably in the military should be afraid of the very forces he had served.

After the interview the asylum officer may have gone to the mountains for the weekend to get away from it all. Not for a moment was he afraid that he would stumble across a mutilated body. Not once did he worry that a passing army patrol would arrest him as a subversive or simply kill him and his wife without bothering to accuse them of anything. He may have hiked, breathed the clean air, and enjoyed the magnificent scenery. He and his wife may have picnicked in a lovely meadow, enjoyed the glorious colors of the sinking sun, and in the fading sunset light strolled hand-in-hand back to their four-wheel-drive car with darkened windows.

Andrés

THE NIGHT BEFORE Andrés's asylum trial was traumatic for all concerned. Andrés lived in a small room in a large house in West Oakland. The landlady was an ancient black woman named Silvie. She was twice a widow, a veteran of Alcoholics Anonymous, and once again she was trying to quit smoking. Tall and thin and with a large, graying Afro that made her seem even taller, she towered over little Andrés. He was not intimidated by her height, however, because she reminded him of his grandmother. Neither was he cowed by Silvie's deep voice made harsh by forty years of smoking, possibly because he could not understand anything she said, or possibly because his dear little abuelita, in her hut in the mountains of Guatemala, also swore like a trooper. For her part, Silvie was protective of little Andrés, possibly because he reminded her of her little brother who had been beaten up by a gang of white boys and then jailed for assaulting them back in Mississippi fifty years ago. Whatever the reasons, a bond of friendship formed between Andrés and Silvie despite their inability to communicate.

Silvie also rented a room to two Franciscan monks who were the only whites on the block. Andrés was the only Quiché Indian. One of the monks spoke a little Spanish, and he laboriously translated for Andrés and Silvie, allowing them to keep up with current events in each other's lives. Silvie's vocabulary was considerably cleaned up in those tête-à-tête-à-têtes. Until that exciting evening before Andrés's trial, the Franciscans had no idea of the depth and breadth that Sylvie's language could reach.

As the two Franciscans were in the habit of retiring early to meditate and pray, the night owls, Andrés and Silvie, were often left on their own. Andrés sought escape by way of Spanish soap operas, while Silvie prowled the living room, dining room, and kitchen, muttering and swearing, letting loose all the words she had politely kept on a short leash while the Nice White Boys, as she called the monks, roamed the property. It was not merely politeness on her part that she let Andrés watch Spanish TV. She had little use for TV in any language, especially the news and the sit-coms, which she found indistinguishable. When she did watch TV, she often swore at the actors. She was just as happy, then, to let Andrés mesmerize himself in front of the electric shrine while she roamed her spotless house hunting dust or long-forgotten cigarettes. Occasionally she would fix him coffee and sit beside him on the sofa while he watched *Las Muchachitas*. Silvie swore at the miniskirted girls Andrés found so sympathetic. "White girls showin their legs like that," was one of the very mildest things she would say.

Sometimes she baked Andrés a coffee cake or a pie while the TV turned his mind to mush. She was glad to have him around the house. She was glad to have the company of the unintelligible TV. She was glad to have someone besides the White Boys who were nice, but too quiet, and went to bed so early, and who made her nervous when they stayed up because she was always afraid of letting rip a few choice words in front of them.

Silvie had not been active in the Civil Rights movement, but as an interested party she had followed the struggle closely. When Andrés told her his story with the help of the

Nice White Boy who spoke second-year high school Span-ish, she had been moved to tears, and she saw that, in many ways, she and Andrés's abuelita had lived parallel lives. The night before his trial she was nearly as nervous as he was.

After the Franciscans had retreated that night, Silvie be-gan her pacing and muttering. She cursed at the crackers and rednecks who wanted to deport her little Andrés; she cursed the friends who tried to help her quit smoking; she cursed A.A. Andrés was so nervous that he couldn't con-centrate properly on *Las Muchachitas'* substantial legs and other not-quite-completely-exposed body parts and began pacing himself. As it was plain that her little Andrés was up-set, Silvie ducked out the front door and dashed to the cor-ner liquor store for a pack of cigarettes. She muttered a string of curses at the three black men who hung out on the corner in front of the store sharing a pint bottle, and she muttered more curses at the A-rab, as she called the Afghani who ran the liquor store, wondering out loud why the crackers and rednecks didn't deport him. Back at the house she and Andrés began chain-smoking. Soon Silvie in-vested her nervous energy in baking an apple pie for Andrés, somehow thinking that such an all-American dish would make up for the all-American effort to deport him. She swore at the government as she rolled out the dough, and she swore at the INS as she peeled the apples. She worked herself into such a stew that by the time the pie was in the oven she needed something to calm her down. She sneaked out the back door and hurried once more to the liquor store. She cursed the three men who were still nurs-ing their pint, and she cursed the A-rab who sold her a pint of gin.

The house soon began to smell of apple pie and gin as she poured herself and her little Andrés generous glasses. By the time the pie was done, Silvie and Andrés had fin-ished their pint of gin. Silvie was calmer, but it was clear that Andrés was more apprehensive than ever. Silvie gave him some money and, pointing at the empty bottle, managed to communicate the idea that he should dash off to the corner store and get another bottle from the A-rab. Andrés was intimidated by the three men on the corner who, having just finished their pint, had nothing better to do than to stare sullenly at him. He was also intimidated by the irascible Afghani who demanded to know what he wanted. And he was intimidated by the realization that between the gin and the sense of impending doom what little English he had command of had completely deserted him. He resorted to pointing, and he pointed in the general direction of the liquor he knew best, rum, rather than the gin he had intended to purchase. When the Afghani grabbed a quart bottle instead of a pint, Andrés accepted his fate and pointed to another pack of cigarettes as well.

Back at the house Silvie and Andrés began on the rum and the hot apple pie. The more Silvie drank and smoked the calmer she got, as opposed to Andrés, who grew more agitated with each gulped glass of rum, each gasped cigarette, and each gobbled slice of apple pie. Halfway through the bottle, the pack, and the pie, Andrés began shouting. Silvie didn't understand a word he was shouting and wasn't overly concerned. She thought that if the poor boy wanted to shout, let him. He had a right.

It wasn't so much that Andrés was a screamer. Normally he was very quiet, shy to the extreme that he was embarrassed by anything that drew the slightest attention to himself. But this was not a normal evening. The booze and the fear that tomorrow La Migra would send him back to Guatemala sent him on a journey—he began reliving the awful events that had caused him to flee.

The Nice White Boys, awakened from their innocent slumber, leapt to the conclusion that entire groups of people were being murdered, which in a sense was the case. They ran to the rescue. In the living room they saw Andrés running around screaming and Silvie sitting on the sofa admiring the smoke rings she expertly exhaled. After determining that the massacre in question had occurred two years ago, the monks grew concerned that someone would call the police (which someone did) and the police would arrest Andrés, who would then miss his hearing and the judge would order him deported. Everyone except Silvie was frantic. The monk who spoke Spanish tried to calm Andrés while the other called La Hermana.

La Hermana arrived at 2:00 in the morning. The police arrived at 2:02. Andrés shouts were clearly audible in the street, but, as he was shouting in Quiché, only the urgency was communicated. The meaning, as with the diatribes of the city's more reliable screamers who regularly shout at beings in other galaxies, was lost. The three men on the corner in front of the closed liquor store heard the commotion and watched La Hermana's car screech to a halt and a little blond woman dash up to the house. The only white women in that neighborhood at that hour were either nuns or hookers, and they had a pretty good idea which of that select group they had just seen slip into the quickly opened door. When the squad car pulled up two minutes later, their suspicions were confirmed.

Inside the house La Hermana was treated to a rare vision. The screaming Andrés was tied to a chair. He squirmed and struggled and bounced the chair up and down as he tried to escape. The monks, using the ropes from their robes, had tied him to the chair to restrain him, and the Nice White Boy who spoke Spanish was standing behind the victim with a cloth that he was about to gag Andrés with. Silvie, who had decided to make another pie, had entered the room at the sound of the doorbell and stood towering over her little Andrés, a cigarette dangling from one corner of her mouth and a rolling pin in one hand.

The instant Andrés saw La Hermana, he stopped shouting. Everyone froze in place for two minutes, taking in the incredible scene. When the police rang the doorbell, all the members of that strange party jumped. The strange party's fears as to who was ringing the doorbell was confirmed when the stillness was pierced by the squawking of the police radio in the squad car outside. The desperados considered not opening the door. Silvie brandished her rolling pin at the door and slurred a stream of oaths.

La Hermana looked out the window and crossed herself when she saw that the one of the big policemen at the door was a Latino. Often Latino cops are harder on other Latinos than are white or black cops. But the young Mexican American, who had grown up in East L.A., moved to East Oakland as a teenager, and attended St. Elizabeth's Church where he had seen La Hermana many times with many refugees in tow, proved to be simpático. La Hermana explained the situation to him in her breathless, incoherent way, and he either understood, which seemed unlikely, or didn't want to get involved with the inmates of that particular institution. In any case it was clear that Andrés had calmed down. The young policeman wished them all a good night and, as he was about to depart, mentioned that it was illegal to tie someone up and that perhaps it would be best if the monks were to wrap the cords around their own waists where they belonged.

Poor Hermana. She sat up all night with Andrés and took him to court in the morning. She did get to taste a piece of Silvie's latest pie, however. Poor Andrés. He was sick from all the pie and rum and cigarettes. In court he was so bloodshot and bleary-eyed, so nervous and frightened, that the judge was afraid to tell him to speak up after being startled by the way he had jumped the first time.

At the end of the ordeal the judge gave his opinion. It was long and in two languages, English and legalese, neither of which was translated for Andrés, who had to search for visual clues with his busy, bloodshot eyes. The judge abruptly finished off his hurried reading by saying that he would grant the petition for asylum but deny the request for withholding of deportation. He then asked Andrés's attorney if she wanted to appeal. This sudden and confusing question caught the attorney off guard. She groped and hesitated and mumbled into the microphone like a president at a press conference who had lost his idiot cards.

She was a pro bono attorney who worked for a large firm, which had corporations for clients rather than that special interest group, people. It was her first time representing a human being and her first immigration case. She had flung herself into the case with all the zeal of a crusader out to free the Holy Land. When the judge said that he was granting asylum, she was elated and squeezed Andrés's hand, but when he followed by saying that he was denying withholding of deportation, she became confused and thought they had lost. Andrés sensed her sudden disappointment and thought they were going to send him back to be killed. He slumped visibly in the chair and moaned audibly. His bloodshot eyes darted from side to side, searching for the men who would soon handcuff him and take him away. The judge, although a good man and a humanitarian, was not amused. He was in a rush to get through with the proceedings as quickly as possible. Looking at the pathetic, twitching Andrés all morning had made him impatient for his mid-morning coffee break. He switched off the tape recorder and informed the confused attorney that he had just granted her client asylum. Why would she even consider appealing?

The three black men on the corner watched as the blond hooker stopped her car and a hungover and wrung-out little Latino emerged. He fleetingly met the gaze of the three men before hurrying toward the house next to the liquor store.

Silvie had heard the car pull up. She had been watching for Andrés. She tried to read the results of the trial in his downcast eyes and shambling figure as he trudged up the front porch stairs. His slumping posture told her that the news was bad, that he had been denied asylum. She was mad enough to wring a few rednecks' necks. She yanked open the front door, slamming it against the doorstop with a bang, causing Andrés to twitch. There she stood, barring the doorway, arms akimbo, looking down on the tempest-tossed Andrés.

Poor, tired, humble Andrés. He raised his weak eyes to meet the statuesque Silvie's stern gaze. He had been practicing a little speech for his landlady, but as he faced the menacing giant his English fled, just as it had the night before in the Afghani's liquor store. All he could manage was a shy smile and an accented, "I'm Juan," which Silvie interpreted as, "I'm one." She was about to ask him what he was one of, when it dawned on her that the sad figure in front of her had tried to say, "I won." She gave a great shout, "Hallelujah!" and, wrapping her long arms around Andrés, lifted him into her embrace. When the three wise men on the corner heard that shout and witnessed that scene, they realized that the little man in the big woman's embrace was special.

The Traditional Family

I CALL THEM THE FAMILY because I can't think of a better term. To show that I am aware of current values, I sometimes add that popular adjective, Traditional. I can't unify them with a last name and refer to them as the Smiths, for example, because as a traditional family there are three different last names involved. When I call them the widows and kids it conjures up the image of old ladies in black tending their sheep in the rocky Italian hills, or worse yet, one of those references in the newspaper articles you find only at Christmastime when your suddenly compassionate local rag tries to drum up donations for the less fortunate—usually there is a graphic thermometer showing the $$$ feverishly raised in the season of giving. So I refer to them as the Family and assume that the listener will not confuse them with that other traditional family, the Mafia, which has generously contributed to the proliferation of the black-clad shepherdesses in the hills of Sicily.

The Family came to us through one of those connections that La Hermana always seems to make. She discovered that a Methodist organization was running an INS Detention Center for families in Texas. When La Hermana spoke in her nonmethodical, stream-of-consciousness manner with the Methodists, she learned about the Family. Her first reaction was, Oh, how horrible. We've got to help those poor people. Her later, more reasoned reaction was, What would we do with them? How could they ever become independent? Self-supporting? Would they be a burden on us forever? We both knew that her first reaction was the right one. We simply had to wait until compassion bludgeoned practicality into surrender.

The Family called one winter night from the San Francisco bus terminal, having, naturally, overshot Oakland. Since my car is small, I asked a friend to help out. Her pickup was low on gas so she drove her small car after I assured her that because refugees have so little baggage we could easily cram all nine of them in our two small cars. I never imagined that disposable diapers could be so bulky or that people who ran detention centers would shop at the Price Club. For their thirty-six-hour bus trip the Methodists had kindly supplied the Family with what looked to my non-parental eyes like a year's supply. I was soon to find out how foolish an estimate that was.

The ten-year-old, the seven-year-old, the six-year-old, and the four-year-old were hyperactive and could not sit still during the twenty-five-minute ride to Casa Esperanza, their new home. How they behaved on the thirty-six-hour bus trip I can only guess. The six-month-old was colicky and the two-year-old had the flu. As the mother of the two-year-old was also the lucky mother of the colicky six-month-old, she was exhausted. As the colicky infant did not want to scream in anyone's arms but Mom's, I picked up the two-year-old. As she was very affectionate as well as being one of the more mucousy babies I've ever handled, she stuck to me like glue, and I couldn't seem to put her down once we arrived at the house. She was infectious, both figuratively and literally, and picking her up was a mistake punishable by aches and fever several days later, a mistake La Hermana made the following day and many of the refugees made in subsequent days until little Guadalupe got well. Perhaps Typhoid Mary was also extremely affectionate and cuddly.

As I watched the children eat a late supper I got an insight into their hyperactivity. They salted down their scrambled eggs as if they weren't going to eat them until the following winter. Naturally they all wanted cola and only grudgingly accepted milk or orange juice.

The Family seems to bring out a certain traditionalism in many of the other refugees. The orphans, the parents who lost their children or were forced to leave them behind, the widows and widowers, they all have their own rigid opinions on how the Family's children should be raised. And I have had to fight down the traditional urge to resort to corporal punishment when the older kids go on hyperactive binges of pinching, poking, and pulling me while Guadalupe affectionately glues her sticky little arms around my ankles. Once, at a fund-raising reception when I was trying to act dignified, they actually gang-tackled me. I have even caught myself thinking that the ten-year-old, a girl who is already developing secondary sex characteristics and in a matter of seconds can alternate between flirtatiousness and bashfulness, would be better off if she were to marry young, say at thirteen or so. The idea is laughable here in the United States where that sort of thing stopped being traditional about seventy-five years ago, but I now understand the impulse to marry off pubescent daughters in turn-of-the-century Iowa or in present-day Guatemala.

The Family is actually a remnant of the traditional family. In Oakland the grandmother and two mothers work outside the home as well as continue their education. They went to school for the first time in their lives when they were in the detention center in Texas. The Methodists taught them to read and write in Spanish. Now that they are learning English, I find it hard sometimes to forgive the Methodists. Not unlike the once-starving person who can't stop eating when she finally finds food, Grandma, the two moms and the older children have become such avid readers that whenever I'm driving them somewhere they read any and all billboards, signs, advertisements, and graffiti out loud for me on the off chance that I might have missed something. NOW OUR $1,000 SLOTS PAY MORE OFTEN.

LONELINESS IS ADDICTING. CALL 1-800-COCAINE. DYS-
LEXICS UNTIE. What does that mean?, they ask.

In Guatemala they were a traditional family. They lived as
traditional extended families in nineteenth-century West
Virginia used to—twelve people in the same small house on
a small plot of land in the country. Grandfather and
grandmother, their two daughters and sons-in-law, and six
grandchildren, all crowded into a three-room house. The
men were traditional men who were superior to their wives
but protected them. They worked outside the home. They
earned money and handled the finances. They took care of
their women and children. The women were traditional
women. They did not work and had no responsibilities. All
they did was have the children, nurse the children, shop,
cook, wash the children, dishes, and clothes, clean the
house, tend the garden, mind the children and chickens,
tend the sick children, men, and chickens, and in their spare
time they sewed and made clothes. Because the women
were not much help in that traditional agricultural society,
the men, although they loved their women very much, may
have wished that at least one of their six children was a boy.

The men did not inform the women of many things that
happened outside the house, partly to protect them and
partly because traditional men simply did not talk to women
very much. The men worked on their small plot of land
where they grew corn and beans, and sometimes they
worked as laborers on other farms, and they became active
in certain dangerous activities. They did things that once
upon a time may have been traditional in Ohio, things like
barn raising, helping their neighbors dig wells, plant, harvest, or sell crops. They tried to organize the poor people in
the area to get them to work together. There was even
some loose talk about forming a cooperative, taking over
some land, and building a school and a clinic. First the
grandfather disappeared. The sons-in-law went to the police
station in town to report the disappearance. The police assured the young men that they would investigate, but they
did nothing. They didn't even make a report. Four days
later the grandfather's mutilated body was found tossed by

the road leading to a nearby town. The hands and feet had been severed and there were over 100 cigarette burns on the body. Several weeks after the distraught family buried the grandfather, one of the sons-in-law was found dead, hanging by his neck from a tree on a hill halfway between the house and town. The remaining son-in-law reported the death to the police who said that it must have been an accident or else he hanged himself. The more recent widow went to the priest who assured her that he did not believe that her husband had committed suicide. The priest warned her not to talk about what was happening. Several weeks later when the remaining man of the house was found murdered the women did not bother going to the police. They simply huddled in their house, terrified to go outside.

Terrified as they were, the women had to work outside the house. They and the children began working in the fields. One day when all but the youngest widow, Ruth, her newborn baby, and Guadalupe were working in the fields, some men drove up to the house in two four-wheel-drive American station wagons with darkened windows. Upon hearing the cars, Ruth grabbed the two children and ran out the back door. From her hiding place in the dense brush by the creek she watched the men ransack the house before burning it. Then they shot the chickens.

Neighbors took pity on the family. They let them sleep in the stable. And they explained to the poor widows that their late husbands had tried to organize the poor farmers to get them to work together. That was their crime. The neighbors were very brave to give the family food and shelter but after the first anonymous note came, warning them that anyone who helped the Family would suffer the same fate as their husbands, the Family decided to journey al Norte, and the good Samaritans breathed a sigh of relief.

The Family has no tradition of adhering to a budget, and they don't manage their money well. They feel that it's their duty to buy everything advertised on TV, the radio, or on billboards. With the grandmother's first paycheck from housecleaning they bought a cassette player. I was afraid to ask what they bought with their second. They eat a lot of prepared foods with lots of salt and drink cola by the gallon. The mothers in many ways are children themselves and seem to have no control over their hypersalted and caffeinated progeny.

Nearly a year after taking them on we still have them on our hands. They are making strides toward becoming independent, but they are more of a burden than we ever imagined. And sometimes when the children playfully tear my clothes because they like to tug at me—they probably think I'm hypoactive—or when they come to the office and speed the decay of our ancient typewriters, I can't help but wonder if we made the right decision in accepting them. Then little Guadalupe crawls onto my lap and hugs me with pure affection, and I stop fretting about whether we have enough energy, resources, or time.

Gulliver

I CALL HIM GULLIVER because he is a traveler, and although he did not urinate on the queen's castle to put out a fire, he was arrested for urinating in public.

Gulliver traveled into the office one morning guided by a Cherokee Indian and a black man. As the escorts were both big men it occurred to me that they might be cops, and as the Indian was dressed in cowboy boots, jeans, and a jeans jacket, and the black man wore an African hat and loose shirt, both bright orange and red, it occurred to me that they might be undercover cops. The Indian did the talking. He said he'd picked up this hitchhiker at Salt Lake City and had brought him to Berkeley and he's got an incredible story to tell, and if I wanted he'd have him take down his pants to show me the scars from his bullet wounds. He called the little guy who'd been blocked from view by the two big men, pushed him forward, and told him in Spanish to take his pants off.

I tried to make it clear that he could keep his pants on and told them to have a seat, all the time wondering if they were cops who wanted to involve me in some illegal scheme.

My weak ears were grateful that Gulliver sat closest to me as he was the one I wanted to talk to, but my sensitive nose was offended as he was the one who hadn't bathed in recent weeks. Despite the filthy clothes and generally unwashed appearance, Gulliver was a handsome man with longish, wavy black hair, clear eyes, and smooth skin. His nose was slightly thick and pushed to one side and the flesh around his eyes was dark, which I at first attributed to dirt. Later he told me that the flat, bent nose and dark eyes were attributable to the Mexican police, who had beaten and robbed him.

Gulliver told me in Spanish with a pleasant Portuguese accent that he was from Suriname. When I confessed my ignorance, he drew me a map, methodically sketching the outline of South America, putting in bays, inlets, rivers. Then he added the northern border of Brazil and above that three little amebas. "Here is Guyana, here is Suriname in the center, and here is French Guiana, you know, where Papillon was imprisoned. You have heard of Papillon? They made a movie about him."

The map was a marvel of accuracy—I compared it to a map in the office—and when I complimented him on it, he told me that he knew about maps because of his travels. He fished a few notebooks out of his overstuffed, expensive French backpack. He flipped through one in which he'd drawn a series of maps of South America and the Caribbean countries and islands, with red lines connecting many of the cities and towns. The red lines, it turned out, marked his travels. I leafed through until I came to maps with odd notes in a strange writing that I at first took to be nonwriting, writing that looked more like the graph of an irregular heartbeat. There was such a simple quality about Gulliver, such a boyish enthusiasm when he talked about his travels in a grocery list recital of place names, that I suspected that he was illiterate but a natural artist, and the writing was his own invention, art imitating literature. The ignorance was mine. He explained that although he spoke many languages, it was the only kind of writing he knew—Arabic writing as he called it. He then told me, with great gusto, which

194

languages he spoke, quickly and even more proudly adding that they were only a small portion of the languages spoken in Suriname. "I speak Portuguese, Spanish, taki-taki, French, and some of the many Indian languages. In my country they also speak Dutch, but I don't speak Dutch, except for a few words." He began to tell me which Dutch words he knew, but I interrupted him. I wasn't sure that I had heard the name taki-taki correctly, and I asked him to repeat it. He did and explained that it was a business language that the traders and Indians used. I waited politely while he then numbered on his fingers the various Indian groups who lived along the Maroni River and clarified for us which were cannibals and which vegetarians. It soon became apparent that his conversational style consisted of strings of nouns, places he'd been, languages he spoke or didn't speak but had heard of, rivers and lakes he'd crossed, and diseases he himself had contracted, seen people die of, or merely lose appendages to. Leprosy seemed to be one of his favorites, and I confess that I inched away from him and the powerful aroma he exuded.

After a number of grocery list conversations, I noticed that with Gulliver, as with so many energetic talkers, it was necessary to interrupt unless one had infinite patience as well as endless time. Unlike other listers I have known, Gulliver always cut off his endless string of nouns with a quick snip of the scissors and waited docilely until the time was ripe to spit out a few more place names.

As I listened to Gulliver's story, how he was forcibly recruited by the military, escaped, was caught by the guerrillas, forced to fight with them, and later fled along with 10,000 other people across the Maroni River into French Guiana, I continued to leaf through his notebook, impressed by his artistic ability and his beautiful writing. The Cherokee became impatient. He said that he had to go to San Francisco to try to sell some jewelry to the American Indian store and could he leave Gulliver with me? The black man had let them crash at his place for a few days but could no longer do so. When I hesitated, he said they could both sleep in his Camaro, no problem. But a July night in San

Francisco can be like a January night during a blizzard on Pike's Peak because of the cold and wind. And Gulliver had no warm clothes. The black man walked home and the rest of us squeezed into the Camaro which, tightly shut to ward off any fresh air, seemed to cherish the scent of Gulliver. Fortunately I live only fifteen minutes from the office. On the way, Gulliver entertained us by listing all the means of transportation he'd availed himself of in his travels—foot, horse, donkey, cart, canoe, steamboat, motorboat, sailboat, liner, car, train, truck, bus, motorcycle, bicycle.

I gave him a heavy wool shirt-jacket, which I was sorry to lose, and we rummaged through several boxes of clothes I'd collected for refugees. Gulliver accepted the shirt reluctantly but was enchanted by a nearly new pair of Nikes and quickly took off his decrepit boots. It was only after our acquaintance had ripened considerably that it occurred to me that smelly, dirty Gulliver had been reluctant to accept my expensive shirt-jacket not because he was overwhelmed by my generosity or because he was humble or because it was too large, but because the garment was not as fashionable as he would have liked.

I stood at the door and watched them as they left— Gulliver, warmly, if not fashionably, clad and newly shod, his old boots dangling from his hand, looking admiringly, I thought, at the garden. I was afraid that he was about to recite the names of all the plants that grew in the Amazon basin when he walked over to the rosemary bush. But no, he merely hid his old boots in the luxuriant growth.

The second time Gulliver came to the office we showed his notebooks to La Hermana. She too was impressed by his maps and his strange writing. She leafed through them more thoroughly than I had done as Gulliver told us about his crossing into the United States. "I crossed the frontier three times without papers. Passports are not necessary. I have crossed many borders without papers. Bolivia I entered without papers. Also Peru. I crossed the frontier into Chile without papers. And Brazil." By that time I was onto the trick of interrupting the unending lists. I asked where he had crossed into the United States. "In the desert," was his sole response. Strange that someone who was so ready to read a list of proper names needed so much prompting to tell a simple narrative. I prompted and prompted and eventually pulled enough teeth to get his story. The first time he had crossed with a Mexican couple into Arizona. The second day of wandering in the desert they had parted company, and Gulliver wandered for two more days without food or water. By the end of the third day he found himself back at the frontier where he had originally crossed. He realized that he'd wandered in a circle. He went back into Mexico and bought a compass before reentering the U.S.

La Hermana came to a primitive crayon drawing in the notebook, a green field with many white crosses and tombstones and a large white cloud hovering over a prone figure. Gulliver explained that he had executed that obra de arte on his third day in the desert when he thought he was going to die. The prone figure was his mortal remains, the cloud his soul, and the tombstone beside him belonged to his late wife. "I was very weak from not eating or drinking and was certain that I would die there in the desert far from my green land where my wife was buried." La Hermana sympathized with his plight and turned the page to a vivid drawing of a barebreasted woman with her skirt hiked up above her hips revealing shapely legs in black net stockings held up by black garters and topped off by black bikini pants. Gulliver and I were embarrassed, but La Hermana, instead of quickly turning the page as we thought she would, calmly looked at Gulliver and remarked, "I see that you were soon feeling better."

La Hermana closed the book firmly and said that she had a few things to do. Her community was having a meeting in Oregon that weekend, and she was to leave the next morning to attend, but first she would find Gulliver a place to stay, and most importantly, a place to bathe. She made a few phone calls, gathered up Gulliver and some papers, and fled the office before something else detained her.

The next morning La Hermana dropped Gulliver and his backpack off at the office and then escaped to the airport.

197

A clean and scrubbed Gulliver loitered in the living room chatting with other refugees and watching TV as I was busy most of the day. I prevailed upon an attorney who agreed to handle his asylum case pro bono. She came to the office in the afternoon to interview Gulliver. Late in the afternoon when I was ready to escape I offered Gulliver a ride to his hotel, little suspecting what I was letting myself in for. As we were driving out of the parking lot, I asked him where he was staying. Had I asked him to name all the rivers in the world, he would have talked until they all ran dry, but to extract top secret information such as his address I had to interrogate him closely. He simply wasn't interested in that type of information. He offhandedly told me that he didn't exactly know where he was staying, neither the name of the street nor the name of the hotel, but he would recognize it when he saw it. Pressed for landmarks, he told me that it was in Oakland where all the tall buildings were and that I shouldn't worry, because he had an even more precise landmark fixed firmly in his mind, a tall building across the street from the hotel that had a U.S. flag flying from its roof.

Well, great.

As we headed toward downtown Oakland I asked him about the building, the neighborhood, the people, etc. I knew from La Hermana that a friend of hers at St. Vincent De Paul's had agreed to let Gulliver stay at a transient hotel for a few days so I already suspected that it wasn't nestled among the prime real estate holdings. Gulliver told me that the hotel was tall, tan, very ugly, and in a very bad neighborhood, and that it was very dangerous in the hotel. He didn't dare leave his pack there because his door didn't lock properly, and he had been afraid to sleep last night. Some people had broken into a room nearby and robbed a student, a woman by herself. They robbed her because she was weak. That kind of information, while interesting, didn't really speak to the problem at hand.

I began driving through the worst parts of downtown Oakland, hoping that we would soon stumble across the familiar, dangerous building. Gulliver got excited whenever we approached a tan building and, unlike me, was never disappointed that it wasn't the right one. As we wandered through depressing streets, Gulliver blithely chattered away, not in the least concerned about whether or not we would ever find the hotel. That was my job, not his. He would help me if he could, but it really wasn't his concern. I speculated that his unconcerned fatalism was somehow a necessary characteristic for someone who had wandered the earth for six years, stopping to sell trinkets to tourists in the Caribbean Islands, hiring on as a sailor on yachts or fishing boats, working in a circus in Mexico. To bring his story more up to date I asked him, as we crisscrossed the downtown ghetto, what he had done last night. In his usual way of getting right to the essentials, he described the cafeteria in the hotel and how he was able to eat with a voucher he'd been given. He had eaten well. Meat, potatoes, salad, bread. Likewise for breakfast, when he had eggs, potatoes, sausages, bread, fruit, and coffee. "One eats well there. Still I do not like it. It is very dangerous. I met a Cuban there last night, and we were able to talk because he speaks Spanish. I speak Spanish as well as Portuguese, taki-taki, a little Dutch. . . ."

"What did you talk about?" I felt like a spy trying to trap a Star Wars scientist into spilling damaging information.

"Oh, nothing."

"Nothing? Didn't he tell you anything about the neighborhood?"

"No. We merely talked. They have a big room in the hotel with comfortable chairs where many people watch TV or play checkers or talk after dinner."

"And you talked there?"

"No. It was full. There was no place to sit, so we went for a walk by the lake near the hotel."

I made a screeching U-turn in the middle of the block and sped toward the other side of downtown. I had tried to cross to the other side a few times but Gulliver had always said, "No, the buildings look too nice here. It was very ugly there." We went to the nice side of downtown despite his protests and shortly found his hotel, a block from Lake

Merrit, just where he'd left it. As we climbed out of the car, he pointed across the street and proudly told me, "See. I told you there was a tall building with a North American flag. I knew I could find this place again."

José Chico

I HAVE A CERTAIN FONDNESS for José Chico, heaven knows why. He's loud, vulgar, and smelly. His unkempt, curly hair makes him look like a wild man. His clothes, no matter how new or recently washed, always seem hopelessly tattered and filthy. He's forever losing his things—his house key, his papers, his money, his radio—as well as other people's things, which as a rule he borrows without asking. He's destructive. He wrecks the furniture in his house, leaves the refrigerator door open, burns pans, never turns out a light, and always turns his radio to full volume. If that weren't enough, his conversation is repetitive. If he wants something, he repeats his request over and over and over until along about the fifth refrain I tune him out. There are those who think that strangulation would be a better solution.

José Chico is just a boy. He's a hyperactive thirteen- or fourteen-year-old. He doesn't know his own age, but on that subject he does show some variation. When he's had it with school—probably when they try to make him sit still and be quiet—he comes into the office to tell me that he's going to get a job, that he's old enough to work, and would I help him get a job? When he wants to get a job, he claims to be seventeen or eighteen, whatever strikes him at the time, and when I ask him to help out around the office by emptying the trash or sweeping up, he says he's too young to work, only eleven or twelve, and anyway he has to go study.

It's neither fair nor just that I should like José, as all the evidence is against him. Perhaps it's because he irritates most people and needs someone on his side. Perhaps it's because the first time I read *Les Miserables* tears came to my eyes when the soldiers killed the heroic little gamin. Well, all right, the second time too. Little José may not be heroic, but he's a gamin. He's a mess. And I'm guilty of liking him.

Little José has been an orphan for a long time. His parents disappeared in the war in El Salvador. He doesn't know what happened to them. They just weren't there one day. In uncharitable moments I suspect that they couldn't take any more and moved away without telling him, perhaps even moving to a more dangerous zone, just to escape from him. José lived for a few years on the streets of his town, and his story, which he tells without much variation, is that the rebels forced him to carry ammunition during a battle. After the battle the army began to hunt for him. He made the long journey north, through Guatemala and all of Mexico, thousands of miles—across what one of our knowledgeable senators called the land bridge to North America—all alone, a twelve- or thirteen-year-old boy. Often walking, stealing food, sneaking onto buses and trucks when he could, running from the police, hiding from vicious adults, befriended by others, José made what would seem an impossible odyssey to me if I didn't know other young children who had made the same journey.

José was picked up by the Border Patrol in Texas, a very frightened boy. He's told me a great number of times that he was very frightened because the Border Patrol wore uniforms that reminded him of the Salvadoran military. He has a phobia against uniforms. He won't ride the bus—perhaps an excuse to ride his bike, his proudest possession—because the drivers' uniforms also remind him of the Salvadoran military. And whenever he sees a uniformed cop on the street, he guiltily plunges his bike into traffic to avoid him. Or her. If his fear is real and not just another of his exaggerations, then perhaps the Salvadoran, Guatemalan, or Mexican military did catch him. If so, it's the one thing he's quiet about.

I have reason to believe that he truly is afraid of people in uniform.

One afternoon he came into the office and before saying hello told me twice that he'd lost the key to his bike lock. I gave him two minutes' attention, enough to shake his grimy hand, ask him how he was, hear him tell me three more times that he had lost his key, advise him to look for it at home, hear him ask twice for a saw, and tell him that I didn't have one. The phone rang, ending round one. A call from the Corralón.

While I tried to listen to a Guatemalan refugee's story, José kept repeating to no one in particular, "If I only had a little saw. Just a little saw. It doesn't have to be a big saw. Just a little saw. With a little saw I could cut through the lock. It's not a very good lock. It only cost three dollars. With a little saw I could cut through the lock in two minutes. I don't care about the lock. If I just had a little saw."

I shut him out the way you ignore a nagging headache, a minor one you can forget about as long as you don't make any sudden movements, hoping that that particular headache would just go away. After the Guatemalan man, there were three calls from Salvadoran women in the Los Fresnos Corralón. I imagined them standing side by side at separate phones, two waiting for their turn at the phone while I spoke to the third. Between their stories and my imagination I was able to completely shut out little José until one of the women asked me why we helped refugees. Her question caught me off balance, and I suddenly brought all four legs of my chair to the floor. The unplanned movement made me aware of the nagging noise at the back of my head. "If only I had a little saw."

During a break in the action about an hour later I noticed that Little José's needle was still stuck in the same groove. I took decisive action. I took him out to my car to get a hammer and screwdriver, thinking that if it really were just a cheap lock we could easily pop it open. When he told me that the bike was behind the student union, I wavered. I didn't want to go that far, a block and a half away, and I didn't want to trust him with my hammer and screwdriver. I was afraid that once his bike was liberated and he no longer needed my tools, he'd drop them with the discarded lock. I hesitated, unable to choose between three simple solutions. I could go with José. I could surrender the tools. Or I could use the hammer and screwdriver on him to prevent the 600th repetition of, "I don't care about the lock. It's a cheap lock. It only cost three dollars. I can easily break it with the hammer."

When the secretary came out to tell me that there was another collect call from a Spanish speaker, probably another refugee in the Corralón, I plopped the tools into little José's dirty hands and ran.

I was busy with calls from the Corralón, filling out forms and applications for ID's, work permits, and social security numbers. I completely forgot about José Chico's latest problem. During a late afternoon lull in the storm, I gathered up some notes and was on the point of fleeing for the shelter of my house where I could type letters in peace, when the phone rang. I didn't want to answer it. It might be an emergency—I should answer it. But nearly all calls on that line were emergencies. Those emergencies could usually wait. Whoever it was would call back tomorrow or leave a message on the machine. I ignored it. I grabbed my papers and folders, turned out the lights and walked out the door, proud of my willpower. As I was closing the door, that universal human weakness, conscience, yanked me back in to grab the phone before whoever it was hung up.

"Hello? I'm not sure how to pronounce it," an English speaker said. I was relieved to hear the mother language as English calls are usually brief, easy to deal with, or, best of all, for someone else. I began composing one of the letters I would write at home as the woman's voice continued, "but is there someone there by the name of Seester?"

"I'm sorry. She's not in today. Can I help you?"

"I'm Sergeant Shirley Simmons of the university police. I was given this number by a young Latino boy we have in custody here."

The university police—the name didn't register. I thought she was calling from the Corralón for minors in El Centro, California, because the letter I was drafting in my partially functional brain was to El Centro. Sergeant Simmons told me that she had caught a young boy named José in the act of stealing a bicycle. That got my attention.

I told her that it was a misunderstanding. I explained what had happened. I agreed to go to the campus police headquarters to identify the young criminal. I strolled over, chuckling, imagining that the campus cops would be glad to get rid of little José because he was probably repeating over and over, "It's my bike. Call Seester. She'll tell you. I just wanted to break the lock. It's my lock. I don't care about the lock. It only cost me three dollars." I hoped that this would be a good lesson to José, that it would teach him to be more careful with his things.

Sgt. Simmons was a big, stocky woman with long, straight hair of white gold, a Brunhilda in a tight, brown uniform with lots of black patent leather accessories—boots, wide belt with holster, walkie-talkie case, mace holder, night stick holder, etc.—all loaded, all adding to her operatic bulges. I was slightly intimidated by her bulk. She showed me the tools the alleged criminal was using when apprehended, and I identified them as mine. She led me to the bike rack behind the student union where the alleged crime in progress had been halted, and I had to pick out José's bike. When I saw the long rack with its three dozen bikes I didn't think I could do it. I knew José's was a mountain bike but so were 90 percent of the bikes tethered to the rack. Fortunately there was a clue. I noticed Sgt. Simmons' card sticking to the handle bars of a bike vaguely similar to José's. That was the one I accused. She smiled radiantly and cut the cheap three-dollar lock with the enormous bolt cutters she had with her. She was friendly and we chatted amicably as we walked back with the bike to spring José.

I signed a paper and another big, uniformed, and accessoried blond woman emerged with dark little José in tow. He'd been crying. Although he kept his head down, his red eyes were constantly active. When the sympathetic police officer raised her hand to pat him on the back to comfort him, he cringed and dashed over to hide behind me, holding onto me, keeping me between him and the uniformed captors. My heart nearly broke when I felt him trembling beneath my arm, and I knew that somewhere, in El Salvador, or Guatemala, or Mexico, he'd been captured.

We sat in the sun on campus for awhile, regaining our strength, watching all the beautiful students parade by. I apologized to José for getting him into that mess. He graciously accepted. When he was able to look into my eyes, we had a talk. Just when I thought I'd convinced him to see one of our psychologists, his batteries got overcharged once again, and he jumped on his bike and sped away, nearly running over several students.

César

ONE SUMMER EVENING in a backyard in Oakland, a series of longwinded speakers, one after another, took center stage to praise César. Because they had nothing interesting to say, they had conspired to use a great many words to say it. It was a deadly combination after the heavy meal we had just eaten.

The yard was small and bare, and the sweaty crowd stood fidgeting or sat nodding, elbow to elbow, hip to hip, under the still-warm sun. I recalled the closed-in feeling and how it had grown tighter, how the temperature had risen, and how what had at first been a barely audible drone had grown to a frightening roar with each step that I took down the narrow stairwell toward the visiting room of the county jail the previous summer. Each step seemed to take me a step closer to the inferno. The inferno was the visiting room, a large gymnasium. A demilitarized zone, consisting of two rows of tables separated by a moatlike gap of three feet, had been constructed along the gym's out-of-bounds lines. Visitors sat on the outside facing in and prisoners on the inside looking out. Because visitor and visited were separated by nine feet of table and moat, it was necessary to talk loudly or even to shout to be heard, and all the shouts echoed through the hollow gymnasium, making it necessary to shout louder and still louder. The infernal roar made it nearly impossible to hear, and the heat, nearly impossible to concentrate. Communication was tedious.

Size seemed to be the motif of the next speaker who waddled to the back of the yard to stand beside the embarrassed César, once patting him on the head, and I couldn't help but notice that the large crowd squeezed into the little yard consisted mostly of middle-aged Mexican American men, nearly all a head taller than César. Like rusted freighters with too much cargo on deck, they had steamed into the backyard, dropped anchor, and were slow to get moving again. Watching them roll with the sluggish waves made me drowsier still, and my mind slipped out with the tide.

A year ago César had told me on the phone that most of the prisoners were black and grandotes (very big), and that they "could kill one." I remembered his words when I watched the prisoners emerge in twos and threes from the far end of the gym. They were happy, smiling, laughing, joking, as they looked around for their visitors. It was a pleasant fifteen minutes for them, a break in the routine. The visitors, on the other hand, were all hard looking and strutting. They seldom smiled and never joked. They had adopted hard personas because they were nervous, perhaps even a little frightened. I know I was. Only the prisoners and the young children were relaxed, and the latter, when they began to have too much fun running up and down the demilitarized zone outside the tables, were quickly intimidated by a rigid police officer. When at last César appeared, I wanted to laugh and cry. Little five-feet-two César, in a baggy, dark blue jumpsuit, walked softly between two enormous, muscular men. When I saw how ridiculous he looked, barely chest-high to those huge men, I suddenly sensed how vulnerable he must have felt. I looked around and saw that all the prisoners were big men. Only César was small, and he walked carefully, like a child in a crowd of adults, trying not to get stepped on.

The next speaker seemed to think that it was necessary to prevent César from escaping as he stood with his arm around César's shoulders, pressing him tightly against his bulging belly. Perhaps he knew that César was something of an escape artist. Over the past six months César had often called La Hermana or me to tell us that he was thinking of running away. In jail he had denied his previous arrest, telling us that he didn't know anything about it, that it must have been some mistake, that someone else must have used his name. He would have denied the second arrest if we hadn't visited him in jail. When he got out, he wanted to pretend that nothing had happened. However, the Lawyer's Committee was having none of his denials and told him that if he didn't get help, if he didn't help himself, they wouldn't represent him in his asylum case. César surrendered. I drove a sad César to the storefront office in East Oakland. On the way there he didn't talk much, merely mumbling a few repetitive phrases. "How am I going to pay? It's a lot of money. I'm going to have to work a long time to pay it back. I owe you $30 that you lent me in jail. I can't pay you back until I get a job. Maybe I should get a job first so I can pay you back." As I didn't respond to the bait, he went on. "But if I don't go they'll deport me. But it's too expensive." And although he didn't say so, he was afraid that it would be like jail all over again. Like César, I had my doubts about the program. I thought it was too severe and expensive. But I said nothing. When we pulled up in front of the decrepit building, I half expected him to bolt from the car and run, but no, sad, drooping César, his little plastic grocery bag with all his worldly goods dangling from his hand, walked into the dingy office. He was eighteen years old.

When César was twelve, he and his uncle had fled Guatemala, walking four days, hiding from the army patrols, and skirting roadblocks, to a refugee camp in Mexico. When the Guatemalan army crossed the border to invade Mexico, César, his uncle, and a friend decided to go to El Norte. When they were stopped by Mexican authorities, they pretended to be Zapotec Indians from Oaxaca who didn't speak much Spanish. The journey took them nearly a year as they stopped to work in the tomato fields in Baja. César's uncle was caught by La Migra at the border, but César and his friend escaped running. He was thirteen when he crossed into California. He worked as a migrant farm worker in the Central Valley, picking tomatoes in the summer, grapes in the fall, broccoli in the winter, running to a new place, a new job whenever he got into trouble or whenever La Migra got close. Despite his expertise at running, La Migra caught him when he was seventeen years old and sent him to a detention center for minors run by a for-profit private company, Eclectic Communications, Inc. At ECI César was interviewed by an attorney from Esperanza Para Los Niños (Hope for the Children), a nonprofit organization that visits the detention center to help as many kids as they can. They contacted Sanctuary, and we got him out and brought him to the Bay Area. We thought he wouldn't have to run anymore, but there are many kinds of escapes, and often we simply substitute one for another.

The first hint of fog rolling in on the bay breeze brought a welcome coolness to the crowded yard as the fattest speaker of all promised us that he wouldn't be long because he didn't want to keep us from the great tubs of ice cream and the huge cake. My stomach was still rumbling from the meal I had been required to eat before the speeches began. La Hermana, who had the misfortune to sit next to me, politely ignored the additional racket. The meal had seemed sizable enough to sustain the crew of a man-of-war on a long voyage, and evidently the ship's officers thought they could make us feel more comfortable by encouraging us to overeat as they brought long trays of fried chicken, big bowls of salsa, corn, potatoes, and salad. "Six months ago," the speaker continued, breaking his promise of brevity, "when little César joined our program, I didn't think he would graduate. I didn't think he had what it took to survive a tough program. And this is a tough program. You see, you start by thinking everyone is against you, that you have no friends. If you can survive that . . ."

César himself had had his doubts. When we talked on the phone he told me that in their meetings some of the old men would tell their stories, how they beat their families, cheated, stole, lied, until they lost everything and ended up living in the streets. Some had lived in the streets for years. Some spent a lot of time in jail. César didn't want to hear those stories. He didn't want to end up like those old men. He made up excuses. He said he had to run away and get a job to pay me back, to send money to his mother. He wanted to escape. He didn't think he would make it. I too had my doubts, but I also knew that César had survived greater hardships. I had been his interpreter when the law school immigration class worked on his case. I knew his story. I knew that when he was twelve years old the guerrillas had killed his father for continuing to work on the plantation of a wealthy landowner. I knew that in that same year the army had come through his village. The army treated all Kanjobal Indians as less than human, as the enemy. They searched from house to house. They stole food and stock. They took many young men away at gunpoint—the Guatemalan version of the draft. They took a few others to the center of town and shot them. Four soldiers entered César's house. One soldier pointed his rifle at César and yelled something but César did not understand. In those days he did not speak Spanish, only Kanjobal. The soldier was angry because César didn't understand and struck him in the face with his rifle barrel. César's mother told him to take his brother and sisters to the school. When they returned home after the army had left, César found his mother on the floor, bruised and bloody but alive. She did not smile or play with the children for a long time after that. The last time the army came through they first burned the village on the neighboring hillside. That was warning enough. César's mother gathered up the kids, the chickens, the corn, and beans, and they hid in a hole in the ground some distance from the houses. These holes were called buzones (mailboxes). They were deep, square holes, which the Kanjobales had learned to dig to hide their food from the pillaging of both the army and the guerrillas. César and his family hid for three days in the buzón, only daring to look out at night to see their village in flames. When the

211

army left after three days, there were no houses, no structures left standing. Because at twelve César was growing big by Kanjobal standards, his mother was afraid that if the army caught him they would press him into service. She sent him to Mexico with his uncle.

It was dark when the last speaker took the floor. He was an emaciated-looking man, a chain smoker. There were many dedicated smokers in the crowd, and the flickering lighters and glowing cigarettes were as numerous as fireflies in the Guatemalan lowlands on a summer night. And like the crickets on a warm Guatemalan evening, the coughing and hacking made a continuous chorus. The one skinny speaker told us in an ancient, rasping voice that he had been around a long time and had seen a lot of men come and go and at first he didn't think César would make it. But he'd learned a lot from César, César who always seemed to have a friendly smile for everybody, even when things got tough, even when everyone else got fed up or lost their tempers. He thanked César nicely for his smile and his friendly attitude and presented him with an oversized graduation card signed by everybody and a copy of *The Twelve Steps*.

A year after his graduation from the alcohol treatment program César is doing well. He runs to keep his weight down. He has two jobs in fast-food restaurants. He paid me back out of his first paycheck and is steadily paying his debt to the treatment center. César has always paid his debts.

Prejudice

I ADMIT THAT I AM PREJUDICED. Why be ashamed of it? All the great people in history, all the prophets of all the religions and the sons of God had certain undeniable prejudices. It seems well documented, for example, that an otherwise forgiving Jesus Christ held an unaccountable antipathy towards tycoons in the temple, one of the few prejudices we seem to have eradicated in modern times. Who then am I to deny that I am prejudiced? The trick is, I think, to be discriminating in one's prejudices.

When I first met Felipe he was fresh out of ECI, which is easier for refugees to pronounce than Eclectic Communications Incorporated. (I don't know about you, but I am NOT prejudiced against people who run prisons for profit. I understand the logic that says that if we have to have misery someone might as well make a profit off it.) Felipe was seventeen at the time. Very short and muscular, he sported a sleeveless shirt, which displayed his development as well as the eagle tattoo on his forearm. While I think that the human body is a work of art, I find certain exhibitions offensive. It's not that I am entirely prejudiced against tattoos, but the ferocious eagle with drops of red blood dripping from its beak and talons on Felipe's biceps would have been more to my liking had it been hidden by a sleeve. I was even more put off by the primitive cross tattoo on the first joint of his middle finger. That would not normally be covered unless the temperature dropped enough to require gloves, which was not altogether improbable as it was July in Berkeley.

Although Felipe dressed like a hoodlum out of a James Dean movie and had the tattoos of someone who'd spent time in stir, he was not a pachuco. He was a Quiché Indian. Because he was a strapping youth he had been forcibly recruited by the Guatemalan military when he was fourteen years old. I would say kidnapped but the INS is prejudiced against the term when the army of a sovereign state does the grabbing. Fear of being kidnapped by government forces can be grounds for asylum, but the INS, while deploring the practice, does not consider forcible recruitment as grounds for asylum. As with so many other actions, it all depends on who's doing what to whom. Miss Reilly, my sixth-grade history teacher, may have misled our class full of innocent minds into believing that forcible recruitment was wrong under any circumstances when she taught us that one of the reasons we fought the war of 1812 was due to the forcible recruitment of U.S. merchant seamen by the British navy. But perhaps my memory of that lesson is hazier than Miss Reilly would have liked.

In modern Guatemala, only males over eighteen can be legally recruited by the army. However, the Guatemalan officer corps does not wrinkle its neatly creased uniforms over legal niceties. Recruitment in that nation of laws means that a military truck cruises the towns, often looking for places where young men might congregate, such as the football field or the market. When likely young men are spotted, the truck stops and the soldiers give chase. Once caught, the new recruits are thrown into the truck. When full, the truck takes its cargo to the military base. The young boys aren't given a chance to tell their mothers and fathers not to wait dinner for them. The recruiters do not check the boys' papers to see if they are of age. They simply take them to the base and sort it out there. Sorting it out means that if a boy's father goes to the base and proves to the commander's satisfaction that his son is under age, then the boy may be released. Poor people and especially poor Indians often lack the means to satisfy the commander.

I admit that I judged Felipe by his appearance, and I judged him harshly. I asked him about the tattoos. He blushed and told me that he had had them etched into his skin when he was in the army because everyone had them. I am not disposed to like people who say they do things because everyone does them, but Felipe's blush softened my judgment. Also, another of my prejudices is that I think the Quiché Indians are a gentle people, and I am disposed to like them. Despite Felipe's appearance he was very much a Quiché Indian, always gentle and shy and an easy blusher. Who knows what he did or was forced to do when he was in the Guatemalan army. You and I cannot imagine the horrible things the Guatemalan army forces Indian boys to do. To his credit, he ran away. He deserted.

Now, when I think of Felipe I cannot help but smile, remembering the lesson he taught me.

I saw him soon after he had gotten his first paycheck in the U.S. He was sitting cross-legged on the floor of his room, wearing a knit cap and an oversized, hand-me-down overcoat, and facing one of the most incredible machines I had ever seen. It was a large ghetto blaster with flashing strobe lights on either end. A red-sequined globe, the size of a softball, shimmered as it revolved on top of the infernal contraption. Felipe was hypnotized and unaware of my presence. I don't know if he was enchanted by the music, lost in thought, or simply enraptured by the knowledge that he owned such a wondrous property. I don't know if he thought his radio was equal in value to, say, Manhattan Island, but, sitting there on the cold floor on that foggy summer day, listening to that Mexican corrido "Juan Sin Tierra," watching the lights flash and the globe spin was a high point in his young life. He, a boy from the mountains of El Quiché, had entered the modern world with his astute purchase. Perhaps he was thinking, if only my family or friends could see me now. Or the officers in the army who used to punch me and kick me and hit me with their rifle butts and yell at me that I was a dirty, stupid Indian, no better than an animal, the officers who made me bathe in sewage, the officers who forced me to eat raw meat that they threw on the ground, the officers who forced me to drink dog's blood to give me courage.

It's a sad truth that we are not automatically immune to the flaws we disapprove of in others. Those who are the victims of prejudices are often disposed to hold the same prejudices against others. In Guatemala there is a tremendous prejudice against the Mayan Indians. People say the same tired old things that they say about any group on the bottom. They are stupid. They are dirty. They are lazy. They don't want to work. (El Salvador avoided much of this problem by massacring a large portion of its Indian population and terrorizing most of the survivors into identifying themselves culturally as Ladinos.) Despite having suffered the slings and arrows of outrageous racism, some Maya find it all too easy to sling a few of their own racist arrows. East Oakland, the barrio where many of the refugees live, is diverse, which is lovely to see, but full of diverse prejudices, which are ugly. During the day it can be like stepping into the American South, Southeast Asia, or Mexico. During the night it's one of the most violent neighborhoods in the United States. Most of the violence is not random but one drug gang member killing another. All too often, however, a gang assaults some hapless person foolish enough to be on the street at night. Since many of the refugees work as dishwashers in restaurants or as janitors in office buildings, they come home late at night, and since they are poor, they rely on public transportation, which means that they always have to walk some blocks from the bus stop to their house. Because they are poor they don't have bank accounts but carry cash, and on payday they carry large sums. And the refugees are small. What easier victims could the gangs ask for? Many of the refugees have been assaulted, and one, who fled the terror in El Salvador, was crippled for life when a gang stabbed him in the back, severing his spinal cord.

Because gangs are made up of young black men, many of the refugees develop an antiblack prejudice.

I lecture the refugees when they make some thoughtless remark about blacks. The beautiful Mayan women who have traded in their handwoven, embroidered skirts and blouses for machine-sculpted nylon pantyhose, polyester miniskirts, and acrylic blouses and sprayed and teased their hair into ridiculous pompadours and the handsome Mayan men who do their best to look like pachucos, I ask them why they aren't prejudiced against Latinos who have persecuted them for 500 years. On the contrary, they want to look as Latino as soon as possible. I ask the Latinos why they aren't prejudiced against whites since the immigration officer who intimidates, threatens, or abuses them is usually white. The people who wrote the immigration laws, the people who want to deport them, are white. If a white post office clerk is rude to them when they try to buy a money order to pay the rent, they blame only that individual, not all whites or all postal employees. When the large, hostile black woman at the social security office rudely refuses to issue them a social security number despite their having the correct documents, some of the refugees start muttering about blacks. That's when I begin lecturing them. That's when they begin edging away from me.

I have known Felipe for three years now. He no longer has the ghetto blaster and blushes when I innocently ask him what happened to it. He is still very gentle. When I am with him in public, I see, or imagine that I see, other people looking, with prejudiced eyes, at his tattoos and slicked-back hair. Once, when I was waiting at the Department of Motor Vehicles for Felipe to take his driving test, I found myself unaccountably blathering about prejudice to the bored black man behind me in line. It was presumptuous of me to ramble on so about prejudice to a black man in North America, but my fountain of babble was triggered by the sight of little Felipe holding out, with a trembling hand, his learner's permit to the examiner, a large, no-nonsense white woman who affected the same persona as the woman in the social security office. The towering woman frowned at

217

little Felipe and frowned at his permit. I surprised my neighbor, a friendly man who wanted to chat about the weather to pass the time, and unless I imagined it, he seemed to edge farther away from me as I went on and on.

I wonder if you have too.

Luz in America

LUZ IS AN ATTRACTIVE YOUNG WOMAN, a widow who earns a living living in. When not living in large houses in well-kept neighborhoods, caring for other people's families, she lives in a small, yet drafty flat in a dangerous neighborhood with her own two tots, her mother, two brothers, one sister-in-law, a nephew, and a sister. Luz and I became phone acquaintances when she lived in for a young couple in the Oakland hills, caring for their infant and toddler as well as cooking and cleaning house. The parents were both working professionals, the wife an attorney for an insurance company, the husband a university professor. They would call me, not when there was a language problem—they got a great deal of satisfaction from working those sorts of things out with the aid of a pocket Spanish-English dictionary—but for ad hoc counseling. They felt guilty about keeping Luz away from her own children five days a week to care for theirs. Their nicer feelings finally got the better of them when the wife was offered a job in politics. The nice young couple explained—I hoped that they were blushing at their end of the connection, otherwise the wife would be admirably suited for her new job in the capital—that their

finely tuned consciences wouldn't allow them to continue
being responsible for keeping Luz away from her own
children. They wanted me to explain that to Luz as their
Spanish wasn't up to it. Although I am no more than an ad-
equate interpreter, I know better than to translate literally. I
told Luz that the fastidious young couple was firing her because they were afraid that in the wife's new job it would be
a liability to have an off-the-books, foreign employee.

I finally met Luz when she came to the office about another job La Hermana had arranged. I was struck by her
beauty and her resignation. During the short drive to her
future employer's house I chatted and joked while Luz
sighed and looked out the window with the sad air of a
prisoner on her way to a windowless penitentiary. The penitentiary we sought was in what was once a working-class
neighborhood of Berkeley, a neighborhood of small, neat
houses that predatory yuppies swallowed up as fast as the
aging inhabitants relinquished their holds on things mate-
rial.

A tenacious inhabitant—a woman I shall always think of
as Mrs. Querulous—greeted us at the sturdily barred door
and thanked me for coming because, "You see, my dear, my
daughters arranged all this, and I don't know how this is
gonna work out cause she don't speak nothin but Spanish
and I don't speak nothin but American."

Having, like Saki, grown up surrounded by aunts and
great-aunts, I am accustomed to the ways of elderly women,
but unlike that illustrious aunt hater, I seldom struggle with
a sweetly stubborn old dear who will not change. I wasn't in
the least tempted to correct her error. Also, I wanted to
keep the interview as brief as possible because it was a busy
day back at the office. I refrained from quibbling, and still
Mrs. Q quashed any hope I had of an early departure. She
sat us at the dining table where she force-fed me the facts
about her husband of fifty years, his death and funeral two
years ago, and her two daughters, who had wonderful
homes and families of their own, incomplete though they
were without Mrs. Q living with them. The daughters were

squabbling over the privilege of having Mrs. Q move in with them.

Mrs. Q was quick to protest that she didn't want to favor one daughter over the other, and besides, she was the quintessential independent woman who wanted to live in her own house, the house where she had raised her remarkable family, the house she had lived in for the past fifty-two years. Mrs. Q had hurt her back reaching for some sheets on the top shelf of the linen closet, which she kindly took the trouble to show me. Sure enough, the top shelf was high as top shelves are wont to be. Stooped over as she was with her injury, Mrs. Q had lost the use of both the top as well as the next shelf down, and as a consequence found herself in a quandary. She needed someone to stay with her who could access the top shelves, cook, clean, help her in and out of the tub, dress, etc. On our edifying field trip to the linen closet I had spied a special toilet, a sort of postmodern throne, next to the more familiar one. I assumed that Luz would have to help Mrs. Q with that. If so, it was the one subject Mrs. Q was quiet about.

Mrs. Q required someone to live in during the week, someone who had a home of her own to go to on the weekends, when Mrs. Q, in strict rotation so as not to needlessly wound, would stay with the doting daughters.

After the oral history came a brief discussion of duties. During the preliminaries, I thought Mrs. Q to have many quaintly interesting qualities. There was little doubt that she was a bit greedy where center stage was concerned, but she was alert, lively, and, at the age of seventy-two, willing to take on a new adventure. Good for her, I thought.

I hadn't translated any of the fascinating details of Mrs. Q's biography for Luz who sat patiently through it all, as that would have inappropriately doubled the soliloquy, and I still had hopes of an early escape. I did translate the duties discussion, omitting the remembered quips of the late Mr. Q or nearly forgotten details from Mrs. Q's life as a girl. Although eager to get away, I didn't rush Mrs. Q because I was equally eager for Luz to get the job, more eager than Luz seemed to be. I listened to Mrs. Q. And listened. And listened. Mrs. Q's quirks were interesting the first time through, but some of the charm began to wear as I gained some insight into what it must have been like to be a family member. I began to suspect that the doting daughters, to say nothing of the sons-in-law, were on our side, that is, they preferred that Mrs. Q live in her own house with someone who didn't speak American to the alternative of having her live with them. They preferred doing their doting every other weekend. Perhaps it was uncharitable of me to think so, but as the afternoon slowly disappeared into the quagmire of Mrs. Q's quips, I had the even more uncharitable thought that Luz was fortunate not to understand American.

Mrs. Q was quite content to reminisce while we, sitting at the dining room table, felt like lifers confined to narrow cells at San Quentin. Our first escape was to the basement to inspect the washer and drier as well as the mountainous supply of canned food—applesauce, asparagus, garbanzo beans, navy beans, pinto beans, beets, corned beef hash, creamed corn, fruit cocktail, peach halves, pineapples sliced, pineapples diced, soups, spaghetti and meatballs, stews, succotash, tomatoes whole, crushed and pureed, Vienna sausages, ad nauseam.

"Her basement seems to be better stocked than most bomb shelters," I observed. Luz did not bother to so much as smile politely. The situation was too serious. After forlornly staring at the cans for some time she sighed. She told me that she did not like canned food and asked me to ask Mrs. Q if she could cook fresh vegetables. Since we were in California where the stores, on special occasions, stock a fresh veggie or two, that seemed a reasonable request. We trudged back up the stairs to face Mrs. Q with all the enthusiasm of French aristocrats on their way to confront the guillotine.

The negotiations had all been settled beforehand, but it seemed that Mrs. Q had questions about some details. Actually, Mrs. Q had some histrionic haggling hidden in her repertoire that was bursting to get out. She suddenly began a loud, nervous discourse on her condition of near poverty.

It seemed that she was afraid that we were going to hit her up for more money. Luz was a lovely girl, she said, and she would love to pay her more but she just couldn't. Mrs. Q's quotidian expenses were too much for her as it was. As it was, she didn't know where she would get the money for Luz's salary. When she stumbled on the recounting of her electric and phone bills, I didn't point out that the totals seemed to be growing even as we spoke. She vaguely knew that she had tripped but didn't know what on. She continued lamely with her accounts until she was able to lean on her rock-solid property taxes. There she rested, allowing me to assure her that we wouldn't dream of asking for more than the $150 a week we had agreed on. It wouldn't be fair, I said, emphasizing the F word.

"That's right, Brother," Mrs. Q quipped. Her voice becoming soft and confidential as suddenly as it had reached near-panic pitch, she said, "I want everything to be fair. That's why I arranged this through Father Conlin. Do you work with him?" As Mrs. Q wasn't completely honest with me, I let her think that I was a Brother.

When Mrs. Q once again complained, "My daughters tell me I'm crazy to have someone in the house who doesn't speak American," I could no longer resist. I mentioned that Luz was American. Mrs. Q merely inquired, "Can she cook American?" I shuddered at the thought of all the American cans, especially the corned beef hash, in the bomb shelter and wondered when in their fifty years of cohabitation the late Mr. Q had stopped dropping gentle hints that merely cluttered the conversation since no one ever bothered to pick them up.

"I can't eat spicy foods. My digestion ain't very good. I just eat American food. I don't know about this whole deal. Don't get me wrong. I'm sure she's a wonderful girl. It's my daughters. They worry about me. They've been nagging me for days. 'Ma, she's not even American,' they say. 'How do you know she won't murder you in your sleep?'"

I toyed with the idea of telling the queasy Mrs. Q that you could count on one hand the number of people murdered by Sanctuary-sponsored refugees but decided that the moment wasn't appropriate for my American brand of humor. Mrs. Q, for all her insistence on being queen of the castle, was a vulnerable little old lady who had a very real concern about the person she was about to live with. I was impatient only because I thought that we had previously discussed those concerns on the telephone. I told Mrs. Q that Luz had worked in several other houses, and all her former employers had raved about her excellent qualities. I also mentioned that Luz was a particular favorite of La Hermana. The references from former employers were like water off a duck's back, but the endorsement of a nun quelled her Texas-Chainsaw-Massacre fears.

When Mrs. Q countered with that old standby, "If only she spoke American," I, trying to give my words a religious overtone, sermonized: "Those of us in the refugee movement, in an effort to keep our hearts and our minds open, as I'm sure we all want to do . . ."

Pause for chorus.

Chorus: "Oh yes. Yes. Amen, Brother."

". . . we try not to fall into the trap of equating English with American, or thinking of the people from the United States as the only Americans, because where would that leave everybody else?"

"Huh?"

"Luz speaks the most common American language, Spanish, and is from the most densely populated country in the Americas, El Salvador."

It was a mistake to say it. I suddenly knew what it was like for a shepherd of souls who, while exhorting the congregation to goodness, looks out on the sea of stubborn faces and experiences the epiphany that the flock will insist on straying toward the same old sins. Mrs. Q quashed my sermon with a look that plainly said, "You religious workers don't know anything about the real world," while sweetly murmuring, "Yes, I'm sure she's a lovely girl. I'm just an old lady who's used to calling our kind American and her kind . . . Is she even Catholic?"

I'm not completely learning challenged. Instead of delivering another sermon to Mrs. Q about how we in Sanctuary did not ask refugees what faith they belonged to, which would have been merely another quixotic tilting at the windmills of Mrs. Q's mind, I came down off my high horse and asked Luz what her religion was. Fortunately I didn't have to consider lying as her answer was Catholic. I did test the elastic quality of truth in another fruitless experiment, however, when I put it to Mrs. Q that it would be good for her to have Luz around the house. It would be a learning experience. I complimented her on her adventurous spirit and her nonexistent willingness to learn another language. When intellectual stimulation failed to get us anywhere, I simply said that I had to get back to the office, and she could think it over and call me if she decided to take the plunge.

Bingo, as the religious community says. Mrs. Q, who on the phone had begged me to find her someone, grudgingly said she would give it a try. I marveled at the way she had turned things around, making it seem that she was doing us a favor.

When at last everything seemed settled, and I thought I saw the light at the end of the dark dining room, Luz told me that she couldn't start on Monday. She was to have an operation instead. That came as a surprise. I had thought that at the office that afternoon Luz had told me that she wanted to start on Monday. I interrogated her. A hostile witness would have willingly surrendered more information. Luz told me only that it was a minor operation, an outpatient procedure, and she could start work on Tuesday. I was reluctant to pry when Luz was so reluctant to talk. Mrs. Q was quick to accept my glib explanation that Luz was too embarrassed to tell me because it was a woman thing. In fact, Luz didn't seem embarrassed at all, merely detached.

Mrs. Q's curiosity was piqued. Already she was planning to spend the first long afternoon quarrying the details with her Spanish-English dictionary from the hard rock mine that was Luz. However, she was also undeniably miffed, not because Luz couldn't start on Monday, or because her quest for information wasn't immediately gratified, but because she, who had entertained us all the long afternoon with a

series of dramatic monologues on her own health problems, suddenly found herself upstaged by a supporting actress with very few lines.

Monday afternoon I called Luz's house to see if she had
survived the operation and to confirm that I would pick her
up at her house the next morning. Luz's mother told me
that they'd kept her in the hospital after all. I called Mrs. Q
at one of the jealous daughters'. She was quite understanding.

Tuesday ditto.

Wednesday Luz came home but was too weak. Mrs. Q
was unquestionably sympathetic and said she would go to
the other jealous daughter's house to spread the joy of
putting up with her. The following week when Luz was still
too weak, Mrs. Q began to get querulous, understandably
so. She worried aloud that perhaps she should find someone else. She didn't want to. Luz was a lovely girl. It was just
that her daughters worried about her. What if she, Mrs. Q,
fell? Luz wouldn't be strong enough to help her, and since
she didn't speak American she wouldn't be able to call for
help. Mrs. Q was momentarily distracted to learn that 911
had Spanish speakers. She thought they only spoke American. Next, she voiced her concern that we didn't even know
what was wrong with the dear, lovely girl. I shamelessly leapt
once more into the breach. I told Mrs. Q, in my most confidential and insinuating manner, that I did not like to
question refugee women. I laid it on pretty thick. I told her
that she and I could only imagine what many women had
suffered and that often they would never tell me, a mere
man, about such things. Mrs. Q's voice quavered as she
assured me that she was on the dear girl's side. It was just
that her daughters were pressuring her.

Luz and I arrived on Tuesday of the following week. Luz
seemed weak. Her pallid color added to the overall impression of weakness. She carried her toothbrush and clothes
in two plastic bags. When everything, including Luz, was settled in the house, Mrs. Q's cousin entered. He was a retired
man, tall and stooped, whose wardrobe had that distinct air
of having been selected in the previous decade by his late

wife. He wore green, plaid golfing slacks, a yellow, checked shirt, and a rust red tam-o'-shanter. He seemed to be quite taken with the pale Luz and gallantly insisted on helping her with her plastic bags.

He had stopped by to take Mrs. Q shopping. It was a once-a-week treat for her to go to Cans R Us, and she seemed to quake with excitement at the impending gratification of her desire to travel to exotic places. However, when she saw her cousin's reaction to Luz, she became quarrelsome. She was suddenly anxious about Luz's salary. She was afraid that Luz expected a whole week's salary even though she would only work four and a half days. Once again I assured her that Luz was fair and wouldn't dream of charging for days she didn't work. Mrs. Q was offended by the F word. Her eyes quickly glistening with tears, her voice quivering like the voice of a misunderstood child—a voice I would frequently hear on my home phone in the coming weeks—she said that she hadn't meant to insinuate that Luz wasn't fair. She was fair too. Why did everybody always accuse her of not being fair? She went on and on about I didn't know what. However, the cousin seemed to have heard it before. Her overreaction left me with the strong impression that she was an actress whose only audience had been the deceased spouse, the doting daughters, and the stooped cousin.

I briefly held Luz's lifeless hand and looked at her downcast, prison-pallor face before I made my escape. I wondered what kind of a sentence I was condemning her to. I would soon find out.

A few nights passed peacefully before the first distressed phone call. Mrs. Q was quite agitated because Luz wanted to bring her children to live with her in that cozy little Berkeley bungalow. Mrs. Q quailed before the vision of a room-by-room displacement by invading hordes of Central Americans. I asked to speak to Luz. Luz was as serene as always. She didn't understand what all the fuss was about. They had been trying to communicate using the dictionary and the little American that Luz understood. Mrs. Q had been pumping Luz about her family and kids, and Luz simply offered to have her mother bring the kids around one day so that Mrs. Q could meet them. When I told her that Mrs. Q had misunderstood and thought that the kids would soon be living there, Luz was not amused. She didn't think the kids would enjoy living with Mrs. Q. Neither was Mrs. Q amused when she came back on the line and I explained the misunderstanding. I thought she would at least be relieved to learn that Luz had only offered to have her meet the kids, but, no, Mrs. Q was equally appalled by the prospect of meeting the little delinquents. I explained her preference to Luz, whom I could almost hear shrugging.

Mrs. Q came back on the line to thank me. That's when I made a grave error. I told her that I was only too glad to help. From that time on the calls came nightly. Sometimes Mrs. Q had a complaint about some oversight of Luz's. Those she invariably prefaced with compliments. "Luz is a lovely girl. I just love her. And she's such a good cook. I'm lucky to have her. But she puts too much salt in the food. My doctor says salt is bad for my heart." Or, "Luz is such a lovely girl. I love her as much as my own daughters. And she works so hard. But when she vacuums and dusts she doesn't look up, and we get all those cobwebs hanging from the ceiling." Most often she complained about her finances. Those calls always included some form of, "My daughters want me to live with them," and generally ended with, "I don't want to be a burden to anybody. Maybe I'll just sell the house and move into a retirement home."

Saturday morning was payday, and Mrs. Q kindly called me at 7:30 to prevent me from oversleeping and to inform me that she was hurt because Luz didn't trust her and demanded her pay in cash. When it was her turn, Luz explained that she hadn't demanded but had merely stated a preference. Like many poor refugees she didn't have a bank account, making it difficult for her to cash a check. Mrs. Q, back on the line, said that she had never heard of anyone not having a bank account. She and Mr. Q had opened a joint savings account after Roosevelt reopened the banks in '33. When I explained to her that many poor people did not have bank accounts because they couldn't meet the minimum deposit requirements, instead of sympathizing, she complained that it would be hard on her as she would have to get her cousin to go to the bank to withdraw the cash.

"Luz is a lovely girl and an excellent cook. My cousin seems to eat with us all the time now. But my food bill is so high and I can't go on like this."

"Luz is a lovely girl and an excellent housekeeper, but she only watches Spanish soap operas when she irons."

"Luz is a lovely girl and we have such wonderful afternoons together but her English isn't improving. It must be those Spanish programs."

"Luz is a lovely girl and I couldn't love her more if she were my own daughter, and I know it's not her fault, but everything is so expensive these days. I just can't afford to pay her $600 a month. I was wondering if she'd accept $500."

Another early Saturday morning Mrs. Q called to run me through a series of quantum leaps in subjects. She complained that she was quite queasy. She didn't feel at all well. Maybe it was Luz's cooking or maybe it was the flu coming on, and she didn't want to accuse Luz of infecting her with a serious disease, but everyone knew that those people didn't practice proper hygiene, not like Americans, "not that it's Luz's fault cause she don't know better, and Luz ain't feeling so good herself. She's in her room, and I don't know what it's all about. It's not my fault. Everything has just gotten so expensive that, really, I don't know what I'll do. I guess I'll just have to go to a nursing home. My daughters don't want me to, but I guess I'll have to. I'm going to my daughter in Orinda this afternoon, and if I'm not on time she'll be so upset and worried. And I don't know what she'll do if Luz don't come back on Monday. I mean, my daughter . . ."

"Why wouldn't Luz come back on Monday?" I interjected.

"I don't know. It's nothing I did. But you know how touchy these people are. And violent."

"Violent? I can't believe that Luz is violent."

"That's right. Take her side. Everybody takes her side and blames everything on me. Ever since I was a little girl everybody's always blamed me for everything. Even my own cousin. Do you think he'd take my side for once? No. Just because Luz fixed him a steak one night. And his doctor told him not to eat red meat. And I'm the one who paid for it. You'd think I'd get a little credit for that. You'd think he'd thank me instead of taking her side. She's not even American. I knew this would never work out. She's a lovely girl. And, really, it's just a misunderstanding. Remember how she got all upset when I tried to pay her with a check?"

Finally the meat-eating cousin got on the line. As for coherency he was but a small step up from Mrs. Q. He was apologetic about the awful thing Mrs. Q had done, and he hoped that Luz wouldn't quit, because Mrs. Q really required someone like her, and he offered to make up the difference out of his own pocket even though he only had a quarter of the money that that old skinflint had.

Luz was tranquil. She said that there was no misunderstanding. Mrs. Q had merely paid her $125 for the five-and-a-half-day week instead of the agreed upon $150 and had hoped that Luz wouldn't notice or wouldn't complain. With quiet dignity she told me that she wasn't angry and certainly hadn't been violent, but she had tried to communicate to Mrs. Q the unfairness of what she had done.

Mrs. Q, with the last word, assured me that it was all a misunderstanding. She was old and her memory wasn't what it once was and she had simply thought that a hunnert 'n a quarter was the correct quantity, and she had just that moment paid the dear, lovely girl the rest of the money, and she hoped that Luz wasn't upset and would be back on Monday as usual, only they couldn't afford to barbecue any more steaks for the rest of the month.

Sunday evening Mrs. Q called from Orinda to tell me that she was ill and wouldn't be back home on Monday. A contented Mrs. Q called Monday to tell me that she was really too ill to return home, and she didn't want to infect Luz who was really a lovely girl. It was better that Mrs. Q quarantine herself in Orinda. Would I please tell Luz that Mrs.

Q would let us know when her services would be needed, possibly next week?

The following week a still-contented Mrs. Q called from the other doting daughter's house, the one in Mill Valley. She asked me to relay the same message. The week after that the apologetic Orinda daughter called to tell me she and her sister were in a quandary about Mrs. Q. She was certain that I would appreciate the fact that they couldn't quarter Mrs. Q with either of them. After all, they had their own families. And Mrs. Q was, well, a bit queer. The sisters were the ones who had encouraged Mrs. Q to find a live-in because they knew she would be happier in her own home. They were still trying to talk her into going back and hoped that Luz would be patient.

The last I heard from Mrs. Q was one afternoon several weeks later when she called from the Golden Sunset Retirement Home in Walnut Creek. She said it was simply lovely there and everyone treated her so well and the food was delicious and there were classes in dancing, art, and even Spanish. Her daughters didn't want her to stay there but what could she do? She couldn't live with both of them at once, and she didn't want to offend anyone. She was that kind of person. And at least in the home everybody was American although there were some kinds she would never have chosen to live with, and it was all so expensive and she didn't think she could afford to stay there much longer and did I think Luz would return if she got out before the doting daughters' husbands sold her house?

The Cemetery

MISS REILLY, IN GRADE SCHOOL HISTORY, drummed it into our little heads that the first child born in the New World of English parents was Virginia Dare. She thought it important enough to make it a question on one of her notorious quizzes because she labored under the misapprehension that the first birth had tied the immigrants to their new land. Yet, isn't it death rather than birth that settles us firmly in? Isn't it the cemetery, the boot hill, the lone fenced grave on the prairie, the family plot on the farm, that makes us one with the land? Isn't the cemetery an archive, the tombstones, filed in orderly rows, the records of our past? Don't they tell us who we are, where we came from?

Walking carefully through the wet grass, the young man approached and held his black umbrella aloft to include me in its shelter from the gentle rain. He stood silently beside me for some time before he whispered, "How are you?" in Spanish. I wasn't paying attention and I responded automatically, without looking at him. After a few more moments of listening to the rain on the umbrella and the words of the priest, my neighbor said in strangely accented English, "You don't remember me?" I looked at him, surprised at how Japanese he looked. Some Latin Americans look Asian, but I couldn't remember meeting one who looked so completely Asian. "I was Madeline's dentist," he said. His words transported me back to the first time I met the family. I remembered those uncomfortable moments we had spent in his waiting room. Señora Colón held her one-year-old, Paz, on her lap while Madeline, then six, sat nervously beside them, using her mother's comfortable bulk as a shield from me, hugging her mother, crying silently. As none of my usual banter could possibly work with the children, I was reduced to talking only to the uncommunicative, nervous mother. And Mrs. Colón was nervous indeed. Just being in the waiting room of an expensive children's orthodontist made her nervous, she who had never been in a dentist's office in her life until the disaster of a few days ago. She was ill at ease because all the other mothers and children were well dressed, while she and her kids, dressed in hand-me-downs, were obviously poor. She felt that she didn't belong there because all the other patients were Japanese American or Anglo, while she and her children were the only Latinos. Because she was nervous she fidgeted with her children. The serene Paz, with great equanimity, put up with her mother's constant ministrations, tugging her dress, pulling up her socks, adjusting her shoes, smoothing her hair, wiping her face, but the clinging, yet rebellious Madeline was another story. She pushed her mother's hand away every time, as if to say, if you're going to do this to me, you can't touch me. Only I can touch you. I didn't know if Madeline realized exactly what the "this" was, but she could tell from her mother's nervous behavior that it was something less than pleasant, something that might even hurt. Just a few days earlier a different stranger had taken the family to the county dental clinic, where Madeline had made such a fuss, screaming and crying at the top of her little lungs, that the startled dentist hadn't been able to examine the tooth that was giving her so much pain. Besides being poor and poorly attired in an obviously upscale waiting room, Mrs. Colón had another very good reason to be nervous. She was afraid that her daughter was going to scream so loudly and horribly that she would frighten the other kids away just as she had done at the clinic.

Frankly, I was nervous too.

Mrs. Colón confessed that Madeline was a crybaby, smiled nervously at the daughter under discussion, and tried to wipe the tears from her cheeks. Madeline pushed her mother's hand away with an angry look that made me fear the worst. She then tried to bury herself in her mother's comfortable folds.

Finally, when the waiting room emptied, the dentist and his assistant called us into the office. Madeline, like a football player who can't quite tackle the opposing fullback but hangs on hoping for help from teammates, clutched the hem of her mother's skirt with one hand and wrapped another around her mother's chubby knee. Mrs. Colón tucked Paz safely in her arms and limped forward, dragging her into the dentist's office.

After a brief consultation, the dentist told us that he thought it best if Mom, Paz, and I put in some more fidgeting time in the waiting room while he examined Madeline's tooth. He assured us that if he needed us he would call. But under the circumstances it was unlikely that he would need us. As she was led into the operating room by the pleasant assistant, I caught a glimpse of Madeline's face. Overwhelming fear of the unknown and the certain knowledge that she was being deserted by her mother were plainly registered. I was sorry for her but sorrier for the dentist.

If I had thought that Mrs. Colón was ill at ease, nervous, and fidgety before, I soon discovered that I had been mistaken. On those occasions when a shrill, inarticulate, animal-like squeal escaped from the nearly soundproof doors of the operating room, Mrs. Colón's eyes widened until mine hurt, and she twisted Paz's dress as if to wring water out of it. I tried to divert Mrs. Colón with a little light banter but failed, and I buried myself in a copy of *Rumpelstiltskin* that the dentist had lying about for us kiddies. Just when I got to the exciting part about baking bread and brewing beer and Mrs. Colón had thoroughly wrung and wrinkled Paz's short little dress, we were called back into the office. A thoroughly wrung-out Madeline was ushered in. She refused to attach herself in her previous leech-like custom to her mother. Clearly she was punishing Mom for the crime of desertion. She stood pouting by the door. The doctor explained to me and I translated to Mrs. Colón that he didn't do anything but briefly examine Madeline. He had simply let her spend the time getting used to the room by playing with some of the toys or doing what she wanted to do. Because of the unusual circumstances he thought it best to proceed slowly. If Mrs. Colón wondered, as I did, why Madeline.had screamed so much if nothing had happened, she obviously thought it best not to ask. Perhaps she didn't mention the shrieks because she knew her Madeline.

The dentist prescribed antibiotics for the infection and made an appointment to yank the rotten tooth the following week. As a rule I didn't take kids to the ice cream parlor after visits to the dentist, figuring that it's somehow counterproductive. However, I made an exception in Madeline's case. Our only line of communication had been glares and stares on her part and a fatuous grin on mine, and I wanted to do something nice. I didn't want her to associate me only with her fears. Everyone relaxed in the ice cream parlor and soon the little girls, with dripping, sticky cones of dangerously teetering scoops of banana and tutti frutti, made even more dangerous by Paz's lack of a firm grip on the law of gravity, made themselves comfortable by sitting on my lap and smearing as much ice cream on my clothes as was possible. I, of course, was gratified by the attention, and Mrs. Colón was only too happy to have the kids on the other side of the table. Free from the terrors she began to talk. She told me that when Madeline was a baby she had had a very high fever, which caused her deafness. They had taken her to a doctor who had told them that there was nothing to be done. No operation or hearing aid could help her.

Madeline lived in a world of silence as well as that strange land, the United States. She had learned to read a few words and phrases from her mother's lips, Spanish words and phrases, and she had recently entered a bilingual school for the deaf where she was learning to read and write, in English only, a language her mother found rather troublesome. She had also just begun a signing program in which she was learning to spell out words and phrases in English. Years ago I had learned to sign letters. I was rusty and awkward and unsure about a few letters, but it didn't matter because Madeline knew even less than I. After gaining proficiency in signing letters she would learn yet another language, American Sign Language, which neither Mom nor I knew anything about.

The following week, when I arrived at their apartment, Madeline seemed mildly glad to see me, no doubt remembering the ice cream and repressing the visit to the dentist. She only became nervous and clingy when we pulled up at the dentist's office. Her inarticulate screams were quite piercing, although the dentist later assured us that she had felt no pain when he yanked the rotten tooth. He gave the usual advice—no solid foods, no chewing on that side, all things that I would let Mom try to communicate to Madeline. I asked the dentist if ice cream was verboten and confessed that we had indulged after our first visit. He laughed. He mentioned that developing the habit of eating ice cream after each visit to the dentist was not the kind of preventive practice the American Dental Association recommended, but he understood the impulse. My childhood dentist had given me a lollipop after each visit. Madeline's dentist stocked the premises with children's books, stuffed animals, and toys. Few are those who wish to be associated only with pain and fear, and they usually find employment in intelligence agencies.

The dentist asked me to recommend a Spanish-English dictionary of medical terms that he could use in case he got more Latin American patients. I promised to send him one.

A month later, when Mrs. Colón ushered me into the living room then fled into the interior of the apartment, Madeline was clearly afraid of me and would have fled to Mom except that she had been told to keep an eye on Paz. Paz sat serenely in her cluttered crib, casually dropping one toy as soon as she noticed another. Madeline wanted to show off her baby-sitting skills and lifted Paz out of her crib, which was quite a feat of strength, and played with her, studiously ignoring me. The move backfired when Paz dropped a toy and noticed me. She smiled and stumbled over to sit on my lap, no doubt expecting ice cream to magically appear. Mrs. Colón ducked into the room to check on us kids. She told me that Madeline was getting good at signing letters. I tried some of my rusty letters with her. While Madeline was fluent—she formed her letters with grace and speed and made fun of my clumsiness—I knew more words and I could spell. We couldn't say much, and I took a long time saying it, but we had fun trying.

Like a general prepared to fight the previous war, Madeline entered the dentist's office with fear in her heart and tears in her eyes, but bravely facing her doom. A half hour passed without screams when finally we were called into the yanking and drilling room. Madeline was on the floor in the corner by the toy box, playing intently. The place was full of toys. Mobiles and little animals were suspended everywhere. Even the diabolical machinery was festooned and decaled. While Madeline took Paz on a tour of the toys, the dentist explained that Madeline was in a good mood because all he did was insert a spacer into the gap where the evil tooth once held sway. That had only taken a few painless minutes, and she had spent the rest of the time playing. He thanked me for the dictionary and told me that he had enrolled in a beginning Spanish class.

Six months later when I arrived at the house Madeline still remembered me and shyly played with Paz while Mom put on the finishing touches to her ensemble. The family was used to me. The first time I'd arrived at the house they'd all been anxiously ready, sitting on the edge of the sofa as if bravely waiting for the Gestapo to break down their door and carry them off. Now they simply went about their business while I sat on the edge of the sofa. On the way to the dentist, Mrs. Colón proudly told me that Madeline wasn't afraid because she had explained to her that the visit was only a checkup, and they weren't going to pull a tooth or do anything painful. She had been able to explain that through signing. Mrs. Colón had learned quite a bit, and Madeline was fluent. Mrs. Colón also explained that now that they were able to communicate Madeline didn't give her a moment's peace. She wanted to talk constantly as if to make up for her lifetime of isolation.

In the waiting room I tried to chat with Madeline by signing letters, but she soon became impatient with my crawling pace. She often interrupted to flash letters much too fast for me to read. She refused to repeat herself and sometimes smugly signed something that I didn't understand and had to ask Mom to interpret for me. Madeline was showing off. And I, like the uneducated uncle who admires his niece's algebra homework, was proud of her. At last she could communicate. There was no crying, clinging, or dress wringing. When we finally ran out of things to communicate, Madeline read a fairy tale. When she was called into the inner sanctum, she went as if she hadn't a care in the world.

She came out, after much mystifying screaming, with tears streaming down her cheeks and her features screwed up into a definite expression of anger. We were in the office by then, and the dentist informed us that he had noticed a cavity, and, as he had time, he had filled it. Madeline glared at Mom, the Mom who had assured her that there would be no frightening operations. She advanced toward that evil betrayer and hit her on the thigh with her fist. It looked like she packed a pretty good punch and it probably hurt, but Mom smiled an embarrassed smile and mumbled that Madeline seemed upset. I mentioned that Madeline seemed to have learned to communicate quite well with her hands. Nobody laughed.

On our way out the dentist mentioned that if I felt the need to take them for ice cream I should at least see that the girls brushed their teeth afterwards. Perhaps that would prevent a repeat performance of the disappointing day.

As we walked to the car, Madeline, still angry with Mom, held my hand and used me as a shield. Children are natural psychologists. She knew that by being nice to me and studiously ignoring Mom she could punish the evil deceiver. I was not the target of Madeline's wrath, no doubt, because she knew the routine, and we were then in the ice cream parlor phase. In the waiting room that very day she had read about what happened to the king who killed the goose that laid the golden eggs, and she was able to apply that lesson to the silly goose who bought ice cream. She was nice to me and knew that Mom told horrible lies. Since Madeline had learned an important lesson about economics and communication, she deserved a double scoop.

The dentist interrupted my reverie to tell me, "I've been studying Spanish for two years now. I speak it fairly well. I have several Spanish patients now and practice with them. But I haven't seen you for a long time. I saw the notice in the paper and thought I would come to the cemetery. It's all right, do you think?"

"Of course, it's all right. The family will appreciate your coming," I told him. I hadn't seen the family for over a year myself. When was the last time that I had seen them? When I took them to Children's Hospital? I could still picture little Paz as she lay unconscious on a white-sheeted bed. She had oversized earphones on and wires taped to her head as the sympathetic doctor and technicians tested her hearing. The bed seemed enormous and Paz seemed such a tiny, fragile creature as she lay all alone in the soundproof room. Madeline held her mother's hand and my hand as we waited. The last time I'd seen the family was when I had dropped in with a chocolate cake and a half gallon of ice cream for Madeline's birthday. Paz was in her crib picking up toys and dropping them. When she didn't notice my triumphant entrance, I noticed that she wasn't wearing her hearing aids. When I asked Mrs. Colón why, she told me that Paz didn't like to wear them.

I didn't know if Paz ever got accustomed to her hearing aids or whether or not she was wearing them when a drunk driver ran over her in a crosswalk near her house. I didn't know if, in her three years of life, she had learned to communicate with her mother or Madeline. What I remembered most about her was the quiet way she had sat on her mother's lap.

I didn't notice that the rain had stopped until the dentist lowered his umbrella. The small gathering around the little grave began to disperse. The sun burst through the clouds and suddenly it was spring. The cemetery sprang to life with the songs of birds and the murmur of people's voices, the sounds of cars starting and driving away on the narrow lanes. Mrs. Colón approached and offered her hand while she tried to stop crying. Madeline held my hand for a moment. When I motioned to the dentist, she half hid, clinging to her mother. I laboriously began to spell out that he was the dentist but she petulantly stopped me before I got going and gracefully signed something. Mrs. Colón translated. "She says that she knows who he is. He is the dentist." Mrs. Colón, who hadn't recognized the dentist until that moment, had a brief conversation with him in Spanish. She thanked him for coming and for all he had done for them. She apologized for Madeline. She complimented the dentist on his Spanish. When we were all out of small talk and the cemetery had grown quieter, Madeline went shyly up to the dentist and held his hand.